Books by Shanora Williams

The Perfect Ruin

The Wife Before

Praise for *The Perfect Ruin*

"A delicious and decadent cocktail of jealousy, passion, and revenge. I was hooked from the very first twist. You'll love this addictive psychological thriller."
—Alessandra Torre, *New York Times* **bestselling author** of *Every Last Secret*

"Twisty and impossible to put down! With a cast of diverse characters, Williams brings to life a twisty thriller that'll leave you reeling long after you've read the last page. 10/10 recommend."
—Claire Contreras, *New York Times* **bestselling author**

"You're going to pick a side, make no mistake. And then you won't put it down until you know the truth. A shocking, sensual thriller with sharp twists."
—Tarryn Fisher, *New York Times* **bestselling author** of *The Wives*

"Williams is an award-winning author of romance and suspense novels; her tale of revenge will find an easy spot in fiction collections. Tailored for book clubs and for those who like to read about the sleazy side of rich elites."
—*Library Journal*

"This twisty thriller takes readers into a high-class, sinfully privileged world populated with characters who will stop at nothing for what they want. Williams stretches out the tension as readers wonder what Lola did to hurt Ivy and whether their shared past will be revealed. With diabolical turns and surprises at every corner, it's an ideal summer read for fans of May Cobb's *The Hunting Wives* (2021)."
—*Booklist,* **STARRED REVIEW**

SHANORA WILLIAMS

THE

WIFE

BEFORE

www.kensingtonbooks.com

To my husband, Juan,
who is nothing like the men in this novel.

ACKNOWLEDGMENTS

I dove deep into writing this book when I was a few weeks postpartum, which meant I was sleep deprived and dying for naps, but this story would not let me rest no matter how much I wanted to. To be honest, I have no idea how I pushed through and completed this book. Some days were really hard and seeing as I had a newborn and two other kids who needed me, I didn't think I was ever going to get it done. Well, I'm so glad I found the time because it turned out to be so much better than I imagined.

I couldn't have done it without my husband. He is the most supportive person I know. He's been on board for my career since I told him about my goals and dreams as an author when I was seventeen. I thank him in every single one of my books because I truly wouldn't be able to do this full-time if he weren't such a wonderful father to our kids and a husband who understands when I need "just one more minute" to finish a chapter.

I also want to thank my sister Dajai for coming over and helping me with my boys during the day so I could write or work on edits. You're such a lifesaver and I love you so, so much.

To my agent Shawanda, thank you for continuously cheering me on and keeping me steady when I feel rocky. You know just how to soothe my soul and I love you!

Thank you to my incredible editor Norma for your amazing skills! Your excitement made this story feel worth all the hard work! I'm so grateful to be able to work with you and hash out the diabolical ideas I send your way.

Thank you, Kensington and especially the Dafina imprint for believing in my work and making so many of my dreams come true! Let's keep delivering the diversity that so many readers crave!

And last but certainly not least, thank you to every single person who is reading this and has given this book a chance. It's because of you that I get to write twisted, over-the-top stories like *The Wife Before* for a living and I'm forever humbled and thankful for that.

PROLOGUE

*H*e *is going to kill me.*

There was a time when I never would have thought such an awful thing about him.

He is not the man I assumed he was. He's different now—or maybe he's not different at all and this is how he's always been. Those eyes that used to look at me so lovingly, now stare back at me like dark coals. The soft lips that would tenderly kiss mine, I haven't felt on my skin in ages.

During late nights when I walk around the mansion, I feel the constant urge to look over my shoulder. Nights like tonight, as I pack my suitcase and then stuff my feet into my shoes, I'm well aware of the footsteps thundering through the hallways.

He's prowling. He hates me and he wants me gone. He's told me so many times before.

You aren't the woman for me anymore.

I'm over you.

Done with you.

I don't feel safe in this house. The air is colder, the light and warmth gone. This is a lonely place, and the terror inside

me is swelling, becoming harder to cope with, with each passing day.

The bedroom door creaks open and I gasp. He stares at me
from across the room, standing in the doorway. Like a wicked
silhouette, he clutches the brass doorknob and I stare back at
him, unmoving. Hardly breathing. What the hell does he
want?

He turns away with a grunt, leaving the door wide open,
those heavy footsteps of his booming through the hallway.
When his dark figure turns a corner and is out of sight, I hurry
to zip my suitcase up and snatch it off the bed. I carry it down
the hallway, avoiding the use of the wheels to prevent any
noise, and make my way downstairs. When I reach the hallway, passing elongated windows, I notice the snow pitter-
pattering, brushing the glass, the moon shining through in a
milky light. I have to hurry before the snow gets worse.

I leave my suitcase at the door and then rush to the mudroom to put on my coat. When I'm at the foyer, I collect my
keys from the gold key bowl and grab the handle of the suitcase, marching for the door and heading outside.

Snowflakes melt on my heated cheeks as I hustle toward
the car parked in the stone driveway. As I toss my suitcase into
the trunk, I hear footsteps behind me and gasp, spinning
around.

No one is around—at least not that I can see. There are so
many trees, so many shadows. So many places for him to *hide.*

"Melanie," a deep voice sings and I gasp again, looking
around. Where the hell is he?

Heart sinking to my stomach, I turn, shoving the suitcase
all the way in and then going for the side of the car. But as I
reach the door handle, the car door locks.

"No!" I scream. He's toying with me. He has my other
key fob! Why didn't I grab that one too? I dig into my coat
pocket, hands trembling, bottom lip quivering from both fear

and cold. I take it out, press the unlock button, and just as I clutch the door, I hear footsteps. They're louder. Heavier.

I yank open the door, panicking, heart racing, but it's too late.

Before I can get inside, a hand clutches a handful of my hair from behind me and a scream rips out of my throat.

I dare myself to look up and face him, and there he is—a dark silhouette in front of me, staring down with angry eyes. His nostrils flare and his hot breaths pass over my clammy skin. I want to scream again, but he and I both know that no matter how much I scream, no one will hear me. It's only us. No one here to save me.

Tonight is the night he will kill me.

CHAPTER ONE

I often think back to the very moment my whole life changed. I was twenty-eight years old, taking each day as it was. I didn't really have much going for me, and not much to look forward to, but I didn't mind that. I was a floater, moving from place to place, going with the flow, not usually one to complain.

But now, I can't help going back to when my life took the slightest turn and paved the way toward Roland Graham.

It all started the day I was supposed to meet my brother, Kell, for lunch. I woke up to the blaring alarm on my phone and groaned, jamming a finger down on the screen to stop the noise. I missed the screen and sat up with a huff, snatching up my phone and pressing the button hard to make the alarm stop.

The label on the alarm said *Work*. I rolled my eyes and flopped back down on my bed, burrowing myself beneath the comforter.

Less than a minute later and my phone rang again. A photo of Kell and me appeared on the screen, both of us smiling up at the camera with alcoholic drinks in hand, and the song "Gold Digger" by Kanye West and Jamie Foxx playing as his ringtone. He'd set it as the ringtone during one of our drunk nights out a couple months ago and I never got around to changing it.

"It's nine in the morning, Kell," I answered groggily. "What do you want?"

"Just checking to see if we're still on for today, sis."

"Of course we are. Every Wednesday, right?" I sat up, pressing my back against the wall. I had no headboard, not even a bed frame. Just a mattress on top of wooden pallets that I'd found, sanded, and painted white. I think of it as bohemian. My roommate, Shelia, thinks of it as a homeless move.

"Right—no, babe." Kell's voice was distant. "That's the tie for my meeting today. Yes, I'll talk to her about it *later*."

"Talk about what?"

"Sorry, I was talking to Ana."

I rolled my eyes at the mention of Ana. "Ah, right."

"Anyway, see you at twelve?"

"Yes, Kellan," I said through a yawn. "Twelve it is."

"Good. And please try to be on time, Mira. I have to meet a client afterward."

"Okay, okay. I'll be on time. Promise."

"Good. See you then."

Kell hung up abruptly and I turned back over in bed, sleeping for another hour.

CHAPTER TWO

"Y ou're late." Kell stared at me from across the two-top table, his dark brown eyes narrowed, and his lips pressed thin. "I told you to be here on time. I literally *just* told you this morning, Mira."

"I know, I know! I'm sorry! I was just really tired this morning because I spent all yesterday job hunting—"

"Job hunting?" he interrupted. "You lost *another* job, Samira?"

"Yeah. I was let go for being late too many times." I waved a dismissive hand.

"Are you serious? I set that job up for you with Miranda. I told her you were accountable and good for her store. She's a client of mine! Do you realize how that's going to make me look?"

"Yeah, I know, but it's not my fault, Kell! And to be frank, your client is a bitch and we weren't meshing, so it's fine. I'll get another job, send her a fancy forgive-me basket or something." I sipped water from one of the glasses already placed on the table for us. "I'm also tired because Shelia wanted to cheer me up for being fired, so we got drinks last night at this new club and we stayed out a little too late—"

"Look, Mira. Just stop." Kell lifted a firm, impatient hand in the air.

I blinked and clamped my mouth shut, staring at him.

"I don't want to hear your excuses anymore."

"Um . . . okay. Noted. What's with the attitude, though? Is this about me being a little late getting here? I'm always a little late, Kell! I'm sorry! What's going on with you?"

Kell looked me over twice and then sighed, the seriousness that was once gripping his features now fading. I took a moment to really look at him since walking into the restaurant.

He wore a navy-blue suit with an olive-green tie over a creaseless tan button-down shirt. His hair was freshly cut, a gold watch on his right wrist.

Kell had been dressing different lately. Before, he'd wear plaid button-down shirts and khakis or black slacks. But now it was crisp three-piece suits, flashy watches, and weekly haircuts when before he wouldn't bother going to a barbershop until absolutely necessary. All of these changes came shortly after he proposed to Analise seven months prior.

Despite my brother's done-up appearance, I could see the tiredness in his eyes. To the average man, they'd see a dapper guy, handsome and alert, but as his only sibling of twenty-eight years I could see right through whatever façade he was trying to put on.

"Kell," I called when he turned his head to look out of the window, at the Miami traffic. He hadn't answered my question and he was avoiding my eyes. Something was clearly wrong. "You're worrying me now. Did something happen?"

"No, nothing happened." He sighed and I lifted my head, relaxing my shoulders a little. "Look, Mira, there's no easy way for me to say this so I'm just going to put it out there, okay? I can't help you out anymore."

I frowned, confused. "Help me out? With what?"

"As far as finances go. I can't keep sending you money every month anymore."

"Why?" I countered quickly. "What happened?"

"Ana is pregnant," he murmured, and immediately lowered his gaze. "I just found out yesterday. I wanted to tell you in person, over lunch."

"Wow!" I stared at him, stunned. "Pregnant? Wow, Kellan, that's—that's so great! I didn't know you guys were planning on having a baby so soon."

He looked away again. "We weren't."

"Oh. But this is good news, right?"

"Yeah—well, I mean as far as baby-related news goes. It's good. But as you know, with a baby comes expenses and not only that, Ana wants to bump the wedding date up now."

"Oh."

"Yeah."

Silence thickened the space between us. "So it was Ana's idea to cut me off?"

"No—Mira, don't think of it like that." He sat forward. "We're just trying to get our ducks in a row here. You have to understand."

I folded my arms and worked my jaw.

"We have a baby on the way and we want to get married, sis. We'll need a bigger house, a place with a yard and all that. I'll be getting a promotion at the firm soon too and it couldn't be coming at a better time."

My head shook hard. "This is all Ana, Kell. I know it! She fucking hates me! I mean she called me a moocher at your Christmas party in front of everyone last year and never even apologized for it. She's been waiting for this day. She's been so ready to tell you to cut me off for something more important. Your *baby* is more important than helping your sister and she knows it. She also knows I'd never stand in the way of you and my niece or nephew. I would never, no matter how much I'm struggling."

"Mira—" Kell reached for my hand across the table but I moved it away.

"No—it's fine, Kell. It's fine." It *wasn't* fine. My eyes burned and my throat thickened from unshed tears, but I refused to cry in front of him. All he would have done was tell Ana that I cried in public, made me look like an even sadder bitch to her, and she'd rub his shoulders with her pasty hands and tell him it was okay—that everything would be fine for me because I'm "so smart" and "so beautiful" and have a whole life ahead of me. She was so full of shit. Our mother would have despised her.

I pushed back in my chair and placed the strap of my tote on my shoulder. "Well, I don't want to hold you up for your important meeting so I'll just text you later."

"We can still have a quick lunch, Mira. I'll pay for it. It's no problem."

I scoffed at him. Pay for what would probably be our last lunch together? He paid for every lunch we had—it was our thing and he never minded taking care of the bill. But with his baby news and knowing that Ana was probably in her cozy, overly furnished condo that *my* brother paid for monthly, laughing about this in between puking her guts out over the toilet, I refused to entertain lunch today. I'd only end up saying something rude about his fiancée that would make matters worse, and neither of us needed that right now.

"Don't worry about it. I'll talk to you later."

I turned and walked out of the restaurant, ignoring Kell's pleas for me to come back.

My brother was all I had left and yes, I was upset about this news. Not about the baby in particular, but the way that it was happening.

I was twenty-eight years old and going nowhere. Truth was I relied on him too much and I knew it. He knew it too, but being his only sister and the only immediate family he had left in the world, he never minded taking care of me when I needed him—or at least he never acted like it.

He always looked out for me. If I needed help with a bill, he gave me money. When I needed a car, he cosigned and helped me buy one. When I moved in with Shelia as her roommate and had a few rough months where I couldn't pay the rent, he helped me out with no problem.

But then he moved in with Ana and all of that started changing. I was certain it was because she was in his ear, saying little things that got to his head and making him recognize my flaws. Making him *resent* me.

Now he's about to get married and has a baby on the way. His career is soaring—big-time manager of the biggest public relations firm in Miami—meanwhile I can't hold a job for more than two months.

In truth, it's only a matter of time before a person cuts off their deadweight so they can evolve, and I guess what hurt most in that moment was that I wasn't at all prepared for it.

CHAPTER THREE

"So, he cut you off? Just like that?" Shelia stood in our kitchen with a knife in hand, slicing through a cucumber. She was prepping salads for her and her boyfriend, Ben, who would be coming over any minute.

She looked gorgeous in her sleeveless turtleneck top and low-rise dark jeans. The top was a light purple that complemented her golden-brown skin. Her hair was braided into two cornrows with gold jewels perfectly spaced throughout each section. Shelia always looked put together, unlike me. I hardly ever wore makeup unless I was going to a club or party, and my wardrobe didn't consist of bright colors like my roommate's. Neutrals were a favorite, but I did love bursts of color in jewelry, and especially loved me a pair of gold hoop earrings. I often wore crop tops, high-waisted jeans, and sandals. My hair had been natural since birth, though I did have it silk-wrapped once and didn't care for it. The unruly look suited me best, but I did love a good perm rod two-strand twist-out. If not the twist-out, I was definitely rocking a springy afro.

"Yep. Just like that."

"I bet you it was that girlfriend of his."

"Fiancée," I corrected, watching her finish off the cucumber.

"Girlfriend, fiancée, wife, whatever! She's a whole mess and I couldn't stand her from the moment I met her. What makes him want to marry that valley girl anyway? Your brother can do so much better than that."

"I don't know, but I'm telling you, Shelia, she's behind all of this. I know Kell, and he wouldn't just spring something like that on me after finding out she's pregnant. He wouldn't just cut me off right away like that. I bet you a hundred bucks she gave him an ultimatum. Her and the baby, or his sister." I sipped my smoothie. "Evil witch."

"Evil indeed."

"What the hell am I gonna do now? I was going to ask him for a little money today to cover the electric bill, but that's clearly out the window."

Shelia looked at me beneath her eyelashes, and as she did there was a knock at the door. "I don't know, girl," she said, placing the knife down and walking around the counter. "But you need to think quick because I'm not your brother. I can't keep covering for you." She smirked over her shoulder before unlocking and opening the door to let Ben in.

I looked away when they kissed, adjusting myself on the stool.

"What's up, Samira?" Ben followed Shelia into the kitchen. Unlike Shelia, Ben dressed down. He always did. His go-to was basketball shorts and a plain, solid colored T-shirt, but since they had a date in the park today, he stepped it up a notch with cargo shorts and a Nike shirt. He was cute, but I could never see the attraction Shelia had to him. He was cute in a little brother kind of way. Twenty-seven and still with a bit of baby face.

"Oh, not much. Just trying to figure out the purpose of my life right now."

He laughed. "The purpose of your life? That's new."

"She needs a job," Shelia said, opening a pack of carrots.

"Another job? Damn, Samira. You'll have about fifty jobs before you turn thirty at this point." He and Shelia laughed, and I rolled my eyes.

"This is not funny, you guys! I need to find something soon. I can't keep being out of work like this. Today was a rude-ass awakening and proof that I really need to get my shit together before I end up in a damn dump somewhere."

"Okay, okay," Shelia said in a more serious tone, but she was still smiling.

"Well, my cousin is bartending for a party tonight," Ben said, opening the fridge and taking out a bottle of water. "He's getting paid ninety dollars an hour to bartend one of the counters at Lola Maxwell's mansion. Ninety damn dollars an hour."

"Lola Maxwell?" I asked, stunned. "Really?"

"Who the hell is Lola Maxwell?" Shelia asked mindlessly, slicing the carrots.

"You don't know who Lola Maxwell is? She runs that nonprofit charity for pregnant ladies? Super rich and super pretty? Over a million followers on Instagram? She's all over the local magazines."

"Don't even try to explain it to her," Ben muttered after taking a swig of his water. "She doesn't keep up with famous people. You'd think she'd know Lola Maxwell though, since she's local. I swear you're so oblivious sometimes, baby."

Shelia pointed the knife at him with narrowed eyes and I laughed. Their banter was always hilarious.

"Anyway, he told me earlier they're looking for waiters and waitresses to serve drinks, bounce around and shit," Ben went on. "I know that's not really your thing, but he told me they're paying three hundred dollars for the whole night. Just gotta be there on time and stay 'til the end to get paid. They need a handful of people and it's an exclusive gig, so you can probably get in if you sign up now. He sent me the link where you need to apply. I can send it over to you. I was going to take him up on it, but I've got a date with my girl and can't bail on her."

Shelia puckered her lips, blew an air kiss, and winked at him.

"Ugh, I hate waitressing. They're the worst jobs and if it's at Lola Maxwell's place, you know there are going to be rich, stuck-up people all over the place."

"It's just one night, Samira," Shelia stated, giving me a stern eye. "You serve some people, show your face, and then hide in the bathrooms for most of the night if you have to. Doesn't matter as long as you get those three hundred dollars."

"Okay—I know, I know." I recognized that tone of hers. If I kept slacking on the bills, she'd replace me. No hard feelings, of course. But paying the bills on time was part of our agreement. Shelia was a stickler about overdue bills. She'd covered me a few times before in order to avoid being late for a bill, but with no job, no more help from my brother, and a looming electric bill, this waitressing gig was the only hope I had right now—at least until I found another job.

I focused on Ben. "Fine. Send me the link."

CHAPTER FOUR

It was so hard for me to stay consistent with jobs, but to be fair, I grew up with a mother who overworked herself because my father bailed on us when I was three. He just up and left, didn't pack any of his clothes, didn't say goodbye to any of us, but he did take the savings my mother had in her safe as a rude farewell.

That burned her and we all know a woman scorned is not one to play with. She had something to prove and she worked hard to earn back every penny he'd stolen.

In the mornings, breakfast would be on the stove or in the microwave for Kell and me and she'd be out the door and headed to work before we ventured to the bus stop. At night, she'd show up at home briefly to swap out her daytime outfit for her diner uniform, kiss us on the cheek as we did our homework, and peel.

The truth was our mother didn't have to work so hard. She'd gotten back the money that was stolen *plus* more within three years, and what she made from her job as a legal secretary was enough to cover the bills, according to what Kell told me. He knew more about what went on with our momma. He always did.

But like I said, a woman scorned is no joke. She had a mission, and that mission was to save up enough money for us to have a cushion *and* for her children to go to college. She'd accomplished that mission too, but it didn't come without repercussions.

She had a stroke when she was forty-nine. Passed away at fifty-two. She's been gone for seven years now but the emotion of that loss still lingers. Everyone who spoke at her funeral talked so fondly about how hard she worked, how dedicated she was, but they didn't see what I saw. They didn't see Momma coming home at midnight or later, bone-tired with bags under her eyes. They didn't wake up to hear her crying at night, asking God how she was going to make it.

Momma never did love again. She hooked up here and there, yes (and always tried to hide it), but she didn't fall for anyone. She just worked. Constantly. Always missing my band practices or Kell's football games. Not there as often to brush my hair or even help me pick a prom dress.

Sadly, my brother is following in her footsteps. Working extra hours and constantly on the move. I worry for him, and that worry is probably why I refuse to stress myself out over working.

A job is a job and money is only an object. Sure, it's nice to have money, but people—Americans especially—have become so numb to working. They get up at the same time every day, slave away for hours, mentally drain themselves, and for what? All so some rich, corporate man can sit in his big mansion and watch the numbers climb in his bank account?

I don't mind working for what I need, and I don't blame the rich for being the rich. After all, we all have our roles and we must play them. It's the circle of life. But my problem with it all is that my mother allowed money to be her end-all, and I refuse to follow in those footsteps.

She raised me and Kell to work hard for what we wanted,

no matter how hard life became, but I could never wrap my mind around such a mentality.

Why kill myself over a check that wouldn't even last a week?

Why trudge through muddy waters when there were so many other options?

Options like the night of Lola Maxwell's party. It was a beautiful Miami night and I had one job—to serve. Serve the rich people standing around the pools and cocktail tables with drinks in hand, get them drunk, feed them, and even compliment them if that's what they wanted for a good night.

I can admit that, though I hated waitressing, I was pretty damn good at it. I knew how to keep a level head when a person got rowdy. I could balance a tray on one hand like an acrobat on a tightrope. I was good at knowing when not to show up, when not to hover, and how to swindle a person to tip more, though tipping wasn't required that night.

It was so easy to me . . . but tonight my skills were against me. I didn't want to be at that mansion, dressed in the itchy collared shirt I'd found in the back of my closet, or the black slacks that were a little too snug on me now. Jazz music was playing and most of the guests were engrossed in deep conversations, which made this feel more like a soirée type of event than an actual party, and it was so humid outside that I could feel each coil of my natural hair loosening and turning into frizz.

I was bothered, but only because I'd gotten a text from Kell right before arriving for the job.

Miranda says she'll give you your job back if you can close for her tomorrow.

I rolled my eyes at the message and shoved the phone in my pocket as I trudged toward the back gate of Lola Maxwell's mansion.

I appreciated Kell for reaching out and trying to make something work on my end. Though I couldn't really blame him for putting his priorities first, it was bad timing and I wasn't ready to forgive the situation yet.

Because of that measly message, I was off my game that night. I normally could dance through a crowd with a full tray in hand like a ballerina, but I kept bumping into tables and walls to get out of the way of the guests.

Some of them frowned at me. Others were so drunk they laughed. I thought about what Shelia said earlier about hiding in one of the bathrooms until it was over, but there was a woman in charge named Abby who was keeping a close eye on all of the waitresses to make sure we were actually doing our jobs. I thought she was kidding when she said she'd be watching, but Abby was like a hawk. Every time I felt eyes on me, I'd look to find them and would see her watching and nodding with a clipboard in hand.

"How about another drink on the house?" I asked a White couple standing near the dessert bar.

The woman, in pearls and a tight black midi dress, quickly placed the mini fruit tart in her hand down on a plate on the table next to her. She reached for a champagne from my tray and grinned. "Keep them coming, girl! It's so humid out here I might faint!"

I laughed on cue but wondered why she was drinking so much if she was hot. Liquor was only going to make it worse. I almost started to ask her if she wanted a water, but our mission as waiters and waitresses was to get people drunk, according to Abby. The drunker someone was, the more money they'd shell out.

My eyes shifted to the chubby man next to her. "Don't tell me you're going to babysit that one?" I teased, nodding to the half-empty tumbler in his right hand.

The man broke out in a drunken laugh and said, "Actually, if you can believe it, this is my third one!" Then he swiped a champagne, spilling some of it on my sleeve as he did. I pretended it didn't happen and allowed the good times to roll, like good waiters do. "Good thing I'm not driving tonight, huh?" he chortled.

"That's right! I'll be sure to keep them coming for you guys!"

They thanked me in an overexaggerated manner and I turned around, only to see Abby standing a few steps away, looking at me. Why did it feel like she was watching me the most? It was like she could sense my *I'm only doing this for a check* mood. She bobbed her head toward more people, and I nodded before turning away and rolling my eyes with a suck of my teeth.

I really had to *work* for that money that night and it felt harder than usual. All I kept thinking about was Kell and Ana. Ana talking to him, facing him with worried blond brows as he spilled his grief about me. He was probably talking to her at that very moment, complaining about how I hadn't texted him back about the job with Miranda and then going on about how I walked out on our lunch. And fucking Ana—she was probably nodding and cooing "Aw, baby," while clasping his hand in hers. He'd share his guilt, she'd let him get it out, and then the subject would change. Just like magic, he'd forget until he thought of me again and, slowly but surely, that guilt would fade and he'd accept that it was the right thing to do.

"Hey—you!" Abby marched my way, pointing a pen at me. "I need you to take more champagnes to table six. Lola's husband is about to share a toast and some of the guests are running low."

"Yep. Will do," I said, but Abby had already turned away to talk into her headset. I rolled my eyes and faced the bartender and Ben's cousin, Roger.

"Stack 'em up, Roger," I said, slapping a palm on the counter.

Roger went straight to work, lining up glasses on my tray

and then uncorking a bottle of the expensive champagne with a loud *pop*. He filled them up until the froth reached the very top, and I was surprised none had spilled over.

"You're good," I noted.

"Why do you think they chose me to get paid ninety an hour tonight?" he said with a smirk.

I grinned. "Fair point."

"Yo, what are you doing after this whole thing is over anyway?" he asked as I slid the tray closer to me. I gave him a once-over before putting all my attention on the tray.

"Why do you wanna know?" I mused, picking up the tray and balancing it on my palm.

"Just wondering. Ben told me you're single."

"Yeah, well, that doesn't mean I'm looking." I turned away, giving him my back. When I was met with the crowd, I smiled over my shoulder and he grinned and shook his head. Roger was good-looking and it would have been fun to go home with him that night of all nights, use him to take away some of my worries. I was stressed and annoyed and I bet if I'd gotten a couple of glasses of that fancy champagne in me, I would have been walking out of that mansion arm in arm with him.

But that night called for other plans.

I was doing fine with the tray, walking through the designated walkways for the waiters to avoid the crowds, but it was as I approached table six that I felt a shift.

My stomach dropped. The floor was wet and I stepped right into a puddle. A gasp shot out of me as my foot slipped and I tried to catch myself from sliding and stumbling, but it was too late.

My tray wobbled and the glasses clashed into one another, the champagne sloshing, causing even more of a mess on the ground. There was a man in a suit right in front of me and the drinks were going to land right on him if I didn't act fast.

As if he sensed what was happening, he quickly turned and shot a hand out my way. His large hand clutched my free arm and I did all I could to save that damn tray, but there was no saving it. It was falling and I was slipping on the wet spot, losing all control. The tray hit the concrete and the glasses went crashing down.

But I didn't fall because the man in the suit had saved me.

CHAPTER FIVE

I was thankful the music was still playing and most of the guests were tipsy or drunk, because a lot of them gasped but then looked past the accident moments later as if things like this happened all the time. And I bet they did. People like them attended events like this often. There was always one waiter or waitress bound to drop a tray or a plate or something, right?

So yes, they all did move on, and not a soul thought to help . . . except for the man in front of me. My heart was beating swiftly and I could hear my pulse in my ears. My mind was racing with thoughts about my mother, about Kell and Ana, about how badly I wanted to run out of there and never look back but needing the money for the bills. I saw the man's sculpted lips move, but his words were incoherent.

All I could think when I saw him was *wow*. I mean, he was gorgeous, and he had nice lips, yes, but what I noticed most were his eyes. Hazel. Despite the lightness of them, there was a gloominess to them—a sadness.

Table six was close to the pool and the blue water made his eyes shimmer. His lashes were long, and his jaw was sculpted. His nose was a perfect sharp angle. Everything about him screamed perfection and suddenly I became aware of how close

I was to him. He was still holding my wrist and my palm was pressed flat to the heart of his suit jacket, my belly against his.

The proximity made me nervous, dizzy, and I pulled back quickly. He released me and his mouth moved again.

"Are you okay?"

The words became coherent, the music louder, my beating heart calmer.

I nodded. "I'm okay."

He studied my face and then looked next to us, at the pile of broken glass on the ground.

"Oh—uh, I am so sorry. I should clean this up." I didn't think as I bent down and picked up the tray. I was still on edge, quickly picking up pieces of glass and placing them on the wet tray.

The man in the suit said, "Oh, I wouldn't—"

But it was too late. A piece of glass caught my finger and not only were there shards of it everywhere, but now my blood was spilling on top of it.

"Shit," I hissed, bringing the bleeding finger to my mouth.

"What the hell happened?" Abby approached and her screech made my ears ring. "You dropped the drinks?"

A woman rushed up next to her in a dress with the letter M monogrammed on the chest. She was brown skinned with her hair pulled up into a sleek bun.

Abby looked at her and her face flushed. "Oh—Georgia, I'm so sorry!"

"What happened?" the Georgia woman asked.

"She clearly dropped the drinks," the man in the suit said. "It was an accident."

"Did anyone get hurt?" asked Georgia, taking a look at our surroundings.

"No. No one got hurt," the man said.

"Okay, well, that's good. Abby, have someone come clean this up, please. And you," Georgia said, looking down at me, "you're bleeding. There is a first aid kit in the guesthouse. Please go take care of that before Lola catches sight of it."

"Okay, thanks."

"What's your name?" she asked.

"Samira Wilder."

"Well, Samira, unfortunately I'll have to dock this from your pay." Georgia winced. "Just standard protocol. It's what you sign up for, in case there are any damages like this."

"I understand." But it didn't make my feelings hurt any less. I was embarrassed on top of stressed, nervous, and all the other things I couldn't help feeling.

I glanced at the man in the suit and he was focused on my chest.

The fuck? I frowned and lifted a hand to cover my chest. "What are you staring at?"

"It's—uh." He pointed at my chest. "It's just the blood. It's getting on your shirt."

"Oh. Oh! *Shit!*"

He reached for the pocket of his suit and pulled out a silky black handkerchief. "Here, wrap this around it. I'll walk you to the guesthouse."

He turned with me before I could protest. I wasn't really going to put up a fight anyway. Despite the fact that I had completely made a fool of myself and was bleeding, I'd caught this gorgeous man's eye. Not for the better, of course, but still. It was something and he was being helpful.

He walked several steps ahead of me and opened the door to the guesthouse. No one was inside, thank goodness, but the bathroom door was ajar, as if people had been coming in and out of the guesthouse all night. Abby had instructed that the waiters use this bathroom if needed and not the bathrooms inside the mansion.

The man headed for the bathroom and started opening the cabinets. I stood in the middle of the guesthouse, peering out of the window, clutching my injured hand with his handkerchief. I could see Lola Maxwell standing in front of her guests, cradling a glass of champagne as a man in a suit spoke into a microphone. He must've been her husband.

"Found it."

I glanced back at the man who stood in the bathroom with the first aid kit.

"I doubt the Maxwells would like seeing blood all over their furniture, so you might want to tend to that cut in here."

"Right." I made my way there, but as I stepped into the bathroom, I noticed he took up a lot of space. It was a spacious bathroom for sure, but he was a large man. Broad shouldered, tall. He definitely filled the room with his presence.

"I'll just . . ." His voice trailed and then he left the bathroom.

I swallowed hard and looked down at the small white first aid kit on the counter. I took the handkerchief off but the cut bled again and blood dripped on the floor.

"No—*damn it.*"

"Everything okay?" the man called.

"Actually, no. It's bleeding pretty bad. I think I might need stitches."

"Stitches?" The man appeared again. "Can I take a look at it?"

"Sure." I removed the handkerchief and he examined my finger.

"Doesn't need stitches."

"How do you know?"

"I've seen my fair share of deep cuts," he said, chuckling. "Trust me, that will be fine. Just needs some pressure to stop the bleeding." His eyes locked on mine. "May I?"

I shrugged. I didn't care as long as it stopped. I couldn't afford a hospital visit right now on top of being jobless.

The man opened the first aid kit, took out a cotton ball, and wrapped it around my finger. He gripped my finger hard, applying pressure and I saw some of the blood ooze through. He grabbed another cotton ball.

"It's one of those days, huh?" he asked, and I was glad he was filling the silence. I didn't know him, and this situation was beyond awkward—a stranger stopping my bleeding.

"Definitely one of those days."

"A rough one?"

"Kind of."

He pressed his lips and nodded. "Rough for me too."

"How so?"

He looked away, focusing on my finger again. "Long story. Better that I don't get into it."

Silence filled the space again. I clicked my tongue before saying, "I didn't get your name."

"You mean you don't recognize me?" he asked, amused.

"No. Should I?"

"That would be a first." He removed the bloody cotton.

"What, are you like some big-time famous guy or something?"

"I wouldn't say all that," he murmured with a smile, picking up a packet with an alcohol wipe.

"Then what is it?" I asked, and I was curious what his name was, even more now.

His eyes flashed up to mine briefly before dropping and tearing open the packet. "Roland. Roland Graham."

My brows drew together. The name didn't register, and yet he was looking at me anxiously, as if waiting for me to react to it. "Sorry . . . I don't know that name."

"Well, believe me, that's a good thing. For you and me."

"Is it?"

"Yes. You've met me before all of the public assumptions have."

"Assumptions?"

He sighed and wiped my finger clean. "Never mind."

"Are you good friends with Lola Maxwell?" I asked.

"More so her husband. We've golfed together a few times. I donated to her cause and he invited me."

"Must be nice."

"Eh, well, when you've been deemed one of the best golfers in America, it makes golfing with amateur friends a little boring."

"Wait. What? One of the best golfers in America?"

"Ah. So you aren't pretending you don't know who I am just to be nice?" He smiled wide and revealed two rows of white teeth.

"No, I'm not kidding. I have no idea who you are and if that's a blow to your ego, sorry, bud. I don't know much about golfing. I mean, I know of Tiger Woods—what Black person doesn't—but I don't sit around watching his games, you know?"

"Yeah. I get that." He opened a bandage and wrapped it around my finger. "All done."

I wiggled my finger. It was sore but not horrible. "Thank you."

He closed the first aid kit and replaced it and then looked at me. He was close again and I hadn't realized before, with all the blood and anxiety swirling like a cocktail around me, but his cologne smelled really good. Expensive, but not too over-powering. Sandalwood with a hint of citrus.

"Well, I should get back," Roland murmured. "Party's almost over."

"Yeah. I should too."

It was funny. We both knew we should have been getting back to it, but this moment felt unfinished. We sort of lingered and fidgeted on our feet. He moved left and I moved right, both of us trying to exit the bathroom at the same time.

I laughed, and he chuckled and then gestured out of the bathroom. "After you."

I smiled and made my way out. When we were outside again, fireworks were going off and the guests were cheering as they stared up at the show, drinks in hand and mesmerized smiles on their faces, their eyes sparkling. The bright colors lit up the night sky and I looked over at him as he stood on the grass, sliding one hand into his front pocket and peering up.

He looked like a god standing there, with his strong shoulders and powerful build. There was a loneliness about him, and I wanted to ask him more questions, like why his day had been rough too. I wanted to listen to him talk some more because he didn't seem like much of a talker, so I bet hearing his voice was a privilege.

But I had priorities that night and I couldn't spend my time standing on the grass talking to some supposedly famous golfer.

Before I could walk away, he asked, "It was Samira, right?" I turned around to him and there was a soft smile on his lips, his hazel eyes gentle yet intense. He looked at me like he wanted to know every single thing about me, and I was sure I was looking at him the same way.

"Yes, Samira," I called out as the music from the party started up again. "And no, Roland Graham. Just because you're a famous golfer and let me bloody your handkerchief doesn't mean I'm going to give you my number." I smiled hard at him and trotted off, and I as I did, I could still feel his eyes on me.

There was a spark between us and if I was right about my instincts, he'd find me again before the night was over.

CHAPTER SIX

I was right. Roland did find me again, but it didn't happen at the party. Apparently, he'd gotten in touch with Abby, who went against the rules and sent my number to him. How do I know this? Because he told me over a drink at a bar.

The day after the party, Roland had texted me asking "Guess who?" and frankly, I had no idea who the hell it was. I gave my number to guys all the time for quick hookups, and since I wasn't in the mood for a hookup and was constantly thinking about Roland Graham standing in front of those fireworks like a god, I spent the better half of the next day ignoring that message.

But then he called around midnight and told me it was him and I felt like a fool. If he hadn't called, I wouldn't have known it was him at all and would have missed the opportunity to see him again. Because that was all I really wanted—to see him again—but he was way out of my league. Women probably flirted with him all the time. I was no different . . . and yet, he'd called. He'd taken the first step.

"A lot of the people who love working for the rich and famous like to think they're doing the rich people favors when we ask for something," Roland said, swirling the bourbon in his glass.

He was seated on the barstool next to me at the bar, his knee awfully close to mine as he faced me. I was leaning toward him, smiling, because I couldn't believe he'd actually found me and I admit, I was flattered.

"Truth is, I would have found a way to get your number regardless."

"Oh, really?" I mused, smirking. "Well, aren't you a cocky one."

I learned a lot of things about Roland that first night out, like the fact that his favorite color is red, and his favorite candy bar is Snickers. I also learned that he was married before, but that his wife passed away, which somewhat explained the sadness I saw in his eyes the first night I met him. He was a widower, and that must have been hard. He's pretty close with his mother, but she travels often and is always on the go, so he doesn't spend as much time with her as he'd like, and his father left when he was seven (which we bonded over, considering my father was absent too), and his favorite movie was *Scarface*, which I made fun of because what guy didn't claim *Scarface* to be his favorite movie?

Even knowing all of that though, there was still so much about him to be discovered. But I left that up in the air that night and instead found myself drunk and clinging to his hand as we made our way to his hotel room.

We drank some more and had sex and it was incredible. I should have been a little ashamed about letting him have me on our first date, but he knew exactly how to talk to me, how to touch me, using just the right amount of control and pressure to drive me crazy. Plus, it'd been so long for me and I was lost in the night with him, wanting to forget about all my worries. There was no shame to be held because we bonded that night, and it'd been so long since I'd bonded with any-one—let alone a man.

Our relationship moved at a steadier pace after our first date. Roland called more often. Sent me flowers every day for a week—all a different bouquet. Shelia wanted to know who my mystery man was every time she saw a bouquet on the counter, but I refused to tell her because I wasn't sure if this was something that would last.

Roland and I ate dinner together and walked the beaches. We'd tried going out for a movie once, but paparazzi showed up as soon as he'd parked the car, and ruined it. He whisked me away apologetically, and then took me to a pristine condo he owned in Miami and let me pick out whatever movie I wanted to watch over popcorn and margaritas.

The whole paparazzi thing was new to me. I didn't think he was *that* famous—not to the point people were ready to snap pictures of him and ruin his dates. After the movie inci-dent, I'd googled him, and his Wikipedia was the first thing to pop up, along with a photo that was taken when he was in his prime during his golfing career. There was also a mention of his wife, Melanie Graham, and the years they were married before she died.

Following that were freshly posted articles about Roland Graham's young, new love interest (me), which I rolled my eyes at. I didn't even bother clicking the links to read the arti-cles. I knew how those things worked. They were probably calling me a random lowlife who was completely out of his league and, frankly, I didn't need to read about that to know it as somewhat of a fact, so I closed the browser and went on about my lowlife day.

I guess it was a good thing Roland didn't feel the need to hide our relationship. If he hadn't been taking me out, then I would have been second-guessing our relationship, but he was showing me off in so many new places and sharing his time with me publicly. He was giving me a lot of effort and so many gifts and it felt good receiving that from someone like him.

I was bothered by the paparazzi—the fact that those hounds with cameras could just disrupt our dates—but I suppose I wanted the world to know we were becoming a thing too—whatever that *thing* was—so I dealt with it.

For three weeks, everything went great with Roland . . . but then Kell called and made me reconsider ever getting involved with a man like him.

CHAPTER SEVEN

The potent scent of coffee beans and freshly baked pastries filled my senses as I drummed my fingers on the wooden table.

Normally, Kell was the first one to arrive for one of our sibling dates, but I was able to arrive ten minutes early that day. I'd gotten a mani-pedi that morning at Betsy's Nails, one of the hottest nail salons in Miami. It was expensive and I never could have afforded it on my own budget, but Roland surprised me the night prior with a gift card to the salon and told me to enjoy myself.

For the record, Betsy's was hard to get into. Betsy French was one of the best nail techs in Miami and she was known for doing the nails of celebrities and big-time influencers. I don't know how he did it, but Roland had gotten me a morning appointment by pulling a few strings, and it was a delightful experience. Fortunately, the salon was only a five-minute drive to the coffee shop Kell and I planned to meet at, so I didn't have to cancel or reschedule.

The bell chimed at the door and I looked up, spotting my brother strolling in with a pink gift bag in hand.

"Mira," Kell said after sitting in the seat across from me.

I had my arms folded but my eyes were on him. "Kellan."

He laughed, placing the gift bag on the table. "Oh, are we using full names now?"

"I may or may not still be upset about the last time we met."

"I know. Which is why I brought you an apology gift."

I side-eyed him and then lowered my gaze to the gift bag. He grinned that same annoying grin he always gave when he was being sincere, and I fought a smile, dropping my arms to reach for the bag.

"It better be something good," I muttered, placing the bag on my lap and then smirking.

"I'm glad you finally responded to one of my texts last week," he said as I dug into the bag and shuffled the white tissue paper around.

"Yeah, well, I was feeling good, so I figured I'd at least say hello."

"Feeling good? You mean about being with Roland Graham?"

I looked up, frowning. "How do you know about him?"

"Who doesn't know, Samira? You're all over the magazines. Publicity is my job. I work with celebrities, and trust me when I tell you, this is not a good look for you, but it is for him."

"What are you talking about?" I pulled my hand out of the gift bag, forgetting about whatever was inside it.

"Samira . . . you can't tell me you think being with that guy is a good thing?" Kell was smiling, but his eyes were serious. I didn't understand what he was getting at, but clearly I was missing something.

"Kell, he's a famous golfer who happens to like me. So what?"

"He's not just some *famous golfer*," he retorted, losing the smile. "Shit, Mira, have you even looked him up? Read about him?"

"I've googled him," I countered.

"And yet you're still with him?"

"I—Kell, what are you getting upset for? I've had plenty of boyfriends and some of them were super shitty and you were never this overbearing about them."

"What did you find out when you looked him up?" Kell asked.

"I don't know." I folded my arms again. "I didn't get past all the articles about him having a new love interest, which was about me, I'm sure."

"So you didn't dig deep? Learn more about him? Because the Samira I know wouldn't be so keen about being with him if she knew his truth."

"What is there to dig about? What great big truth is there to know, Kell?"

"He was married before."

"I know that. I'm not an idiot. He told me he had a wife who passed away."

"Yeah, Mira." Kell pressed his lips, and his eyebrows drew together as he sat back against the back of the chair. I knew that look, and had a feeling that whatever he was about to say next wasn't going to be good. "And do you know that he *killed* her?"

CHAPTER EIGHT

"What?" I shrieked, sitting forward. "What are you talking about, Kellan? Why would you say something like that?"

"I'm not just saying it, Mira! There were stories circulating around years ago of people saying he killed his wife. They never could prove that he did it—not enough evidence, apparently—but everyone has this hunch that he did. The case had too many holes, didn't make sense."

"I—*what?* That's ridiculous! He would have told me about something as serious as that!" I sat back in my chair, chewing on my thumbnail, thinking back to the first night I met Roland. I didn't know who he was, or that he even golfed, but he was at Lola's party, so I did know he was important in some kind of way and that he clearly had money. I found out about his deceased wife through him, but he didn't exactly go into detail about her death, and I didn't ask how she'd passed because it felt too soon to get into such a heavy topic. When I googled him, a part of me thought to look deeper, especially since he'd mentioned there were rumors floating around about him, but I didn't think to bother because fuck rumors. Everyone had a rumor floating around about them somewhere, but that didn't make them true.

"What? Did you expect for him brag about the fact that people think he killed her?" Kell scoffed. "Why would he bring something like that up? He's not an idiot."

"No, I didn't expect that, but this *killing* her thing sounds really far-fetched! He's good to me, Kell. He's a great guy. Why would people say that about him?"

"Like I said, her case had too many holes. Her car supposedly rolled off a cliff only a couple of miles away from the mansion he owns in Colorado. They found her body in the lake and when they did, they saw she had fresh bruises on her thighs and arms, as well as cuts on her wrists. Like she'd been abused or beaten prior. They also found heroin in her system."

"What?" I wheezed.

"Yes. That's part of the reason I've been trying to reach out to you, Samira. I wanted to see you and check on you after last time, yes, but then I saw the articles about you and Roland Graham and I couldn't believe it. There's no way in hell I could just let you be with him without saying anything."

"You could have called!"

"You weren't answering!"

"Well, then you should have sent it in a text to warn me!"

"First of all, you wouldn't have believed me, and this isn't something I wanted to risk texting you about. I didn't know when you were around him. What if he'd seen my message to you? What if he hurt you too because of it?"

"I doubt he would have done anything to hurt me, Kell. He is such a different man compared to the other guys I've dated. He's kind and patient with me. I've never even seen him get upset about anything while we've been together. I like being around him. How can anyone think he did something like that to his wife?"

"A lot of people out there think he did it, Mira. Just do your research. Read about what happened with him and that

case. All you have to search for is 'Roland Graham wife murder' and it'll show up. And after you do, cut him off and lose
his number because he's no good for you."

"But I have a date with him tomorrow," I told him, lowering my gaze to the pink gift bag.

"Then cancel it, Mira. Look, you can't go out with him
anymore, okay? Even if he is innocent, which I doubt he is,
it's not a good look for you. And now that I know you don't
know about his past or the stories with his wife, it's also clear
to me that he's using that to his advantage. He wants the
world to think he's a good guy who has moved on and is
happy, so he's doing all these things for the public eye, like
taking you out on dates, buying you expensive things, walking the fucking beaches of Miami. He wants people to see you
two together. It makes him look better."

"No." I shook my head and closed my eyes. I didn't want
to believe Kell about any of this. Roland was good. He was
sweet and witty and giving. He liked me and I liked him. We
had a spark—a connection I had never felt before. There was
no way he was a murderer.

"He's *using* you, Samira." Kellan's voice was firm enough
for me to pop my eyes back open and look at him. "Like I
said, I know publicity and I've worked with my share of
celebrities. Stunts like this are a part of my job and clearly his
agent has him doing this to rebuild his reputation as this nice
guy, and he can do that all he wants, but I won't let it happen
with my sister. So cut it off *now* while you're still alive and
breathing and everyone sees you, 'cause I'll be damned if anything happens to you while you're with that demented motherfucker."

CHAPTER NINE

As soon as my little meetup with Kell was over, I drove to my apartment with a knot in my stomach. We didn't stay at the coffee shop long. I grabbed a coffee and bagel at the counter but couldn't stomach it after the newfound information on Roland.

How was it possible that he was involved in something like that? Better yet, why the hell didn't I think to dig deeper into his past? It made sense that Roland would use a woman who didn't know much about him to his advantage if there were dangerous stories and rumors floating around about him. No wonder he was giving me funny looks in the guesthouse bathroom at the party, trying to see if I was serious about not knowing who he was. He saw an opportunity and ran with it.

"Ugh. I'm so stupid," I muttered, climbing out of my car and locking it up. I headed to the front door, keys in hand, peering over my shoulder.

As I stepped into the apartment and saw the lights were off, I was glad Shelia wasn't home. I flipped the kitchen light switch on, tossed my bag on the countertop, and went to my room to change into a pair of sweatpants. I eyed my laptop on my desk, sighing. I was devastated, and curious to know the truth.

I went back out to the living room and curled up on the suede sofa with the laptop, wasting no time searching for the exact words Kell told me to use.

Roland Graham wife murder.

My heart pounded harder with each click of the keyboard and for a moment, I hesitated, a finger hovering over the enter button. Doing this was going to change *everything* between me and Roland. It'd only been three weeks, but we'd already done so much together. We had sex, and that really changed things between us. What if I had slept with a *murderer*?

I groaned, feeling the knot tighten in my belly, and without giving it another thought, I hit enter.

There were so many results it made me dizzy. Several articles had catchy headlines, but there was only one that made me quick to click.

Did Roland Graham REALLY kill his wife?
By Henry Caldwell

Not too long ago, the world loved Roland Graham. He was America's best man, the professional golfer with a graceful swing and beautiful poise. But overnight, he has become the most hated man in America.

On February 10th, 2018, the Sageburg Police Department reported that an unidentified woman had driven herself over a cliff and into a lake. The woman was Melanie Graham, the wife of professional golfer Roland Graham. This was initially reported as an accident, but as more of the story unfolded, sources revealed that Melanie's body had been found bruised with cuts along her wrists.

The toxicology report later revealed there was also heroin in her bloodstream.

Suddenly, it was no longer ruled an accident. It'd become a homicide case, which sparked an investigation and the number-one suspect was her husband, Roland Graham.

Graham's attorney told reporters that Roland Graham was on a solo golfing trip the night Melanie died, at the Vista Golf Club in Colorado; however, staff members of the on-site hotel reported not seeing Roland Graham the night of February 9th. One of the staff members said his room was still booked for two more nights, but that his Do Not Disturb sign was hanging on the door the duration of his trip. Graham also denied turndown services, which made police question why he didn't want anyone in the room.

Footage shows Roland Graham exiting the room on February 9th to visit the ice machine. Footage also shows him leaving the hotel at 6:13 PM and returning at 6:47 PM with a bottle in a brown paper bag, which was reported to be a bottle of bourbon that he'd picked up from the nearest liquor store.

Melanie Graham's time of death was approximately 11:00 PM, and on the night of her death, there were no more reports of Roland Graham leaving his room after his trip to the liquor store, but there is footage showing Roland Graham leaving the room the next morning at 7:02 AM to go to the golf course.

So did Roland Graham really kill his wife? There is no footage showing that he left his room after buying the reported bourbon, and given that he was only gone for thirty-four minutes, how could he have possibly gotten back to Sageburg, Colorado—a fifty-five minute drive away—to beat his wife, put her behind the wheel of a car, and cause her to drive over a cliff that is six minutes away from his home? There was simply not enough time for him to accomplish that, which is most likely why he was never arrested or charged in her death.

The bruises on Melanie Graham's body could have come from anything or anyone. With drugs in her system, her husband out of town, and family members of Roland Graham as well as locals reporting that the Grahams' marriage had been on shaky ground for months, she could have been with anyone that night, so why, after all of this conflicting evidence is the world targeting Roland Graham and accusing him of her death?

Is there more the police haven't told us? Is it because the world can't accept that perhaps Melanie did kill herself? Or is it because, in cases like this where a young wife dies tragically after being found with bruises and cuts on her body, it is always suspected that the husband either did it or is behind it?

We may never know, but the case remains open and the whole world has their eyes on Roland Graham.

I drew in a shaky breath, clicking back and scrolling through the next article. This article had two images of Roland and Melanie on a yacht. In the first one, her arms were laced around his neck, her head thrown back mid-laughter. She was pretty with straight black hair, golden brown skin, and a wide white smile. In the second images, I could see her eyes were the shape of almonds, and she wore a short royal-blue dress with strappy white heels. Roland's hand was locked around her waist as he gazed at her lovingly, a subtle smile gracing his lips. His eyes weren't sad then. He looked genuinely happy with her.

There was no way he could have murdered her. And like the previous article said, when would he have had the time? Still, what Kell said was right. Something about this didn't add up, and as I continued reading article after article, falling deeper and deeper down the rabbit hole of the Melanie Graham tragedy, I felt an unsettling twist in my belly.

There were videos of people ranting about Roland, screaming all kinds of theories, and then there were others supporting him, claiming his innocence and that his reputation had been ruined for no reason at all.

I couldn't believe it. This man was a walking OJ Simpson case—you either thought he did it or you didn't—and then there was me. A woman who was falling for him, and was torn about which side was the truth.

CHAPTER TEN

After all the information and articles I'd found on the internet, I started ignoring all of Roland's text messages. I didn't know what to think about the situation or him. All I knew was that Kell was right—whether Roland was innocent or not, it wasn't a good idea for me to be with him.

It sucked. I missed him, ached for him, but I had to be strong. So his reality was harsh and he'd been dealt a bad card. I'd had enough bad luck in my life. I didn't need to bring this man into it and carry all of his baggage too. He was going to be in Florida for the next month for work purposes, but he'd be gone soon and I had to keep that in mind.

I lay in bed, staring up at the ceiling fan as it whirled slowly. It was just my luck to meet a guy I really liked only to have to abandon him. Sighing, I turned over just as there was a knock at the door.

Shelia popped her head in with a smile. "Can I come in?"

"Always."

She smiled as she passed through the doorway and gently closed it behind her. That was a bad sign—her shutting the door. She never closed my door to talk to me unless it was something serious, like the night she cried on my shoulder when her father passed, or the night she and Ben had a hard falling-out and had broken up for a month.

"What's up?" I asked, sitting up and resting my back against the wall. She sat on the edge of my mattress, close to my feet, and sighed.

"How's job hunting going?"

Oh, shit. I should have known it was going to be about this.

Money. Bills. A stable job.

"It's . . . going, I guess."

She nodded, pressing her lips and gazing at me sympathetically. "Did you like the waitressing gig Ben set you up with?"

"Oh—yeah, it was good." It was how I met Roland, so yes, it was good . . . for a while. Shelia knew of Roland now after all the flower deliveries and seeing a picture of him and me together on my phone, but she didn't know how close I was getting to him, and after finding out the rumors about him—well, I was glad I hadn't gotten all gooey about him with her. She and Ben would have just teased me about it and looked deeper into him than I had, which would have made me paranoid.

"Good. Good," she said.

I sighed, placing my phone down. "What's up, Shelia?"

"What do you mean?"

"You came into my room and closed the door. You didn't come in to talk to me about that waitressing gig. Something is clearly on your mind, so what's up?"

She studied my eyes a moment before finally releasing a sigh and placing a hand on top of my bare foot. "Well, I've been talking to Ben a lot," she started, avoiding my eyes.

I nodded, even though she wasn't looking at me.

"And . . . we've been talking about moving in together."

I blinked. "Oh."

She peered up at me. "Don't take it the wrong way. I love having you as a roommate. You're my girl and you know that—but . . . well, when Ben moves in, I'm thinking maybe we'll need more privacy, and if we have a roommate then . . ."

"No, no. I get it."

She rubbed my leg. "I'm sorry, Mira."

"No—stop it, Shelia. Seriously." I grabbed her hand and squeezed it. "This is good news! You guys are taking your relationship to a new level and privacy is so important. Trust me, I get it. I really do."

She smiled, squeezing my hand back. "I don't want you to think I'm kicking you out or anything though! You can stay here for however long you need to until you find a steady job and a place of your own."

"Thanks, Shelia. I appreciate that."

"Of course, babe." She gave my hand one more squeeze before standing. "I was thinking about hitting the Crab Shack if you want to join me? My treat," she sang.

I smiled. "Sure. Let me get ready."

I watched her leave the room and my smile immediately faded. I got dressed and met her at the door. She drove to the Crab Shack, where we had unlimited crab legs and shrimp along with lime margaritas. It was a fun night, but there was a little voice in the back of my head, screaming at me about where my life was headed.

Shelia may have said I could stay however long I needed until I found another place, but Ben would be moving in soon, and she would want privacy as soon as possible. I couldn't stay for long, no matter how nicely she put it. I couldn't be too upset either. Ben had a steady job. He could help pay the bills with Shelia, no problem, but nothing about me was steady.

Kell damn sure wasn't going to let me stay with him, not after the way Ana basically had him shut me out, so that left me with only one option—to find a job and get my own place.

God, being an adult sucked.

CHAPTER ELEVEN

After Shelia told me her plans with Ben, I woke up at eight the next morning, hopped on my laptop, and searched for jobs. I spent five hours applying, submitting my bland résumé, and hoping for the best. When I felt satisfied enough, I left my apartment to get lunch.

I ate lunch in my car, and realized the gift Kell gave me was still on the passenger seat. Placing my sandwich down, I dusted the crumbs off and then picked the bag up by the white ribbon. I dug into it, felt something hard, and pulled it out.

My eyes widened as I studied the gift in hand. It was a pink pocketknife and pepper spray kit. A card was attached to it:

Just in case he doesn't take no for an answer.

I shook my head, crumpling the note into a ball and shoving it back into the bag, then tossing the knife and pepper spray on the seat. Kell was such an asshole.

★ ★ ★

After lunch in my car, I went to a nursery to go plant shopping, which wasn't the wisest thing to do considering I needed to be saving my money, but retail therapy always pulled me out of my funk, not to mention one of the stores I shopped at was hiring.

I pulled into a parking space in front of my apartment building—the apartment that wasn't going to be the place I called home for much longer.

I sat a moment, watching a silhouette pass by our window on the second floor. A man. Ben was there, and normally I wouldn't have cared, but things felt different now. The apartment was going to be his now. I couldn't saunter around like before, sprawled out on the couch, or pick at Shelia's leftovers. All that she had would be his, and I would be the third wheel.

Head shaking, I shoved the thoughts aside, collected my tote bag and the stupid knife and pepper spray kit, and climbed out of my car. As I started tucking everything into my tote bag, ready to move to the back seat to grab my plants, I heard footsteps and whipped my head up.

A familiar person was walking toward me and I gasped, my back bumping into the open car door.

CHAPTER TWELVE

"Samira, I need to talk to you," Roland said, walking closer.

"R-Roland?" I gasped as he kept walking toward me. "Wh-what are you doing here?"

"I've been trying to get in touch with you. You haven't responded to any of my messages in days." I panicked, looking around the empty parking lot before peering up at the second floor, where my apartment was. Maybe if I screamed, Shelia or Ben might hear me.

"I . . ." I didn't know what to say, but I could feel the knife and pepper spray in my hand.

Roland stopped a foot away, as if he sensed my unease. "Samira, please . . ." He let out a long sigh and I couldn't believe it, but beneath the light of the lamp posts, his eyes glistened. "I . . . I knew this day would come, and I know I should have mentioned it to you but I . . . I didn't know how."

My grip slacked around the kit, only a little. I still didn't know what to say.

He sighed and looked up at the sky before lowering his hazel gaze again to focus on me.

"Is it true?" I asked, looking him up and down.

"No, it's not true."

"How do I know that?" I countered, tightening my fist around the kit again. I could feel the Velcro that separated the knife and pepper spray. One yank and I'd have the knife in hand.

"You don't know it," he said. "All you can take is my word for it, and I know my word doesn't seem like shit with all that's out there about me, but I want you to know that I didn't do anything to Melanie. I loved her and I never would have done something like that to her."

I softened again. Damn my weak heart.

"Listen." He sighed, rubbing the top of his head. "I *really* like you, Samira, and I haven't felt like this about a woman since . . . well, since Melanie."

I pressed my lips, watching his eyes burn with sincerity. Damn. There was no way he could have done it. No way. He loved her—I could tell by the photos that were posted of them. I could also tell right now, with how he talked about her. That, or he was a damn good liar.

"You swear?" I whispered.

"I swear," he promised.

I loosened my grip on the kit. "I'm sorry, I'm just . . ." I sighed. "I'm sorry, Roland. I saw those articles about you, and I freaked out a little. I shouldn't have judged you without hearing your side of the story."

"Don't apologize. It's human nature to guard yourself after finding out something like that." He smiled at me.

"I just . . . why would they say that about you?"

"I ask myself that question every day." His feet moved as he shifted his weight. "The day that I met you was her birthday," he murmured.

My eyes stretched. "Oh. That's why you were having a bad day?"

"Kept thinking about her." He shrugged. "But you were a

good distraction, bloody finger and all." He smiled and I couldn't help but laugh. When his face turned serious again, he asked, "Do you think I can take you somewhere? It can be public, if you want. We don't have to be alone. I just think I really need to talk to you about this, so that you don't have the wrong idea of me. Even if you decide you never want to see me again, I'll understand. I just don't want another person in this world to think of me as this vile man who is ready to kill."

I swallowed hard, then I glanced over my shoulder, noticing Ben and Shelia's silhouette. They were dancing arm in arm. They did that sort of thing when they drank too much. Ben's mom had put him in salsa classes once so that he could dance at her wedding. He'd never forgotten the moves.

My eyes swung back over to Roland's and he had this hopeful yet completely worn-out look about him. He was probably so tired of defending himself to people, and here I was, adding even more fuel to a fire he couldn't put out.

"Sure," I said, finally releasing the kit and closing my car door. "But let's not go out where everyone can see and bother us. I'd rather talk in private."

CHAPTER THIRTEEN

There was a reason I wanted us to talk in private. For starters, you didn't talk about *murder* in public, especially when so many eyes could be watching and ears could be listening. Secondly, I needed to digest what was going on and how I felt about the entirety of the situation. I don't know why, but I couldn't bring myself to believe any of the stories that'd been fabricated about Roland.

Roland took me to his place but we didn't go up to his condo. Instead we hung out by the pool, which was vacant. The blue water rippled with the pool lights, casting a blue glow on both of us. He took a seat in one of the chairs at a table and I sat across from him, keeping my bag perched on my lap, the kit still inside. I didn't think he was guilty, but I could never be too sure about my own judgments lately.

"I'm sorry for sneaking up on you," he said.

I smiled. "It was a good way to get my attention, that's for sure."

"Yeah." His eyes shifted down to the tabletop. "So . . . ask me anything."

"About your wife?"

"Whatever you want."

I studied his face, the seriousness in his eyes, and then looked away, toward the pool. "Okay . . . umm . . . so what really happened to her?"

"She drove over a cliff."

"Why?"

"I don't know," he said with a sigh. "I ask myself that every day—why would she do something like that? She never seemed suicidal to me."

"I read somewhere that you were at a golf resort or something when it happened . . ."

"I was."

"How soon did you find out about her being . . . dead?"

"Not soon enough. I played a round of golf the morning she died, not knowing that she was dead, and was called twenty-two hours later, once she was identified."

"Wow. I'm so sorry, Roland."

He shrugged.

"Do you do drugs?" I asked.

"Never have and never will. My father did them heavily. I don't touch any of it."

"So why did they find heroin in her toxicology report?"

"I don't know the answer to that, honestly. I've never seen Melanie do drugs of any kind. Did she drink? Sure. But never drugs."

"Do you think . . ." I paused, looking around the pool area. "Do you think she was with someone else?"

His jaw ticked and he avoided my eyes when he said, "I don't really know."

We sat in silence, listening to the waterfall trickle into the pool. "My brother works in PR. He thinks I should stay away from you."

"And he has every right to think that, considering he doesn't know the *real* me."

"I don't want to believe any of it is true."

"Then don't."

"But how do I know that it's not? I mean—I really like you, Roland. How do I know that it's not true?"

Roland looked me in the eye for a moment, then he stood up and walked around the table. Taking me by the hand, he gently tugged on it and brought me to stand. His arm wrapped around my waist, his fingers clasped my chin, and he looked down at me with warm eyes.

"If you feel like you aren't safe with me, I get it, Samira," he said. "But I want you to know that I really like you too, and I've enjoyed spending time with you. I want more with you. But I can understand you not wanting the extra attention or the stress of all of this. But I promise you, I did not do it. I did not kill my wife. I don't have that kind of evil in me."

I sighed, unsure what to say.

"I've been single since my wife died," he confessed. "Not because I wanted to be, but because no woman is brave enough to be with me after the accident. Doesn't matter if I know I'm innocent, the whole world thinks I did something bad to her." His eyes saddened, glistened, and I really felt for him. I wanted to hug him, comfort him. It had to hurt knowing a large percentage of the population hated him based on assumptions and rumors.

"But you were with me," he went on, smiling. "For a few weeks, you accepted me even before knowing any of this and . . . I don't know. I guess I wanted to cling to that feeling. The feeling of being *wanted* by someone after so long."

I dropped my eyes to his mouth. "I hate that for you."

"Mmm."

"I don't want to believe any of it is true," I whispered again.

He tipped my chin higher and dropped his lips on mine. His lips were soft, and the kiss deepened, and I melted into him, moaning.

"Then don't."

CHAPTER FOURTEEN

Maybe I was a fool for what I did after my run-in with Roland, but I couldn't help it. I didn't believe the rumors about him. I ignored all of the articles that ridiculed him. I didn't believe any of it because I liked being with Roland. I enjoyed my time with him. He treated me so special, and I felt I could talk to him so much more than any guy I'd ever been with.

We laughed at the same jokes, enjoyed the same TV shows and movies. Our sex was off the charts hot, and our relationship was so dynamic and powerful. We could carry on a conversation for hours, never getting bored or tired of each other's voices. There was no denying he was the man for me—but why did the man for me have to be a former suspect in a fucking *homicide*?

Life never played fair for me, but if these were the cards life was dealing me, then I'd play them right. And by that, I meant that if I wanted to be with Roland, I had to keep it quiet. We couldn't be out and about so much anymore. If we wanted our relationship to work and for our bond to be impenetrable, people literally couldn't know anything else about us. We couldn't feed paparazzi any more intel about our whereabouts unless we weren't together, and I damn sure couldn't have Kell finding out that I was still with Roland.

He was mine and I was his. I didn't feel any danger or threats while around him. I only felt his kindness and affection, and damn it, I was happy.

"You still job hunting?" Roland asked me one day as I sat on his bed, scrolling through my phone. I was on a job-search website and none of the posted jobs seemed promising.

"Yes. My roommate is pretty much kicking me out so her boyfriend can move in, so I need a job and a place to stay, really soon."

Roland placed a glass of wine down on the nightstand next to me and sat on the edge of the king-sized bed. As I scrolled, my back pressed against the upholstered headboard, I could feel him looking at me, so I looked up and fought a smile. "What?"

"Nothing," he said, but he was smirking, and when he smirked, he usually had something he really wanted to say.

"No, tell me." I placed my phone on the nightstand, replacing it with my own glass.

He smiled, then sipped his wine and looked into my eyes again. "Well, I was just thinking . . . if you move in with me you wouldn't have to worry about bills or finding a job."

"Oh." My eyebrows shifted up and all I could do was blink at him.

He sipped his wine. "That's why I didn't want to mention it."

"What do you mean?"

"Because of that exact reaction. It's outrageous, is what you're thinking, right? We've only been together for a month and a couple weeks."

"No—I'm not thinking it's outrageous." And I really wasn't. I took a look around his bedroom, the floor-to-ceiling windows, the polished hardwood floors, and the little things that made this place his, like the watches on the dressers and the self-healing books on the nightstands.

I ran a hand over the fluffy gray comforter on the bed I sat on. Truth was I could really see myself living in luxury with him. Being with him, in our own private world, sharing morning coffees together and dinners at night.

"I have some upcoming trips and events that I've been invited to, but I can stick around in Miami when I'm not traveling so you aren't alone. Do you think that's crazy?" he asked.

"No," I responded quickly, smiling. "No. I don't think it's crazy at all. I could stay here a while—at least until I get a job and find my own place."

He took my wineglass from me, placing both of the glasses on the nightstand and then turning to me, maneuvering between my legs.

"While you're with me, Samira," he murmured on my lips, "you won't have to worry about any of that." He kissed me once. Twice. "I've got you." Another kiss. "You won't ever have to worry about another bill or place to live so long as you have me in your life."

CHAPTER FIFTEEN

Here's the thing about me—I have a bad habit of not thinking things through. I can be both impulsive and impatient and I get overly excited about the smallest things, so imagine what it's like when a big event or opportunity turns up in my life.

Because of this little personality quirk of mine, I don't always make the best decisions. Therefore, when Roland asked me to marry him five months after moving in with him, I said yes.

Seriously. I wasn't thinking. He and I were traveling together, and I was attending events as his plus-one. Despite the negativity he'd received due to his previous wife's death, it was hard for many to lose respect for Roland, and he was still a man in demand. Prior to losing her, he'd created his own children's charity, donated to good causes abundantly, and hung out with very famous people. Not to mention, he was worth a lot of money and, according to Roland, it didn't matter what a person did wrong, money still talked and he had a lot of it. We were living a dream, so by the time I had room to think, it was already too late.

Things moved fast the night he asked. We ordered takeout from a local Chinese spot. When we were walking to his car, he came around to my side and dropped to one knee. It was so unexpected, and yet, I said yes. After I did and we'd had several drinks back at the condo, he told me about a mansion he owned in Colorado.

"You know, we don't have to stay here in Miami," he said, placing his chopsticks down.

"What do you mean?"

"I own a mansion just outside of Sageburg. There are less eyes there. It's mostly populated with nice, elderly people. It's a quiet place, everyone minds their own business."

"That sounds nice."

"I'd like us to get married there."

I straightened my back. "In Colorado?"

"At the mansion." He smiled. "We'd have more privacy there. I can call in a local priest. You can buy a nice dress. We can keep it small, simple. Just us."

I couldn't help but look away when he said that. I immediately thought of Kell and what he would think if I ran off to another state that was hours away with a man who he thought was a wife-killer. I'd still been meeting him for lunches every other week, purposely avoiding the topic of boyfriends and relationships. Kell still paid for lunches, but lunch wasn't the same. He seemed so stressed and uptight now, and I was sure it was because of his pregnant fiancée or his exhausting, fast-paced career.

"But I understand if you don't want to," Roland said abruptly. "I don't want to whisk you off if you're not ready. We can stay here too."

"Roland, stop." I grabbed his hand across the dinner table and squeezed it tight. "I paused because I thought of my brother. There isn't much in Miami for me. Only my brother and my best friend, Shelia, and I can always come back to visit them whenever I want."

He nodded. "That's true."

"I love you," I said. "And I want to be with you. I also

want to make you happy. I can tell this mansion brings you joy so, if being in Colorado is where you feel happiest, then I'll go with you. I'll go anywhere with you."

I'd never seen him smile so big. I'd made him happy, despite feeling a little nervous about the whole idea. He kissed me, we shared another bottle of red wine, and he talked about how beautiful the snow was in Sageburg during the winter, and with winter coming, he'd take me to explore the city on a snowy night. After we celebrated by drinking more and turning on some music, he took me to the bedroom and we made love several times that night.

But I admit that when I woke up and the drinks had worn off, I started second-guessing the idea of leaving the only place I had family and friends, to be alone with him in Colorado. I was going to be with him in the mansion that he used to share with his now dead wife. He'd told me that was where they lived and that he never sold the place—that he felt connected to it.

To anyone on the outside looking in, they would have called me a fool. And perhaps I was a fool—a fool in love. I don't even know why I loved Roland, or why we were moving so fast, but I did. And though sometimes it didn't feel right to be going at such a fast pace, I couldn't say no to him. There was something about him that intrigued me, lured me in. Whether it was fast or not, I needed this. I had no place to stay and no job, and he was willing to provide it all for me. There was no way I was going to reject it.

It only took one morning kiss and Roland's hands on my hips for me to forget about my doubts and worries and realize that I would be okay in his hands.

He was willing to give me everything I ever wanted.

All I had to do was become brave enough to take it.

CHAPTER SIXTEEN

I had never traveled outside of Florida. I'd lived in Miami my whole life, born and raised. I'd always endured long, hot summers and hasty winters that we couldn't even really call winter.

To know that all of my things were being sent off to another state—a state that was a thirty-one-hour drive away (yes, I checked)—was a little daunting. Fortunately, Roland and I were flying to Colorado in first class seats, but I couldn't stop my mind from churning.

I loved Roland. We hadn't been together long, but I loved him. And that was also a fact. But what if this was a mistake? What if I should have waited just a little longer? Maybe I should have told Kell. I'd told him that I ended things with Roland, which I did at one point, but I didn't tell him we picked back up, that I'd moved in with him, and was now *engaged* to him.

I hadn't told Shelia that I'd moved in with Roland either. She knew I moved out, but I told her I was temporarily moving in with a friend I used to work with. To her knowledge, I was still crashing with that friend. I'd met Shelia for lunch a week after Roland asked me to marry him and I wanted to tell her all about his proposal, but I couldn't bring myself to do it. What if she knew Roland's story and figured he *wasn't* innocent? What if she called me crazy for saying yes to his proposal? Insane? A lunatic?

She also knew I was dating someone, but my relationships were never serious, so Shelia most likely assumed I was messing around with some guy I'd met on a dating app.

All of my choices were irrational at best, and yet there I was, sitting next to my soon-to-be husband, embracing this next chapter in my life that I wasn't one hundred percent certain about.

I mean, of course I wanted to be with him. Sure, I loved his money and his cars and the way he spoiled me. Hell yes, I loved the sex, the candlelit dinners, and our endless conversations. But I was sure there was more to Roland that I didn't know. And I had a feeling I was going to learn all of it in that mansion.

When we landed, Roland's cousin Dylan picked us up from the airport. Dylan was also Roland's errand boy, according to Roland, though he told me to never call him that. He was also Roland's caddy.

During the car ride, I'd learned that the two of them had grown up together. Roland was an only child and Dylan had siblings, but he was the youngest of them all and there was a large gap between him and the second youngest, so he wasn't very close to them. He and Roland were around the same age, and by the way they cracked jokes on each other, I could tell they were practically like brothers. Being around them and all their banter felt good. Roland was much more relaxed than I'd seen him in a long time and I immediately understood why he wanted to come back. This was his happy place.

"Did Roland tell you that I whipped his ass in a golf match once?" Dylan asked, looking at me through the rearview mirror.

"What?" I laughed, looking from his eyes to Roland. "No, he never told me that."

Roland laughed and rolled his eyes. "Here we go."

"Yep! It was right in his backyard. He has a mini practice facility and driving range back there, right? Beautiful range with putting green and sand bunkers. Anyway, we were drinking and we made a bet. If I won, he'd give me a thousand dollars. If he won, I'd clean all his golf clubs, which is a lot 'cause he has about eight sets. That's a lot of iron to be cleaning."

I giggled. "And you won? Against the best golfer of our time?"

"Damn straight I won," Dylan said proudly. "Roland shouldn't have had so much to drink. Those thousand dollars came in handy too."

"All he did was spend it on stripper booties."

I looked at Roland and snorted a laugh.

"Come on, man! She just met me. Don't go telling her all my business like that!"

When we pulled up to Roland's home, I couldn't believe my eyes.

The mansion was beautiful. But really, beautiful was an understatement. It was absolutely *stunning*, and I couldn't believe a part of me was thinking *not* to come to this place. I hadn't even set foot in it yet and I was in love with it. And the architecture of it was so . . . *Roland*.

The exterior of the mansion was made of soft-brown brick and taupe fieldstone, donned with dark gray shutters that matched the towering roof. Even beneath its thin layer of frosty dew, the broad green lawn was pedicured to perfection and there were four garden beds at the front of the house, each consisting of tiny green hedges and a mix of red and yellow flowers that limped sadly, most likely because of the cooler weather. Regardless, the landscaping was impeccable.

As Dylan continued driving, passing through an archway built into the home, four garages came into view, which reminded me of the time Roland told me he owned three vehicles—a Cadillac, a Maserati, and a Subaru for the snowier days. The extra garage was used as his entertainment space, where he hosted his guests or hung out with his closest friends.

"Wow." I gaped.

"Nice, huh?" Roland said, and I felt the heat of his body as he slid across the back seat to get closer to me. "I had it built nine years ago."

"It's so gorgeous, Roland."

"It's a French Country home. When I was thirteen, I remember riding around with my mother as she pitched signs in yards that she'd gotten a sale on. She was a Realtor. Anyway, there was one house that she took me to and I couldn't believe my eyes when I saw it. It looked just like this one. I remember telling myself that one day I would own a home like that one, and now I do."

"It definitely suits you." I looked over my shoulder at him. "Where is your mom now?"

"She's living her best life in Rome right now," he said, sighing. "She'll probably be calling me soon so I can send her money for her next adventure."

I smiled as he did. "That's sweet of you to take care of her."

He pressed his lips and grabbed my hand.

I looked ahead and noticed Dylan's eyes flicker up to look at us before dropping down and peering through the windshield again. He parked in front of one of the garages, sighed, and said, "We made it."

"You'll love it here," Roland murmured. "I promise."

CHAPTER SEVENTEEN

The inside of the mansion was perfection, and it screamed Roland Graham in every room. Everything, from the black and gray furniture and cherry hardwood floors, to the mounted TVs in almost every single room. This place was all his and it showed. It was manly, not an ounce of a woman's touch, which I found odd since he'd once shared this place with his last wife.

I brushed the last thought aside and told myself I'd add my own feminine touch to it. Maybe Roland got rid of whatever Melanie added, so as not to remind himself of her too much. Then again, as I roamed the long hallways, taking in picture after picture of Roland either swinging a golf club in perfect pose or standing with one, I couldn't help wondering why he didn't have a single photo of him and his wife on the walls.

"Think you'll love it here?" Roland asked me as we entered the bedroom. The master bedroom was on its own wing, separated from the rest of the home. It was spacious as hell, with a fancy bathroom to match. The bathroom was all marble and silver, with a wide clawfoot bathtub and a standing shower with a rainfall showerhead that I couldn't wait to use.

I turned to face my fiancé with a smile. "Yes," I murmured. "I know I'll love it."

He grinned. "Good. Now let me show you the place where you'll always find me if I'm not in the house."

"Where's that?" I asked as he draped an arm across my shoulders.

"My range."

The driving range was behind his house, beyond the back deck, which consisted of a built-in firepit and cushioned chairs beneath an exotic-looking pergola.

"It's several acres of turf with three greens and four bunkers," Roland said as we stood at the start of the course. "We'd need the golf cart to see the whole area, but I won't break it out on your first day here." He laughed. "Maybe I can teach you how to golf one day, though."

I smiled up at him. "You'd love that, wouldn't you?" I faced the range again, taking in small hills and curves and the waving flags planted in the holes of some of the nearby bunkers. There was a small station not too far away with a slanted white roof above it. From the turf on the ground that I could see, and how it dipped and rose, it reminded me of a miniature golf course. He probably did a lot of putting there— he'd talked about that often. Benches were built into one of the walls of the station, which probably made it a place where Roland could take a break after being on the range.

I looked to my right, and not too far away was a burgundy shed. I frowned at it. There were two windows on either side and a rocky path led to it. It didn't look too well-kept, which made it feel like it didn't belong there. The wooden shutters next to the windows appeared to have had too much sun and the roof was fading and covered in leaves. Naked tree branches hovered over the shed like witch fingers, gently tapping the side of the house and the roof as the wind blew.

"What's that for?" I asked, pointing at the shed.

Roland looked with me. When he didn't answer right away, I faced him again. He was staring at the shed, his jaw clenching. "Melanie's," was all he said and I frowned, confused. "It was her she-shed. Her go-to place. It's where she did a lot of her hobbies."

"Hobbies? What all did she do?"

"She designed clothes," he said through a sigh. "Read a lot. Wrote."

"Those are cool hobbies."

"Hmm. Yeah. All of her things are in there. My mom put it all in there when she passed. I didn't have it in me to do it. I tried calling her sister to come and pick it up and go through it, maybe sell some of it, but I couldn't get in touch with her, so it all just sits in there."

"Oh." I chewed on my bottom lip. I wanted to ask him if his mother had put any photos of him and Melanie in there too, but thought against it. I'd just gotten there, and I didn't want our first night together in his mansion to be filled with tension.

"Come on. I'll order us some lunch and then we'll get you settled in." Roland grabbed my hand and turned toward the mansion and I walked with him, but I couldn't help looking over my shoulder at Melanie's shed.

CHAPTER EIGHTEEN

It took no time to settle into my new home. All of my things were delivered the next day and Roland helped me unpack and unload it all. By the third day I was acquainted with every room of the mansion.

We immediately began discussing the wedding. He'd called a pastor who had agreed to wed us, and then Roland took me on a three-and-a-half-hour drive from Sageburg to Denver to shop for wedding gowns. I didn't want him to see the dresses, so he went to find a place that could fit him in last minute for a tuxedo.

It felt nice trying on dresses, but also lonely. I wished that I'd had someone else to share this moment with, like my mother or even Shelia or Kell, but I had refused to tell my brother about my relationship with Roland, and even if I'd told Shelia, she wouldn't have been able to drop everything to come be with me. We were going to get married that follow-ing weekend.

Before I knew it, the weekend had come and as Roland said, our wedding ceremony was very simple. It was only us and a pastor named Reverend Taylor, a kind, older Black man with russet skin and graying hair. Dylan was also there, as well as a woman who I came to know as Yadira, who was Roland's personal chef and part-time housekeeper of eight years. She was nice, didn't really talk unless spoken to. Roland's mother was there via FaceTime. She didn't smile much, and I had a feeling that I didn't need to take that personally. His first wife died three years ago and he was getting married again to a woman he'd only known for half a year. She probably thought it was too soon for us.

These weren't the people I knew, but it was a great night. We kissed hard after our I do's and drank champagne under the pergola with a hot fire going. We filled up on rotisserie chicken wings, baked macaroni, and hors d'oeuvres, and it was a romantic evening, all things considered.

Roland allowed me to hire a local wedding photographer to capture our special moments, and once it was all said and done and the night had stretched to day, we went up to the bedroom I could officially call ours and made the sweetest love as husband and wife.

But, despite having such a great night, my mind constantly reverted back to one little thing.

Melanie's old shed. What all was in there? And why did I care so much to find out?

CHAPTER NINETEEN

For our honeymoon, we didn't go far. It was a good thing we'd had a winter wedding because we were able to stay local and visit a ski resort close by. The resort was nice and cozy and though I didn't know how to ski, Roland assisted me. We had an amazing time and shared some incredible meals, but the trip was almost ruined when a group of people recognized him and started taking pictures of us. We decided to spend the rest of our honeymoon in a cabin, far away from anyone else.

Before I knew it, we were riding back home in his SUV, the heat cranked up and blasting on us as snow flurries fell down from the gray sky.

"I could really get used to this," I sighed.

"Oh yeah?"

"Yeah. I mean, at first I didn't think I'd like the snow but I actually really love it. It makes this part of the world seem pristine—majestic."

"That, I can agree with. I'm glad you like it here. Melanie didn't really care for snow."

I looked at him, the sharp angle of his nose and the stubble along his jawline and chin. "She didn't?"

"No. She didn't want to move here at all, at first. I met her in North Carolina."

"Oh. That's a long way."

"Yeah. She lived in Raleigh, so it didn't really snow much there."

"Well, how did you rope her into moving to Colorado with you?"

"It took a while, but she eventually decided that there wasn't much left for her there, so she moved with me right after we got married."

Wow. That sounded awfully familiar. So Melanie and I had something in common—well, other than marrying the same man. She left her hometown and everything else behind to be with him.

"But what about her sister?"

"What about her?" he asked quickly.

"Did her sister visit often?"

"Yeah. Sometimes."

I waited for him to say more but nothing came of it.

"Oh."

The car fell silent and I noticed his grip tighten around the steering wheel. My brows stitched together as I looked from his tight knuckles to his face. His eyes were ahead, focused, but there was a crease between his eyebrows. He was agitated.

When we got home, I took a hot shower, walked across the heated marble floors, and stared at my reflection in the mirror. I couldn't end up like Melanie—working in a shed, doing drugs, driving over cliffs. I wasn't sure what had possessed her to do any of that, but I knew for a fact that I needed a purpose. It was nice that Roland was taking care of me, and that we were in love, but I couldn't center all of myself around him. I needed to find something worth doing. Leave a mark of my own in this world. Now that I had his resources, I would take some of the opportunities.

I'd always wanted to get into graphic designing and drawing again. I had started school for it but never finished, just like I did everything else in my life. Sometimes I hated that about myself. This time, I wanted to fulfill one of my own dreams. Perhaps with a little assistance from Roland I could purchase an iPad and stylus pen, kickstart my passion again, and sell some prints. I wanted to create an Instagram account specifically for my designs and figured Kell could help me market it. He was very good at social media marketing—he had over twenty thousand followers on his personal account.

The thought of my brother made me pause during the middle of my skincare routine. I hadn't told him anything about my marriage. We'd kept in touch while I was secretly dating Roland, but I never spoke about my love life with him. If I had, he would have known I was talking to someone. He always sensed those things, and I would have found it extremely hard not to confess. When he asked me about work, I told him I'd found a simple retail job. He was proud of me . . . and I couldn't stand myself for betraying his trust.

I hadn't heard from him in about a week and a half. I assumed he was busy with his pregnant fiancée now, catering to her, trying to buy a home, and also adding more hours at his job to care for his soon-to-be bundle of joy. He traveled a lot too, so I was sure he was busy.

I was going to tell him . . . I just had to give it time—prove to him that Roland and I were okay. I wanted to give our marriage half a year before telling Kell, then he'd see that Roland was good. That I was happy.

I opened the drawer to look for my toner and shuffled around for cotton pads. My finger landed on something cold and hard and I picked it up.

It was a gold earring, a dangly one with the shape of a dove on the end. I blinked twice as I studied the earring, knowing damn well it wasn't mine. It had to be Melanie's . . .

I sighed, carrying it to a container on a shelf on the wall

and tossing it in there. Knowing her stuff was still lingering in this house, hiding in some of the nooks and crannies, was bothersome. His first wife was still lingering around, staking claim, not only of the home, but Roland too.

He loved Melanie. I could tell. It hurt him to talk about her and that pain cut him deep—so deep that I was sure when he felt it, his only wish was to see her again.

How the hell was I supposed to compete with that?

How was I supposed to be better than the wife before?

CHAPTER TWENTY

Last night I'd asked myself how I could be better than her. I figured the only way to become better was to actually *be* a wife. To me, it meant adding my own touch to the mansion, so I started shopping, in person and online. I had Dylan take me to the town to browse some furniture pieces at a local furniture store.

Whenever I had downtime, I'd sit in the den with a fire going and watch YouTube videos about renovations and interior design. There was one young woman I really liked named Evie King, who flipped houses, and I took a lot of home designing tips from her.

Roland didn't mind it. He liked giving me money to go out. He liked that I was settling in and making the house mine too.

Everything was going so smoothly for us . . . but I also wanted to feel accomplished with my own life, so I decided to bring my plan up to him.

"I was thinking . . . maybe I can clear out Melanie's things from the shed for you?" I couldn't even look at my husband as I put it out in the air. But I had been thinking quite a lot, and not only did I want to see what was in there (and possibly see if we had anything else in common), but I also wanted to renovate the shed and make it my own.

We were seated in the den in front of a fire with glasses of rum. Roland was sitting next to me on the leather sofa with a motivational book by T. D. Jakes in his hands.

"*You* want to clear it?" he asked, lowering the book.

"Yeah. Well, I remember you saying you tried to get her sister to get rid of some of it. Maybe I can go through and organize it to sell some of it and whatever money we get, we can donate to a charity she would have liked."

He stared at me blankly for several seconds before sighing and tucking a bookmark into the spine of his book. "I was going to get around to clearing it myself one day . . . just wasn't sure when. Plus, I still have money being donated to a charity she chose when she was still alive." He paused. "I kept the money going to honor her in a way."

"Wow. That's really sweet, Roland. And I get it about not having the chance to clear it yet. It's probably tough for you to go in there. That's why I don't mind doing it for you. I know how hard that might be for you, to go through everything that reminds you of her."

"Yeah." He dragged a palm over his face and then tossed his head back, resting it on the sofa. "I don't want you to do it if it'll make you uncomfortable."

"It wouldn't," I said, sliding closer to him and smiling. "I'm a big girl. I'll be fine."

His eyes shifted over to focus on me and he smiled.

"I also want to maybe make it over, if you think it's okay? Do a little renovating on it, make it a place of my own? I've been watching these videos by this really good renovator named Evie King. She's very detailed and I'm sure I could spruce the shed up."

"What would you use it for?" he asked.

"Well, I told you about how I'm really into drawing and

graphic designs. I could turn it into my own little space to work. I've already got my iPad, already have a laptop. I wouldn't call it a she-shed, though. I really don't like that title for it. Maybe I'll call it the *Samira Escape* or something."

He chuckled and opened his arms to me. "That is actually very fitting for you."

I moved between his long, toned arms, resting my head on his chest.

"Do whatever you want with the shed, Samira," he said, then kissed the top of my head. "Her stuff can't stay there forever. And I know you'll take care of it."

"I will."

CHAPTER TWENTY-ONE

I'd decided to wait until the weekend to go through the shed. It was still snowing, but the snow was slowing down over the weekend and the sun was making an appearance after several days of gray skies.

I asked Dylan if he could take me to town for supplies and he had no problem doing so.

"So why are we shopping for trash bags?" he asked when we got into the warmth of the store. He loosened his scarf, taking a look around as I went for a shopping cart.

"I'm clearing out Melanie's shed." I pushed the cart ahead and went to the aisle for the trash bags.

"Roland is okay with that?" Dylan asked, following behind me.

"Yeah." I shrugged. "He gave me permission. I'm gonna clear it out so that I can make it a working space for myself."

Dylan fidgeted at my side as I browsed the gallon-size bags.

"That's a lot of work. Should just burn the whole thing and be done with it," he said with a nervous laugh.

I glanced at him, but he was no longer looking at me. His

eyes were distant, looking past me at the end of the aisle, as if deep in thought.

When we got back to the mansion, Dylan left without coming inside, which I found surprising because he always came in to hang out a while and even ate with us sometimes. Roland was on a phone call anyway, so I kept my coat on, collected the bags, and stepped out of the sliding glass doors to get to the backyard patio. I was dressed in a chunky beige sweater, a scarf, leggings, and polka-dotted rain boots. I could see the shed from where I stood, the burgundy a stark contrast against the bare branches and distant green pines. It seemed so far away, and yet it was only a short walk. It was about thirty yards or so away from the mansion. I liked that it wasn't too close. It ensured privacy.

I left the deck, stepping onto the slush-like snow, feeling the warm rays of the sun beam down on me and caress my cold cheeks.

I made my way up the path toward the shed, my boots crunching on the pebbles. As I got closer to the shed, taking note of the naked tree branches and the ice droplets that clung to them, my heart started beating harder.

I swallowed and then drew in a breath, not stopping until I was right in front of the brown door. The gold doorknob was rusty, and the paint on the door had faded. There was a brown floor mat on the step with the words *I hope you brought wine.*

I took the step up onto the mat and clutched the door-knob. It was loose, jiggly. I gave it a light twist and it opened up right away. The door creaked loudly on its hinges, clearly not having been used in a long time. Stepping inside, I noticed the floors were made of hardwood. They were in great condition, which was wonderful news. Evie always said checking the floors was one of the most important things when renovating. Some floors had mold beneath, some had holes.

I stepped in and closed the door behind me, taking in the stacked boxes all over the room and on top of the L-shaped desk. There was a light green rolling chair in front of the desk with a coat of dust on it. Against the east wall was a built-in bookshelf full of books. The two windows were behind me, giving the inside of the shed ample light. Dust motes floated and drifted, some of them moving as I did. I looked up and there was a simple copper chandelier above me.

I smiled. This place wasn't so bad. She didn't seem to have much stuff—well, not as much as I'd originally thought. There had to have been at least fifteen boxes, big and small. I noticed a built-in heater near the wall by the shelves and walked between some of the boxes to turn it on. It roared to life and I waved a hand over the vents as cool air blew from it. When the air transitioned to heat I smiled again. I unwrapped my scarf, weaving my way through the boxes and hanging it on one of the built-in hooks by the door.

None of the boxes were labeled, which meant I was most likely going to have to sort everything out before making do with it.

I opened the box closest to me and inside it were dresses, skirts, and a few silk blouses. The box beneath contained the same thing. I checked the smaller boxes beside those and they also had clothes in them. A smaller box had jewelry, scarves, and purses. All of the boxes on the left were filled with clothes and jewelry. That was good to know, and clothes were easy to deal with and pretty simple to sell or donate.

I walked across the shed, checking one of the boxes to the right, and it was full of ivory shirts. I took one of the shirts out and there was a green dove on it. The dove drawing looked just like the earring I'd found in the bathroom drawer.

The tag inside the shirt said Lovey Dovey Raine Company. That was the name of Melanie's clothing line. I checked more of the shirts and they were all ivory with doves in a variety of colors. Jackets were in the next box with the dove logo on the heart of them.

I moved on to the boxes in front of the bookshelf. Books. Office supplies. Papers and documents were in a tan bin. I huffed a breath. This woman hadn't given me much to work with at all. This would be easy. Most, if not all of it could be donated or trashed. Auctioning it would cause too much trouble. Sure, I could have hired someone to take it all away and sell it, but what was the point when I could just drop it off at the nearest Goodwill or Salvation Army and be done with it? Roland clearly wasn't going to make use of any of it, and if Melanie's sister hadn't come by now, she clearly didn't want anything to do with it either.

I browsed the names of the books on the shelves. A lot of them were romance novels—mostly historical. There were some contemporary, and a handful of paranormal, but her taste was definitely in the historical. I guess we didn't have much in common in the reading department. I was more a contemporary romance reader.

The bottom shelf was blocked by boxes and I moved them out of the way, only to discover two rectangular green bins. I took one out, wiped off some of the dust, removed the lid, and then a gasp fell through my lips.

CHAPTER TWENTY-TWO

This bin was full of photos. A large stack. I took a handful out, placed the bin on top of a box, and shuffled through the pictures. All of them were of Melanie.

She smiled in a lot of the pictures. Some were taken of her eating dinner. Of her reading. Of her drinking. She wasn't doing much of anything in these photos. Sometimes she'd look at the camera and give a subtle smile. Sometimes she'd be looking away, focused on something else.

I switched out the stack in my hand for a new stack and shuffled through them. Melanie in the snow. Melanie sitting next to a fireplace. Melanie holding a glass of wine. Melanie eating a hotdog. *Weird.*

I kept flipping through, but the images had slowly stopped being so simple. Suddenly, Melanie was on a bed, dressed in only a bra and panties. Then Melanie had a shot glass in hand. The next photo she was drinking from the shot glass. Next, she was laughing as she refilled her glass.

In the following photo Melanie stood on a terrace with no bra, only lacy green panties, with her arms thrown in the air, as if she was screaming *"Hey, world! Look at me!"* The next, she was facing the camera, shirtless, biting into her bottom lip, her eyes lazy and seductive as she cupped her full breasts in hand. A necklace hung around her neck with a dove on the end—the same dove as the earring and the one on her designer shirts.

I stared at that image the longest. The way she bit her lip, the way she stared into the camera. For the longest time, I had this image of her in my head of being this quiet, shy housewife who may have been looking for a good time but got caught up with the wrong crowd, but I was wrong about her.

There was more to her—more to *this*. Roland said she drank, but did she drink all the time, or was it occasional? She seemed awfully comfortable being drunk in front of the camera, as if she'd done this sort of thing many times before. She had to be taking these pictures with Roland and he was her husband then, so that was fine, but why was my heart racing again? Why did these photos suddenly *concern* me? Was it because I didn't know my husband had this side to him? Or was it because ever since being with him, not once had I seen Roland pick up or use a camera? Not even on his phone.

I took a look around the shed, at all of her things that surrounded me, and I felt claustrophobic. Stuffing the images back into the box, I closed it with the lid, picked up my scarf from the hook, and left the shed as quickly as possible.

CHAPTER TWENTY-THREE

I didn't tell Roland about the images I'd found, but he could tell something was bothering me as he cooked for me that night.

As we ate dinner, he asked me what was on my mind, and I told him that I was fine, that nothing was wrong. He brushed it off and spoke of one of his contacts wanting him to sign golf cleats soon for a children's charity he'd donated to, and my mind kept going back to that photo of Melanie. Her breasts cupped in hand. The lip bite. The crimson lipstick. The dove necklace.

"Babe?" Roland called and I looked from my untouched food to him. "You okay?" he asked.

I forced a smile. "Yeah, I'm fine, babe." I forced myself to take a bite of the fish to satisfy him.

When we were in bed, I couldn't sleep. Roland had practically fallen asleep as soon as his head hit the pillow. I stared at him a while as the milky light of the moon cast its glow through the slits in the curtains. What was he not telling me about Melanie? About his marriage with her?

I looked from him to the ceiling fan. It wasn't on, but I

imagined it spinning, spinning, spinning . . . and then I imagined lacy green panties. A red lipstick print on the blade of the fan.

I closed my eyes. Rolled onto my side, my back to my husband.

I was overthinking this. Melanie died by accident. Roland was a good man. Everything was perfectly fine.

Everything was *not* fine.

I needed to go back to that shed. I'd walked out and felt like things were left unfinished, plus I needed the shed for my own personal use. Those photos were just photos. That's what I'd told myself so I could fall asleep the night before, but now that it was daytime again and I was roaming the halls of the mansion—halls Melanie used to roam too—I had this unsettling feeling rooted deep in my gut. A knot had formed and was so big I couldn't eat.

"Are you not hungry, Mrs. Graham?"

I blinked twice and looked up. Yadira was on the other side of the table, giving me a concerned look. "Roland told me you like rolled oats, that's why I made it, but I understand if you don't like it. Is there too much cinnamon?"

"No—no, Yadira. It's not that at all. I'm sorry. I'm just a little exhausted. I didn't sleep well last night. And please, I told you to call me Samira. Seriously. Mrs. Graham is way too formal."

Yadira laughed. "Okay, *Samira*, well, you know I have a tea for that? For a good night's rest? It's a very soothing caramel blend. I can leave you a canister behind for tonight if you want it." I watched her walk to the stove and stir something in a silver pot.

Yadira was a gorgeous woman with natural ebony hair and skin like Jhené Aiko. She was tall too—almost the same height as Roland. She honestly could have passed for a model and I'd told her that the night I got married (because I was drunk and loose tongued) and she told me she was too nervous to model because of the gap between her two front teeth. I told her she was ridiculous, that her gap made her all the more unique and beautiful.

"I'd love the tea. Thank you." I dug into my oats, which were actually *very* tasty, but I only had three bites before I scraped the rest out and took the bowl to the sink.

"Any requests for lunch?" Yadira asked, taking out a bundle of carrots from the fridge.

"Whatever you want to make me. I'm not picky."

"You got it."

I left the kitchen after grabbing a bottle of water and went to the mudroom to put my boots on. I grabbed my olive-green trench coat, a scarf, and then went back to the kitchen, heading for the sliding doors. "If Roland comes back before I get in, can you tell him I'm in the shed?"

Yadira stopped cutting the carrots and snapped her eyes up at me. "The shed?"

I paused with my hand above the door handle. "Yes, the shed. Why? Is something wrong?"

"No—no. Of course not." She went back to chopping carrots. Her shoulders were tense now, her lips pursing.

"I feel like you're not telling me something." I watched as she kept her eyes down, avoiding mine completely.

"I guess I'm just surprised Roland is letting you in there. The only person he's let in there is his mother. I helped her out for a day or two. She straightened things in there for him, offered to throw it all out a couple years ago, but he told her no." She side-eyed me quickly before looking away again. "Guess he wasn't ready to let it go then."

"I see."

Yadira's gaze lifted to meet mine. "He is very happy with you. It's nice to see him like this."

"Yeah." I smiled, and then turned away to slide the door open. I thought it strange the way she tensed about the shed . . . but then I figured maybe talking about Melanie was a touchy subject for her too. She was here when Melanie was. Surely all of this change must have been a little weird for her—serving one wife and now another.

CHAPTER TWENTY-FOUR

I separated all of the clothes by category. Dresses in one pile, blouses in another. Jewelry in one box, and scarves in an empty bin. I figured I'd take all of the clothes to town, sell what I could and donate the rest. The jewelry looked expensive and I was tempted to keep some of it, but it was enough taking her shed. I didn't want to take anything else, let alone walk around in her hand-me-downs for Roland to remember her by.

As I cleared everything and revealed more and more of the built-in desk, my eyes kept wandering to the bin of photos. I had no idea what I was going to do with those. Throw them away, perhaps? Burn them? If Roland knew about them, he would have kept them, right? They seemed very private. Also, if Yadira and his mother were here and had organized things for him, they had to have come across the photos too. Did his mother ask her son about them? Or did they both do what I did and pretend they never saw them?

I brushed all of the thoughts away, sliding the boxes to one side of the room and then going to the bookshelf to take down books I most likely wouldn't read and could donate. A room without books was a room without a soul, so yes, I'd keep some of them on the shelf. No point in hauling them all away.

When I reached the fourth shelf, I noticed there was a collection of black books, all neatly lined up. They probably wouldn't have caught my attention if they'd had words on the spine, but none of them did. They only had numbers on the bottom of the spine, ranging from one to six.

I placed the books I was holding down on the floor and pulled out the book with the number "1" engraved on the spine in gold. The journals were thick, with hard covers, and on the front was the word *Confessions* embedded in a thread-like gold font. I opened it to the first page and there was a note.

This journal belongs to Melanie Raine.

Oh, shit.

I flipped through the pages quickly and each one was filled with words, all seemingly handwritten by her.

Something in the back of my mind screamed for me to close it and throw it away, burn it along with the photos, but I couldn't bring myself to do it. I read the first line—*When did everything between me and Roland go wrong?*—and then the next line, and then I sat in the dusty green chair, and kept reading.

Before I knew it, I was completely riveted.

CHAPTER TWENTY-FIVE

When did everything between me and Roland go wrong? I've been asking myself this a lot lately. I used to be so in love, so happy. But now my marriage is in shambles and I cry every night. I miss the old me—the old us. But then I think . . . maybe there was never really an old me. Maybe I've always been this way, and so has he.

Funny enough, I still remember the moment I fell in love with him. It was May 12th, 2015, and I was working the front counter at Bailor Golf Club. I'd gotten the job by luck, courtesy of an ex-boyfriend of mine, and I couldn't stand it, only because my manager was an overbearing asshole and the polyester uniform was itchy. But it paid well, and I didn't have anywhere else to work, so this was fine for now.

It was the weekend of an all-star golfing tournament. The hotel was busy and full of guests, and all staff were on duty. I'd been checking people in all day and eventually they'd all become a blur of features—big eyes, little eyes, bulbous noses, thin noses, dry lips, glossy lips—but then he showed up. Roland Graham. And of course, if he'd caught my eye, he had to have stood out amongst the crowd.

The first thing I noticed about him were his looks. What woman wouldn't have? He was extremely handsome—one of those rare people with a rather proportionate face—but I could tell he was very modest about his looks. He didn't walk around with a boastful air like some men did. He exuded confidence, yes, but there was a slight dip in his chin, and his eyes wandered. He kept his head down but his eyes vigilant.

He walked right up to the counter, said his name, and I checked him in. While I did, I snuck a glance at his fingers. No wedding band. That was a surprise.

"You'll be in room 1303, Mr. Graham."

"Oh, come on now," he said, sliding his credit card into his wallet. "Mr. Graham was my grandfather. Call me Roland."

I laughed. "I'm almost certain every man has used that line—Mr. So-and-So is my father slash grandfather."

"I believe that's because thirty-year-olds don't want to be called mister." He smirked and cocked his head at me.

And I remember saying something along the lines of, "Okay, then. Mr. Roland. Enjoy your stay, and good luck in the tournament." I smiled way too hard and he laughed, clearly amused.

His smile was easygoing as he turned away with his rolling suitcase. I watched him go, and as I did I remembered something a friend in the past said to me: "If a man looks back when you meet him, he's interested."

And sure enough, as Roland stood in front of the elevator and waited, he peered over his shoulder at me. Our eyes connected, his a beautiful hazel pool that I could have stared into all day, and then the elevator doors parted open for him.

I worked all weekend, and just so happened to bump into him several times inside the hotel. I'd see him at breakfast, eating grapefruit and oatmeal, or he'd pass by the front desk as he spoke to some of the guests of the tournament, but not without swinging his eyes over to me as he did it.

Sometimes he'd call the front desk, which I assumed was on purpose, and request extra linens. I would pretend to be professional, and he'd thank me in his warm voice, and I'd hang up with a smile that I couldn't push away.

Eventually, with all of our running into each other, he asked me out. He wanted to take me to dinner after he won—which he was sure he would do—and had asked me just as I was wrapping up my shift for the night. He'd caught me about to leave the hotel, my purse strapped around me and my work jacket folded over my forearm.

"You're a smug bastard, aren't you?" I teased in response to his bragging about winning.

He laughed in return, looking me in the eyes. "I will win."

"How are you so sure?"

"Because I'm that good."

"So cocky."

"Wanna bet on it?"

"Depends on what we're betting."

"Dinner," he said. "I win, and you have to come out to dinner with me after the tournament."

"Okay." I grinned. "And if you lose?"

He collected his bag of golf clubs. "I won't."

His confidence was delicious. I swallowed it down like fine wine, absorbed the encounter in my mind to replay for the rest of the night.

And sure enough, he did win. And when he did, he didn't wait around to take pictures, didn't stop to talk or speak or celebrate with his peers. He came straight back to the hotel, found me fixing the display table, and spun me around with his trophy in hand. And then he said, "Told you I'd win." And he kissed me. Just like that. Right in front of every person who'd watched him play, every sports journalist (because they'd all followed him inside too), every staff member.

And that's when I fell in love with him. He was so bold. So daring. So confident. So . . . perfect. And he was one hell of a kisser. That night, he took me to dinner and used his prize money on me.

And then the tournament was over, and he had to go home.

His home . . . all the way in Colorado.

CHAPTER TWENTY-SIX

I slapped the journal closed.

"No, Samira. No." I shook my head and stood. *No.* This journal was personal. She was writing about her marriage . . . about *Roland.* This was clearly sacred.

But I had so many questions. Why was she asking when her marriage went wrong? How could it have gone wrong? They were happy and in love. He loved her and she loved him, right?

I looked down at the front cover of the journal, then my eyes lifted to the bookshelf. I took down the rest of the journals, and all of them had her name and were numbered on the spine.

She had these journals made specifically so she could write in them about her marriage. Why? Who did something like that?

Did she want to share these one day? Was she writing a personal memoir? Roland told me she liked to write but never told me she was writing anything like this. So what the hell was she going to do with these? And why were they in the shed? Had Roland read them? Had his mother? Had *anyone?*

★ ★ ★

Later that night, as I washed my face and brushed my teeth, I watched Roland shuffle about in the walk-in closet. He pulled down a pair of plaid blue pajama pants and yawned, and I finished up just as he walked out of the closet.

I sat on the edge of my side of the bed as he did his and rubbed lotion on my arms and legs. While tucking my hair into my bonnet, I thought about how to approach him about what I'd found without upsetting him.

"Melanie liked to read," I said, and I felt so stupid saying it. Lots of people liked to read. I liked reading. Roland liked reading. He was about to read a book right now, his back against the headboard and a pair of reading glasses on the bridge of his nose. It was too late to retract the statement.

I looked over and noticed him pause, his book halfway open.

"She has a lot of books in the shed," I added.

"Yeah. She was a voracious reader."

"I can tell. She has a nice collection. The used bookstores will feel like they've won a jackpot when I donate them."

"Hmm." He smiled, but it didn't reach his eyes. He opened his book to the bookmarked page.

"Do you know if she wrote often too?"

"Wrote?" He was scanning the page. "Well, I know she used to write in some kind of journal, but from what she used to tell me, she never wrote anything too serious in them. Mostly just about her day, I guess. How she was feeling. Her therapist had her writing in it every day."

"Her therapist?"

"Yes." Roland lowered the book. "Why so many questions about her tonight?"

"I'm just asking," I countered quickly. "I've been clearing her things out and noticing by what she owned that we would have had a lot in common."

Roland studied my face, then he sighed and closed his book, placing it on the nightstand. "Come here." He opened his arms to me and I crawled across the bed and onto his lap. I draped my arms around his shoulders and smiled down at him as he looked up at me.

"Are you having second thoughts about clearing the shed? If so, I can build you a new one."

I laughed. "Don't be silly. That one is fine. I just can't wait to use it."

"So just toss all that stuff then." He kissed my lips. "It meant something to me before to have it there, but I realize now that it's just stuff. I have no use for any of it."

"Yeah."

He kissed me again.

"I just want to be careful with it. Take my time. Maybe I'll find something that you actually might need. I saw a couple business documents in there. Never know when they might come in handy."

"Well, bring those in and we can go through them together." He ran his palm down the curve of my back. "Samira, I don't want you to feel out of place here. This house is yours just as much as it is mine. You don't have to tiptoe around me or be afraid to ask for what you want. She's not here anymore so . . ." He swallowed hard and looked away.

I cupped his face in my hands and brought his eyes back to mine again. "I know, baby." Then I kissed him. "This is all just so new to me. I've never stayed in a place like this before—a place with *so much*. But I'm warming up to it."

He gave me a crooked smile, then he flipped me onto my back and kissed me deep, and I laughed as he moved between my legs.

In a matter of seconds, all thoughts of Melanie had faded, and I was his.

CHAPTER TWENTY-SEVEN

I didn't see the harm in reading the journals. Surely, if they were still in there, it was fine. It wasn't like my reading them was going to change much of anything anyway. She was gone now. It wasn't like she could just pop up and shout at me for it . . . but I suppose she could haunt me in a way if she wanted to.

Still, the fact that Melanie had to ask herself when everything went wrong . . . that didn't sit well with me at all. Roland was suspected of murder as a result of her death. What if things *did* go wrong? What if, somehow, Roland was the reason Melanie drove off that cliff?

He may not have actually murdered her—that I believed—but what if he led her to suicide?

It was ridiculous to think . . . and yet I needed to know.

So back to the shed I went the following day, pulling down journal number one again and picking up where I left off.

CHAPTER TWENTY-EIGHT

I didn't know when I'd see Roland again after the tournament, but I had his number and he had assured me before leaving North Carolina that he would text and call me often. He was going to be in Colorado for a week and a half and then back to traveling again for another tournament.

At this time, Roland was a rising star. Everyone wanted their hands on him and he was getting personally invited to golfing competitions now. He really was that good. They called him the next Tiger Woods. The King of the Green.

I had no idea when he was ever going to make time for me. With all that fame, it was bound to go to his head, so I didn't take him or our dating life that seriously, and yet . . . he kept calling. Kept texting. And then he started making surprise visits.

We'd spend weekends together getting to know one another, drinking, eating, having sex, and doing it all over again. I was falling for this man hard and I couldn't stop myself, no matter how much I tried.

I'd fallen in love before and it was ugly and cruel and I vowed to never do it again, but Roland swindled me. He got to me. I really had fallen in love with him, so I don't think it came as much of a surprise to either of us when we both agreed to run off to Vegas and get married four months later. It was so cliché, and Roland had only invited his mother, a cousin, and a few close friends, but it was so damn romantic and the wedding ceremony was one I will never forget.

In Vegas, we gambled, drank, made love in a honeymoon suite. Then, suddenly I'd found myself quitting my job at Bailor to travel the country with him and watch him play.

And, not long after, my husband became an A-list star and there were more and more cameras around him—around us—and the privacy we had before quickly disappeared. But it was fine. We had nothing to hide. We were in love, he was insanely talented, and I was his loyal trophy wife who stuck by his side and cheered him on.

For almost two years, we were in bliss. I'd moved with him to Colorado, we built a mansion in Sageburg, I took care of the home, hired a housekeeper/chef, and had dinners ready for him when he returned home from his trips. I wanted to be the perfect wife who carried no guilt and had nothing but good intentions for her marriage.

Everything was going wonderfully . . . until my sister called.

CHAPTER TWENTY-NINE

Miley is my sister . . . and she has issues. A lot of them.

I wasn't expecting her to call me—I hadn't heard from her in months—so when her name popped up on my screen, I froze. I was in the middle of prepping myself some tea, about to head off to my Pilates class, when I saw it.

The last time I'd seen Miley, she'd thrown a china plate at me and screamed at the top of her lungs until I was left with no choice but to run out of my own apartment crying.

She only called when she wanted something, so I didn't answer. I ignored it, finished making my tea, and went to class.

But during all of class and even on my drive back home, I couldn't stop thinking about her call. And not only that, she'd left a voicemail. I hadn't listened to it, too worried that she was only calling to deliver bad news.

When I got home, Roland was at his range, prac-

ticing. I recall him coming into the bathroom as I was showering, and entering the shower with me.

"Hey, beautiful," he murmured on my lips.

"Hey." I forced a smile.

He tipped my chin and brought my eyes to his. "What's wrong?"

"Nothing," I responded, and then I smiled again, laced my arms around the back of his neck, and kissed him.

Making love with him was a temporary distraction, and thankfully he'd let it go. That was a mistake. I should have told him that very moment what was going on.

But . . . see, the thing was I hadn't told Roland about Miley yet. He had no idea I even had a sibling. Truth was, I was embarrassed to claim Miley as my sister and if I'd told him about her, he would have wanted to meet her. I couldn't have that. Because Miley would have taken one look at Roland and ruined everything good that we had.

Miley called for seven days straight. Each day, she left a voicemail, and on the seventh day, I finally cracked and listened to her messages:

Hey, sis! It's Miley! I thought I'd give you call, check in with you. I, um . . . I'm doing a lot better. I'd really love to see you. Call me back. Love you.

Hey, Mel. So, um . . . just checking to see if you got my first voicemail? I really need to talk to you.

Mel, please pick up. I promise you I'm better.

Melanie. I'm your fucking sister. Answer me! I know you're getting my calls!

So, guess what? I'm on your Facebook page right now and I can't believe I had to find out through a social media app that you got *married*! What the fuck, Mel? This is not like you. I see he golfs. Didn't know you were into golfers too but whatever. He's older? He looks older. Anyway, call me back. I need to talk to you.

Mel, if you don't call me back, I don't know what I'll do. I need you. Call me back please!

All right, you know what? Fine. I see how it is. You run off and get married to some rich fucker and forget where you come from. Cool. Just know if I do something crazy, it's because my sister didn't answer her goddamn phone. So much for family.

After listening to her last message, I sighed and went to her number. My finger hovered over her name, and I don't know why I felt a sudden wave of dread, but it struck me hard.

Still . . . I called back. And I regret that I ever did.

CHAPTER THIRTY

A *week later and my sister was in Colorado. My husband was away for work in Florida, so I had the mansion all to myself.*

I waited in front of the door outside the house, watching my sister climb out of a yellow taxi with a dent in the front passenger door. She waved and I waved back. Then she walked up to me, the handle of a suitcase on wheels clutched in one of her hands, and hugged me tight.

"I missed you so much," she sighed over my shoulder.

"Yeah. Missed you too."

I told her that she could only stay one night in the mansion, and she relished in that. She ventured around the place, taking in every nook and cranny. She gaped over the kitchen and the firepit in the back. The den and how I'd furnished it, and even the relaxation room that I'd set up so Roland could de-stress during his breaks between golfing. She was in complete awe.

"So, this golfer guy is legit?" she asked.

"*Depends on what you mean by legit,*" *I said with my back to her, fixing us both tea in the kitchen.*

"*I mean . . . like, he's got money, right? You have money.*"

I sighed and turned with the tea tray, carrying it to the table. "*I don't see why that matters, Miley.*"

"*I'm just asking.*" *She grinned and watched me pour the tea. When I was done, I slid a teacup over to her on a saucer.*

"*Bitch, this is fancy!*"

I huffed a laugh. "*It's just a tea set.*"

"*You remember when we used to beg Momma for tea sets. Bitch hated us.*"

I lifted my chin and cleared my throat, picking up my teacup and sitting in the seat across from her. I was not in the mood to talk about Momma. "*I'm glad to see you're better,*" *I remember saying.*

"*Oh, yeah. Much better.*" *She sipped her tea, then placed it down. Then she started tapping her knuckles on the tabletop. She was jittery that way—could never be still. I always told Momma that I thought she had ADHD, but she never took her to get an official diagnosis. She didn't believe in any of that stuff. She always called mental health issues and crises "bullshit."*

"*So why are you here?*"

"*Ah. The million-dollar question.*" *She always made everything a joke and it irritated the hell out of me.* "*I need a place to stay,*" *she said and I frowned.*

"*Where were you staying before?*"

"*With a friend from the clinic. He told me I could stay with him until I found a place.*"

"*Hmm.*"

"*'Hmm'? What does that mean?*" *She flashed a*

smile. *I couldn't help noticing her smile wasn't as innocent as it used to be. It was strained, sad.*

"I don't have a place for you to stay, Miley."

"What?" she scoffed, then she looked around the mansion and then back at me as if I was an idiot. "You literally have a whole fucking mansion, Mel!"

"Yes, but it's not just my mansion."

"Okay . . . then just ask your little husband if I can stay."

"No, Miley, I can't just spring something like this on him."

"Why the hell not? I'm sure he wouldn't have a problem with you letting your only sister and sibling stay with you for a couple weeks."

I immediately looked away and folded my arms defensively.

"Oh. Oh wow!"

My eyes slid back over to hers. Her jaw had dropped, her brown eyes wider. "You haven't told him about me, have you?"

"Miley, it's not that—"

"Yes, it is! You're so ashamed of me that you haven't even told your husband about me. Wow. Do you realize how fucked up that is?" She pushed back in her chair, the legs of it scraping the marble floor, and glared down at me.

"See, this is why I didn't tell him about you! Because you blow everything out of proportion!"

"Oh, what the fuck ever." She stormed out of the kitchen.

"And what are you gonna do now, huh?" I asked, chasing after her. I found her in the mudroom, stuffing her arms into her coat. "You gonna scream and run off and throw a fucking tantrum like you always do?"

"No—I'm just going to run off and be fucking homeless, Mel! That's what I'll fucking do!"

"As if I'll let you be homeless, Miley! Miley—just stop!" I caught her by the elbow before she could turn away, and gripped her upper arms. *"Look at me!"*

She breathed hard through her nostrils, staring me in the eyes. Sometimes I hated how alike we looked, because I saw that anger on her face and knew that was what I looked like when I got angry. Or sad. Or hurt.

"I'm not going to let you be homeless. But I also can't let you stay here. I just . . . I can't, okay? Things are good here. I don't want to risk or ruin anything that I have going on."

"Why? Because you don't trust me?"

"Actually, no, I don't."

She grimaced and snatched her arms out of my hands. *"Fuck this."*

I grabbed her again. *"I'll rent out an apartment for you instead."*

That caught her attention. She lifted her gaze back up to mine, the anger transforming to confusion.

"It'll be close by and I'll check on you every single day, but I swear to God if you fuck up even once, Miley, I will cut you off. Do you understand? I will kick you out and send you back to North Carolina so fast."

"I won't fuck up," she countered quickly, and a smile formed on her lips. *"I told you I'm better. I'm so much better. I just need some help getting on my feet. That's all."*

I nodded, wanting to believe her, but feeling in my gut that she'd fuck this up one way or another.

Even so, I did what any good sister would do. I helped Miley get back on her feet. We found an apartment within the next two days, a studio with a mountain view.

For ten weeks, Miley was great. She'd found a job in town, paid all the bills except the rent, which I took care of for her, as it was kind of steep.

And as promised I checked on her every single day, but I didn't tell Roland about it. Nor had I told him I even had a sister in town. Or about the apartment I purchased for her. None of it.

That was another mistake.

CHAPTER THIRTY-ONE

I couldn't help it. After the way the first journal ended, I took the second journal with me into the mansion. I hid it under the sofa in the room Roland called the relaxation room—the room I just found out was created by Melanie. It was a room where he came to unwind, meditate, and practice yoga, though since I'd moved in, I hardly saw him in there. That was a good thing because if he wasn't going to use it, I definitely was.

A navy-blue suede sofa was perched against the wall across from the door, a Moroccan theme going with rugs and wall decor I didn't care for, but there was something about the room that was relaxing in itself. Maybe it was the candles and the diffuser that automatically turned on when a person entered the room, pumping out eucalyptus in the morning or lavender at night, or maybe it was the oversized floor pillows that I didn't mind sitting on.

Whatever it was, it was the perfect hideout. I had no idea if Roland knew about the journals, and I couldn't read them in plain sight. I hated that I was even hiding it from him, but as I said before, there was a niggling at my conscience, something telling me to keep this little piece of discovery to myself for now, so I did.

After dinner with him, we went up to bed. He curled his large body around me, spooning me from behind and I sighed, clinging to his hand.

"I love you," he rasped in my ear.

"Love you more," I said back. But would a wife who loved her husband hide the fact that she was reading his dead wife's journals?

I worried that he'd throw them away if he saw them and I'd never get to finish them. Or maybe I worried that he'd look at me differently for having read any of it at all.

Either way, it was too late to go back now, and as he fell asleep, I kept that in mind. *Too late to turn back now. Too late to turn back now.*

At two in the morning, Roland had rolled over to the other side of the bed, lightly snoring, and I climbed out of it, making my way to the relaxation room.

CHAPTER THIRTY-TWO

*R*oland began to look at me funny around Miley's third month in Sageburg, which was right around the time I was planning on having a dinner so that he could meet her. I remember the conversation going something like this . . .

"Why are you looking at me like that?" I asked him as we ate breakfast. I had looked up and he was staring at me, head cocked, hazel eyes slightly narrowed.

"Like what?"

"Like I have something on my face," I said, then laughed as I wiped my cheek.

"Nothing's on your face. But clearly there's a lot on your mind."

"What do you mean?"

Then I remember him saying, "I feel like you aren't telling me something, Mel."

"What?" I asked, ignoring the tugging in my gut.

"I checked your bank statements." He placed his fork down.

"Okay?"

"And it says you've been making monthly payments to Stone Creek Apartments. Wanna tell me about that?"

I didn't think he'd look through my bank statements. Roland and I had separate accounts, but he still had full access to mine, as I did his. We just liked it that way. He'd transfer money into my account and that was that. I never felt the need to check his transactions unless it came down to taxes or to inform Jeff, our accountant, about something, and he never asked about or checked mine either . . . until now.

"I'm going to ask this as calmly as possible, and I want you to be honest with me, Mel. You've been so absent lately, coming home late, not answering your phone, and whenever you do, you always sound like you're too busy to talk to me." He inhaled before exhaling and I braced myself for the backlash. If he'd gone through my transactions, surely he'd found out about Miley. *"Are you cheating on me?"*

"What?" I stared at him, flabbergasted. *"Cheating on you—Roland, what kind of question is that? How could you think that?"*

"Well, it would explain all of what's been going on with you lately," he snapped, and his jaw clenched.

"I—what? No—I am not cheating on you! Why would I ever do that?"

He looked down at his plate. *"I don't know,"* he mumbled. Then he peered back up. *"That's why I'm asking. I know I'm not home much. And sometimes I have issues communicating . . ."*

"Baby, no." I pushed out of my chair and walked around the table to sit on his lap. "Are you kidding me? No."

"So, then what is it, Mel? I feel like you aren't here with me anymore—that your mind is somewhere else."

I sighed as he tightened his arms around me. "I . . ." I studied his face—his hazel eyes. I had to tell him . . . but telling him was going to make my unstable world collide with my secure world and the thought of it already gave me anxiety.

But he was my husband and I didn't want him having any doubts about our marriage or have him thinking I was having an affair, so I told him all about Miley and how she'd first come to Sageburg to visit while he was away for a work trip. I told him about the apartment I'd bought her and how I visited her every day and during some nights. It all made sense to him, but of course he asked, "Why didn't you just tell me all of this in the beginning?"

"Because, Roland, my sister . . . she's not okay. I mean, she has a fun personality, but she has a lot of problems. She's very unstable."

"Wow. Didn't even know you had a sister. What else are you hiding from me?" he asked jokingly.

"Nothing." I smiled, wrapping my arms around his shoulders.

"I'd like to meet her."

I figured that was coming too. "That can be arranged."

"Okay." He smiled, but the smile didn't meet his eyes. It was almost like he still didn't believe me about Miley—that he needed confirmation with her physical presence.

"I'll have Yadira make us a dinner," I said. "But

I'm warning you, Roland. Miley has no filter. And she knows you have a lot of money, so don't let her throw any kind of pity stories at you to feed into them. She has an addiction problem. Before she came here she was in and out of rehab. She seems better now, but . . . I have a feeling it won't last."

"Ah. Have a little faith." He grabbed my chin and smiled at me. "And I know how to handle an addict. My father? Remember?"

"Yeah." I got off his lap and he stood, carrying his plate to the sink.

"I'm gonna go practice for a little. Dinner tonight?" he asked, on his way to the mudroom.

"Yeah. Tonight."

The following night, I told Yadira to hide the valuables and anything that could be pawned or sold. I know it was extreme, but I really couldn't trust my sister with things like this. She'd stolen from me before and it broke my heart. My mother had given Miley and me matching gold necklaces. It was the only thing my mother had ever given us that meant something to me, and that said a lot considering I practically hated my mother. She'd put me through a lot of shit, but that necklace had been given to me on one of our mom's good days and it meant something to me. I cherished it. Miley took mine and sold both necklaces for a baggie of coke. I still haven't completely forgiven her for that.

As I was coming down the stairs, I heard the doorbell ring, then checked my wristwatch. It wasn't time yet, and Miley wasn't the type to show early for anything. I headed for the door, checked the camera, and saw a young Black man on the other side with his head down.

I cracked the door open, and realized he was

taller than I'd expected, and very familiar. He wore jeans and a black button-down shirt. His hair was cut low and wavy, his skin like brown suede.

"Hi. Dylan, right?" I asked when his eyes found mine. "What are you doing here?"

"Dylan!" Roland's voice boomed through the hallway. I looked back and Roland was hustling down the steps. "He just got in town and I invited him over for dinner." He opened the door wider. "That okay?"

"Yeah, of course it's okay!" I looked from Roland to his cousin and smiled. "I remember you from the wedding! Come in!"

Roland had told me a lot about Dylan, and he was at the wedding but I really hadn't shared more than a few sentences with him before we ran off to our hotel for the night and then to our honeymoon the next day.

They were cousins, but more like brothers. Their bond was special, and I'd only seen one photo of them together that Roland showed me, back when they were teenagers. Dylan was a man now, grown and mature, looking nothing like the boy in the photo.

Dylan had always believed that Roland would make it, when no one else did. He supported him, sent him text messages every game to wish him luck. He was a good cousin, from what I gathered, and I was partially elated that he was there that night because it meant Roland would cut the evening short to show Dylan around and hang out with him. Which also meant less time for him to be around my mooching sister.

Dylan walked into the house and as he did, he pulled a bouquet of roses and baby's breath from behind his back and handed it to me. "I'm glad to know you're still treating my cuz well," he said, handing me the bouquet.

"Oh—wow. Thank you!" I took the flowers from him and he smiled down at me with perfect square teeth. "Yeah, he's a handful, but he's a great man." I smiled up at Roland and he gave me a close-lipped smile and a wink.

"Come on, let me show you around while we wait for Mel's sister." Roland clapped Dylan on the back and walked deeper into the mansion with him. "How was your drive?" I heard him ask as they turned the corner.

As I was putting the flowers in a vase, the doorbell rang again and I froze, knowing exactly who was at the door this time.

CHAPTER THIRTY-THREE

*M*iley was in jean capris with rips in the thighs and fishnet stockings underneath. She also wore a black leather jacket with a red T-shirt underneath that said F*ck Everything.

She was not presentable, but this was to be expected from my sister. And as expected, Roland looked at her oddly when introduced to her, and then at me, as if he were wondering how the hell we could have ever been related. Despite how alike we looked, I could understand. My sister and I are polar opposites. We dress different, act different. Our tastes in food, hobbies, and even self-care are different.

Dinner wasn't so bad to get through. Roland would ask a question and Miley would give a straight answer. Whenever Roland turned to ask Dylan something that was most likely golf related, Miley would look from her end of the table at me and smile, as if everything was going wonderfully. I'd smile back . . . but something told me things were going to get out of hand soon. If not that night, then eventually.

After dinner, Yadira brought out her infamous chocolate cake and we each ate a slice with a cup of espresso. We eventually moved to the den, where Roland had lit a fire. He and I sat side by side, while Dylan and Melanie took the stretched sofa opposite of us.

"So, you're Roland's cousin," Miley said, side-eyeing Dylan.

Dylan smirked with a small cup of espresso in hand. "That I am."

"Are you freeloading too?"

Dylan laughed at that and I fidgeted in my seat. Roland tightened his arm around me and I looked up. He was already looking down at me, giving me a look that said, "Everything's fine. Stop worrying."

I relaxed in my seat and had to take a sip from my wineglass to calm my nerves.

"I wouldn't say freeloading, but . . ." Dylan turned his head quickly to look at me, as if a thought had just occurred to him. "Melanie, I already spoke to Roland about this, but he told me I had to confirm it with you."

"Oh." I blinked twice, looking from him to Roland, then back at him again. "Okay?"

"I offered him a job," Roland said.

I looked up. "You did?"

"Yeah. He's going to be my new caddy."

"But what about Freddie?"

"I already let him go." Roland shrugged. "He's not much of a mentor and I need someone who can help me bring my A-game—someone who gets me. Dylan has always been that person for me."

"Oh."

"I'll also be helping out around your house, be a groundskeeper and all that," Dylan said, *and I turned my head to look at him.*

"You will?"

"Yeah." He hesitated, looking between Roland and me. *"It would be beneficial to both of you guys,"* he went on. *"I'd fix things around the house, run some errands for you, drive you anyplace you need to be if you don't ever feel like driving. I'll make sure Roland's golfing facility is maintained and that nothing around here goes awry. Caddy for him if he needs me to. Basically, I'd be the guy you two call if you ever need anything."*

"Oh. I see. So how much is the pay?"

"Well, that's the thing," said Roland. *"I wouldn't exactly pay him, just take care of his bills and whatnot. He'd also get a room here."*

"A room?" I blinked twice at my husband, stunned. *"Roland—I . . . um."* I had to think carefully before speaking. Who was I to reject this? This was Roland's mansion. He'd built it for us, yes, but it was the home he'd bought with his hard-earned money and though I was his wife, I was really just another occupant. My name wasn't on the mortgage or the bills. His was.

But still, I was his wife and I'd only just met his cousin and knew nothing about him. I didn't even want my own sister moving in with us, mostly for privacy reasons, but now this guy was? I understood they'd grown up together, but this was the first I was hearing about any of it. My eyes shifted over to Miley, who I thought would be upset, but she was amused by the conversation, smiling and sipping her espresso, waiting for me to speak again too.

"That sounds great," I said, and then I put on a smile that I hoped would show that I was okay with it. The men fell for it and Roland went straight into how excited he was to have Dylan be his new golf caddy, but as I sipped my wine and looked at my sister again, I recall her simply shaking her head and smirking.

Roland ran off with Dylan to one of the garages, which had been converted to Roland's entertainment room, where he played pool, watched sports, and other things. I was left with Miley, so I took her outside by the firepit. Since we were so far away from the city and on several acres of land, there weren't many lights around, which made the sky appear pitch-black, minus the twinkling stars and distant crescent moon. A slight chill was in the fall air so we wrapped up in thick sweaters and sipped more wine by the fire, sitting in silence.

For sisters, we often didn't have much to talk about. We were opposite in a lot of ways . . . and in the ways we were the same, well, they weren't exactly healthy, so we never discussed them.

"You don't want that guy to move in, do you?" Miley asked.

"No, I don't."

"So why not just tell Roland that?"

"I don't know. It's his house and that's his cousin. I don't think he has much."

"I didn't have much either."

"Yeah, but I gave you your own apartment."

"True." She shrugged, like she always does. "Roland should pick up some pointers and buy Dylan his own place too. Don't tell me he's one of those cheap-ass rich people."

I laughed. "He can be frugal. But I don't think that has anything to do with his cousin. He probably just wants him here so they can be close, especially if he's going to caddy for him."

"How long is he even going to stay?"

"I don't know."

"Hmm." Miley sipped from her glass. "Well, if Roland's cousin ever feels like he needs another place to live, I should probably tell him there's space at my apartment."

"What?" I laughed.

"Come on, Mel. You can't say he's not sexy."

I focused on the flames again, refusing to look at her. "I wasn't looking at him in that way."

"Yeah, fucking right. I mean, Roland is nice looking in the handsome, gentlemanly way, but his cousin is legit sexy. Like fuck me right now sexy."

I rolled my eyes. "You shouldn't even be worrying about that right now," I said, pointing at her.

"I'm just saying." She threw her hands in the air. "Hopefully he's single."

I wanted to laugh as she did, but I couldn't. Because once Miley showed interest in someone, she didn't leave it alone until she had the person. And this was Roland's cousin. He was going to be living with us, which meant Miley would try and come around more often than she needed to, just to find ways to bump into him.

I thought of them possibly hooking up—of the chaos it would cause with all of us under one roof. I was going to have to talk with Dylan about my sister as soon as possible.

CHAPTER THIRTY-FOUR

*D*rugs weren't the only thing Miley was addicted to.

She was also addicted to love. But when love fucked her over, she did everything in her power to numb herself and forget about it. That's why I had to talk to Dylan. But I didn't talk to him right away. I waited three weeks after he'd settled in.

It wasn't so bad with him around the house. Roland gave him the attic, which was a loft, practically built like a studio apartment. He stayed out of the way for the most part, only doing requested errands and work around the house, like painting rooms for us or moving new furniture around that I'd ordered for a particular room. He caddied for Roland on the course a couple times a week. He never complained, never griped, never made a face. He did all that was asked of him with a smile and a pep in his step, and I appreciated that.

So, to thank him, I set up brunch with Yadira in the sitting room that had the skylights and invited him by leaving a note taped to his door. He came on time, dressed in black jeans and a gray pullover hoodie.

"What's all this?" he asked, smiling as he studied the spread on the table between us.

"It's for you." I put on a smile. "I thought I'd thank you for how hard you've worked and, most of all, for putting a smile on Roland's face."

"Well, that's no problem."

I shifted my weight in my nude stilettos, then pointed at the ivory recliner next to him. "Sit, please. Join me."

He sat and looked at me for reassurance as he reached for a green china plate. I nodded and smiled, then reached for my own plate. I chose my good plates—the green ones were my favorite because green had recently become my new favorite color. Green represented new beginnings, peace, and harmony—all the things I wanted in life. After Dylan prepared his plate and placed it on the table between us, he slid to the edge of his seat and dug in.

"So how are you liking it here?" I asked.

"Oh, it's nice as hell," he said, chewing a slice of bacon. "It's like being on permanent vacation. I really appreciate you letting me stay, by the way. I know you and Roland just built this place and all and probably wanted more time alone in it."

"Don't worry about that. He's really happy you're here."

He stopped chewing and cocked his head only slightly. "Are you happy I'm here?"

"Doesn't matter how I feel."

"Of course it matters. Roland didn't run any of this by you. He kind of just sprung it on you, but I was under the impression that you two had at least spoken about it before I'd arrived."

I pressed my lips.

"Did he even tell you I was coming to visit?" he asked. "That he wanted me to caddy for him?"

"No, he didn't."

"Hmm. Guess he wanted to surprise you. Roland is all about surprises." Dylan flashed his perfect white teeth at me. That was probably what Miley was attracted to. His smile. He had a beautiful smile. Naturally straight, clearly took care of his teeth.

"You grew up in Colorado, right?"

"Denver," he said, nodding.

"Roland tells me you two were like brothers. What was that like?"

"He is like a brother to me. I have two sisters and one older brother. My brother is the second youngest but there's a big age gap between us, so we didn't grow up as close to each other as I'd hoped. Nine-year difference."

"Wow."

"But me and Roland hung out every weekend. Used to spend the night at each other's houses." His brown eyes flickered up from his plate to me. "I came here because my mother died."

"Oh—oh my God, Dylan. I'm so sorry." I pressed a hand over my heart.

"It's okay. And if you're wondering what from, lung cancer. She was bad about cigarettes. Told her so many times to quit," he said with a shrug and half a smile. "That was my mom though. Ready to gamble anything, even her own health."

I didn't know whether to smile with him or remain serious, so I didn't react at all.

"Roland heard the news and that's when we discussed me moving in with him and all that. I lived with her, but her house has a lot of debt that I can't

afford, so my oldest sister, Yvette, took it over. Basically kicked me out so she can try and clear the debt herself, renovate it, and then sell it."

"Oh. Well, it makes sense that Roland took you in then. He didn't tell me about your mother passing though."

"That's because I didn't tell him until a week ago. She passed almost two months ago. While she was sick, he had tournaments and was traveling and I didn't want to throw him off his game, ruin that big win for him."

"Wow. Well, that's considerate of you, but I'm sure he wouldn't have minded since you two were so close. He was close with your mom, right? Wasn't she his aunt?"

"She was his aunt, and no, they weren't really all that close. She always made stuff up about him—always said he acted like he was better than us, that his momma acted like she was better than her. His momma and mine had an on-going feud that I never understood. Mine always complained about Aunt Cathy, Roland's momma, and her real estate job—called her a lousy mother because she didn't stay home with her kid all day like she did." Dylan huffed a laugh. *"But my momma lived off government assistance and child support up until I was eighteen."*

"Wow. They didn't get along, huh?" I suddenly felt uncomfortable knowing this.

"Yep. Not sure when the feud started between them, but I do know that when Roland's talents started to shine through, matters only got worse with them. There came a point where she stopped letting Roland spend the night at my house and everything when we were in high school."

"Wow. That's horrible."

"Yeah. I'm surprised he hasn't told you any of this."

"Well, you know Roland. He likes to pretend everything is fine and dandy when really everything is shit."

We both laughed at that sad truth.

"Other than caddying for Roland, what else do you want to do?"

"Well, I talked with my sis a lot about starting up a renovation company. We're good at it. We could be like those people on HGTV who knock down walls and refurbish old houses—well, if we had enough money for it." He chuckled. "Before she kicked me out last minute, I was helping her fix up the place."

"So, you should get some of the money too, right? If she sells it?"

"Not exactly. My mom left the house in her name. She's the oldest, so she's calling all the shots."

"Oh."

Dylan's eyes narrowed and he looked me up and down in my jeans and blouse. "Something tells me you didn't just invite me in here to ask me about my family and what I want to do though."

"No, actually, I didn't."

He sat forward, elbows on his knees, and said, "Tell me what's on your mind."

"It's about my sister."

"Miley? Yeah, she seems cool in an I don't give a fuck kinda way."

"I guess so. It's just . . . she mentioned to me how she's attracted to you."

His eyebrows shot up. "Is she, now?"

"Yes. And I want to tell you that if she tries to

make any advances on you or anything, I would love it if you kindly show her you're not interested."

"Why is that?" he asked, his head cocking again. He was smiling, amused. I didn't like that smile. It was arrogant, like he demanded a challenge.

"Miley is an addict. If one bad thing happens in her life, or she feels like she's not worthy enough, she loses herself."

His smile rapidly faded. "Oh. Damn."

"Yeah, so I would really appreciate it if you did this for me. Especially if you aren't looking for anything serious right now, or don't think she's your type. She's not really the kind of woman who goes for one-night stands or quick hookups. She dives in headfirst and always has a hard time resurfacing."

"Right. I understand."

"She keeps calling me, asking if you're around. I have to tell her you're not, that you're busy."

"Mmm." He pressed his lips, then he said, "Melanie, I'm in your home, so I won't disrespect your wishes. You clearly know what's best for your sister, so I understand. If she advances or tries anything, I'll let her down gently. I promise."

"Okay." I sighed, relieved, and he smiled. Then, as we dug back into our brunch and the tension had faded, he asked something like, "So how did my corny-ass cousin end up getting you to marry him anyway?"

All seemed well with Dylan. He was a charming houseguest. I kept Miley away from the house unless absolutely necessary and whenever she did show, I'd text Dylan and tell him to either stay in the attic if he was home, or to stay out a little longer if he was away from the house so that Miley couldn't magically bump into him.

I felt bad about it, I did. Who was I to control what my sister wanted or to tell him what to do? I don't know. Maybe I was doing it for selfish reasons.

Or maybe, deep down, I knew Dylan was attracted to me from the first moment he saw me— and not Miley—and I liked that someone other than my husband found me attractive. Maybe I was fucked up for even thinking such a thing. Whatever it was, it didn't matter because it didn't last long.

Dylan could only hide from her for so long. Eventually the holidays arrived, and we all had no choice but to come together. Break bread. Drink wine. All that good stuff.

And that promise Dylan had made to me? He'd broken it just as quickly as he'd given it.

CHAPTER THIRTY-FIVE

"Samira?" Someone pounded on the shed door and I gasped, slapping the journal in my hand shut. I hopped up, shoving it into one of the boxes and then hurrying for the door.

Roland was on the other side, still dressed in his pajamas, along with a puffy black coat. Just behind him, the moon was wading its way through the fog, revealing a ground still peppered in snow.

"Hey," I breathed, holding the door halfway open. "What are you doing up?"

"Me? What the hell are you doing out here? I was looking for you all over the house."

"Sorry—I wanted to get an early start on clearing more of the stuff out."

"At three in the morning? Last I checked, you hate mornings. Samira, what the hell is going on? Why are you out here?"

I hesitated, unsure what to tell him. Last night, I left the bed and went to the relaxation room to read more of the second journal. But then I finished the second journal and it left me with more questions, so I went back to our bedroom and to the closet, changed into thermal pants and a sweater, and then hit the mudroom for my coat and boots.

I ended up in the shed, pulling down journal three to read more while sitting on the green desk chair.

"I'm sorry." I sighed. "I'll come back to bed. I just can't stop thinking about this shed and making it my own."

He gave me a funny look, one that made me think for a moment that he didn't believe a word coming out of my mouth, but then he sighed too and extended his arm, offering a hand to me. "Come on."

I left the shed with him and made the trek back to the mansion, but not without giving the shed one last glance back.

CHAPTER THIRTY-SIX

I ate breakfast in town with Roland. After our three AM bump in the night, I really needed to give him all of my attention. And after reading Melanie's journals, I felt guilty and icky about all of it—sorting her things, selling it, reading her words—yet and still, something about what she was writing didn't feel right. But now, it wasn't so much about Roland. My thoughts had shifted to Dylan.

I had no idea Dylan lived in the mansion before. While I lived in the mansion, Dylan had his own place in town. Neither of them had mentioned Dylan staying here, which you'd think would have come up in conversation at least once since marrying Roland.

"You can't scare me like you did last night, babe," Roland said when our meals arrived at the table.

"I know. I'm sorry."

"No, seriously. I get déjà vu with situations like that."

My brows peaked. "What do you mean?"

He picked up his fork and sighed. "Melanie used to have a lot of moments where she'd disappear."

I froze at the mention of Melanie. "She did?"

"All the time and it really used to annoy the hell out of me."

"Moments like when?"

"I don't know." He shrugged hard and cut into his omelet. "Closer to when she passed away, I guess."

"Wow. Do you think something was wrong? Or that she was hiding something?"

He gave me a stern eye. "I *know* she was hiding something."

"Like what?" *An affair?*

Roland brought a cut of the omelet to his mouth. "I don't know. But she became distant and I don't want that with you, Samira. I want you to be open and honest with me. Always."

I nodded, lowering my gaze to my pancakes. "Why do you think her sister never got back to you about getting her things?"

I risked the chance of looking up and he was already staring at me. "Why do you have so many questions about her today?"

I stacked my spine defensively. "I'm just asking."

He lowered his fork. "Did you find something in the shed I should know about?"

"No—no, nothing like that. I'm just curious. There are a lot of valuable things in there, is all." I used my fork to cut my pancakes. "I'm going to call my brother tonight." No, I wasn't going to call, but I had to change the subject to something more important. Something current. Roland knew about Kell and how much my brother hated the idea of me being with him, so this was relevant to both of us. No Melanie. No Miley. Back to us.

"Are you?"

"Yes. I miss talking to him. And I think I should finally tell him about us."

"He'll be upset, Samira. Not only because you went against his word about staying away from me, but also because you got *married* to me and didn't even let your own brother know."

"I know." I dropped my head.

"Hey." He reached across the table, tipping my chin with his forefinger to lift my head back up. "No matter what he says, you'll always have me, babe. I've got you."

"I know," I said in a low voice, and I couldn't help wondering if he'd used those exact words with Melanie when it came to her sister.

And now look at her. Dead.

Roland had a friend in town named Felipe who was going to be around for the next three days. Roland decided he'd set up a lunch for him that same afternoon after getting the call, so we hurried back home and informed Yadira. She went to the grocery store for what she needed and while we waited for him to arrive, Roland and I changed clothes and got ready.

Yadira had put together steaks, potatoes, and steamed vegetables, and we all ate at the dining table, our glasses of wine being refilled every so often by her.

Felipe was a handsome guy. He was about an inch or so shorter than Roland, who was six-foot-three, and he had warm tan skin, like he bathed in sunlight frequently. His hair was curly and shoulder length, two dimples in his cheeks.

At the six-top table, Roland sat across from me, and Dylan was sitting to my right. Felipe was sitting next to Roland, diagonally across from me. I noticed Yadira had asked Dylan if he wanted any wine and he passed, requesting sweet tea instead.

"You know Felipe does graphic designing too, Samira?" Roland looked at me, his wineglass in hand.

"Yeah?" I put my attention on Felipe.

"I do," Felipe said, his Colombian accent thick. "Roland tells me you do it as a hobby."

"I do." I smiled. "I'm not a professional by any means, but I do love to put designs together. I was thinking of making digital prints and selling them online. I want to start up my own small business or something, sell stickers, decals, prints—all that." I smiled.

"That would be nice, and I know many people who are making a killing doing that right now." Felipe flashed his smile and I smiled in return. "I'd love to see your work—if you have any."

"Do you have any work to see?" Roland asked. "You have the iPad now, right?"

"I do. I've tried my hand at some things, but I don't think they're good enough to show yet." I pressed my lips, fighting the urge to grin.

"You're modest," said Felipe, smirking and then sipping his wine. "Modesty in a woman is good for Roland."

Roland slid his gaze over to Felipe and I noticed a moment of tension spark between them, but Roland simply nodded and sipped his wine again.

I glanced at Dylan, who was using his fork to move his vegetables around on his plate.

"Did you know his first wife well?" After I'd asked, all of their eyes were on me. None of them smiled. They appeared almost stunned by my question. "What? Is talking about her forbidden now that I'm around?" I joked.

Dylan dropped his fork and Roland's jaw ticked. Felipe cleared his throat and sat up in his chair, placing his glass down. "I knew her well enough—through Roland, of course. But do not worry, there is no competition to be had. You are a much better wife to him. Nicer on the eyes too."

Felipe chuckled and swung his eyes to Roland, who huffed a laugh. Dylan sipped his tea with a straight face, staring at a wall across from him and avoiding everyone else's.

When lunch was over, the sun had sunk beneath the horizon, the leftover rays streaming through the floor-to-ceiling windows. Roland took the guys to the garage, where they played darts and drank some more (except Dylan), and while they did, I dismissed myself and figured I'd help Yadira clean up.

But my mind kept going back to those journals. I had been thinking about them all day, even while trying my damnedest not to. Now, Roland was occupied, and the shed was calling my name.

"Lunch was good?" Yadira asked, washing the last of the dishes.

"It was. Thank you for that."

"I was thinking fish for dinner. I'm not sure if Felipe is staying, but I'll make extra, just in case."

"That'll be good."

"And strawberry shortcake for dessert."

"Mm–hmm." I tossed some potato peels in the trash and then went for the broom on the hook. I looked out of the double doors, past the back deck, at the desolate shed in front of the trees.

"Oh—don't worry about that, Samira. I've got it." Yadira turned, wiping her hands off on her apron and then extending an arm, reaching for the broom. "I'll sweep."

"Oh. Okay." I handed it to her.

One of her brows peaked as she stepped closer. "Are you okay?"

"Yeah. I think I'm just going to go out to the shed while Roland is hanging out. Clear up more of her things."

Yadira's smile fell for a fleeting second, but then she nodded. It was the second time she'd reacted that way when I mentioned the shed.

"Okay." She turned away with the broom and started sweeping. I headed to the mudroom, putting on a coat and boots, picking up a scarf, and walking to the doors while wrapping it around my neck.

I closed the doors behind me and when I looked up, Yadira's eyes were on me. She quickly looked away and went back to sweeping.

CHAPTER THIRTY-SEVEN

After the way Yadira looked at me, I decided not to go back into the mansion with the journals. I had no idea what she knew, but I didn't want her seeing me carrying anything inside and alerting Roland about it.

When dinner was ready, I didn't miss the looks she passed at me and then Roland, as if she had questions for us but didn't want to intrude. Instead, she served and mostly stayed in the kitchen unless needed.

I was glad when dinner was over and Roland told me he was going bowling with Dylan and Felipe. Yadira was gone now, the kitchen spotless and the countertops clear, other than the dessert sitting on a gold platter on the island, covered with a clear dome. The house was vacant and clear of bodies other than my own, and relief swirled in my belly. I had other plans that revolved around an old shed and handwritten notes.

Perhaps if I'd had friends of my own in this town, I wouldn't have felt the need to run to the shed so quickly. But I was a woman alone in a mansion with nothing else to do. I had no job and the hobby that I did have, I couldn't really focus on at the moment because thoughts of my husband's dead wife were consuming me. I wasn't going to let it go until I knew more about what'd happened before her death.

On my way to the shed, I couldn't help thinking about Dylan. He seemed like a nice enough guy, but nice guys made mistakes too. Did he sleep with Miley? Why would he do that after promising he wouldn't? The only explanation I could think of was that he badly wanted to get laid, since he had been new to the area and Miley was his only convenient option.

Then I circled back to Melanie, and how desperately hard she'd tried to steer Miley away from Dylan. But if he'd broken his promise, clearly that meant he and Miley did something together. And if Melanie was writing about it, clearly that had upset her way more than it should have.

This wasn't just about protecting her sister. Her sister was a grown woman who could make her own choices, addict or not, and a woman Melanie had ignored for seven days straight because she was ashamed of her. Not to mention she didn't tell her husband—*my* husband—about her only sibling for *years*. There was so much more to this story and I needed to know *everything*, so I made my way to the shed to collect the next journal.

As I shut the door of the shed behind me, glancing downward so I didn't miss the step, someone asked, "You found them?"

I gasped, leaping backward and pressing a hand over my heart.

"Oh, shit! Yadira!" I cried, finding her in the dark. "You scared me! What the hell? I thought you were gone!"

"I was, but I forgot the grocery list for tomorrow and came back." She stepped forward, her head at a slight angle and a worried expression on her face.

"You found the journals." She wasn't smiling. In the dark her face was serious, almost frozen.

I clung to the journal in my hand.

She sighed. "I'd hoped this wouldn't happen. I had hoped you would just throw them away."

"You knew about them?"

"Of course, I knew about them. His mother found them along with some other books while clearing out her stuff in the closets, but I don't think Miss Cathy knew they were journals, and if she did, she didn't care. She just put them on the shelf with the books to get them out of the way." Yadira rubbed her cheek. "I was helping organize the shed during times Miss Cathy wasn't around. I read a couple pages but knew better thanu to read all of it. You shouldn't be reading them, Samira. It'll only cause trouble."

"Well, why did you leave them in there? Why not throw them away yourself if you knew they'd cause trouble?"

"Because I figured Roland would have wanted to see them or that he would have come across them himself. I don't know." She shrugged hard, her shoulders hiking. "It seemed like something he was supposed to discover himself to make peace with . . . but not something the detectives were supposed to find, so I hid them when they started digging around after she died."

"Why?"

"Because Roland has only ever been good to me, and Melanie was good too, but . . . some of the things in there would have made him look like a horrible man if the detectives had read it, and he was already grieving. He didn't need their personal matters getting out too."

"Yadira, there are things in here that I think would hurt him if he ever read them . . ."

"Which gives you all the more reason to stop reading them while you can." She moved closer, so close I could feel the heat of her breath on my cold cheek. Her eyes studied mine and she touched my hand. "I worry that if you keep doing this—sneaking around and hiding these from him— *lying* to him—"

"How did you know—"

"I worry that your marriage with him will end up like theirs was, Samira. And that's just me being honest. I heard their arguing. I saw both their tears. I saw Melanie at her lowest right before she died, okay? You don't want to get to that point too."

I swallowed hard, looking her in the eyes.

"I know I can't tell you what to do here. I know you're curious about her. Just . . . please, be careful." She pulled her hand away and gripped the collar of her jacket. "And, for the love of God, don't believe everything you read in those."

I watched her walk away, the cold ground crunching beneath her, then I turned toward the mansion when she was gone. I went straight to the relaxation room, sat on the sofa with a blanket and, despite Yadira's warning and clearly a glutton for punishment, I cracked the new journal open to the first page.

CHAPTER THIRTY-EIGHT

*W*hen *Dylan's betrayal happened, it was during that odd gap between Christmas and New Year's, when you don't exactly know what to do with your-self after the high from opening gifts and spending time with loved ones, pigging out on homemade food and desserts and alcohol. You sort of coast through the days like a plane passenger while life is the pilot, and wait in anticipation for the landing of New Year's Eve so that you can scream resolutions, get drunk, and pretend the next year will be your year.*

On December 29th, I texted Miley and asked what her plans were for New Year's Eve. She didn't respond. So, I sent her another text the following day, to which she didn't respond until later that night. It was strange for her to respond so slowly, so at first I thought maybe she was working late—the stores were busier during the holidays with longer hours and she was working retail—but then I re-membered a specific moment after Christmas din-ner, when she and Dylan were sitting in the den in front of the fire.

I brought tea to share with her instead of another glass of wine that she'd requested, and she had her hand on top of his. When I walked in, he quickly snatched his hand away and looked away from her, as if nothing had happened. I had been drinking, so of course I brushed it off and pretended it was nothing—that Dylan would never betray me, a woman he'd made a promise to—but that night, he drove Miley home because she'd drunk too much and he didn't like to drink at all, and he didn't come back until the next morning.

When I asked him where he'd been, he told me he'd gone to a bar to meet a friend. But there were no bars open in Sageburg on Christmas night.

Still, I brushed it off, pretended it was nothing. Maybe he'd gone somewhere else and didn't want to tell me and it was none of my damn business to know. That's what I told myself.

But then the next night, he got home late again.

And the next.

And I realized Miley had stopped asking about Dylan completely.

When she did get back to me about New Year's Eve, she declined and said she had other plans, which I found really fucking odd because my sister had no friends in Sageburg that I was aware of.

So I watched the ball drop with Roland and expected Dylan to celebrate with us, but he'd slunk his way out around eleven that night. I saw him with his coat on, a black beanie on his head, and he didn't stop to say goodbye, didn't even look our way, he just walked past the living room and left the house.

All of it was fucking shady, so when the night

was over and the New Year had arrived and my husband had passed out on the sofa from too many bourbons, I got in my car and drove to Miley's apartment.

And sure enough, Dylan's car was parked in the lot. I remember my grip tightening around the steering wheel, my face getting hot, my throat thickening with emotions that I couldn't quite understand at the time.

I had to drive away—go anywhere other than home. I needed to think and figure out how to approach Dylan about this.

He'd lied to me. He was with my sister, fucking her, I was sure, when he said he wouldn't get involved with her.

That fucking sleazebag.

CHAPTER THIRTY-NINE

I waited an entire week before confronting Dylan. I needed proof. Pictures. So I followed him every night when he left, parked in the lot as he did at Miley's complex, and took photos of him with my phone.

Photos of him climbing out of the car. Walking up the stairs. Knocking on her door. I even had a photo of him standing on the balcony with her as she smoked an e-cigarette, both of them laughing like they were the best of fucking friends.

It was a little overboard, but I needed all the proof I could get, not just for myself, but for Roland too. I wanted Roland to kick Dylan out after this because if he could break my only rule, imagine what else he could do.

I waited until Roland went to his golfing facility before going up to the attic. I wanted to give Dylan the chance to explain himself, at least. I felt that was reasonable enough. After all, maybe I had the wrong impression. Maybe he was meeting her just to hang out because he felt bad for her. Maybe he wasn't sleeping with her at all.

Ugh. Who the fuck was I kidding? He was defi-nitely sleeping with her. There was no way Miley was inviting him into that apartment without sinking her claws into him.

I knocked on his door and drew in a breath, my cell phone with the photos clutched in hand. He answered the door, wearing only a white towel around his waist. His brown skin was still damp, his abs defined. I quickly swung my gaze back up to his face, ignoring the fact that he was half naked in front of me.

"Mel," he said, smiling. "What's up?"

"Don't call me Mel. I need to talk to you."

"Okay? What about?" He leaned against the door and I breathed in slowly, taking in the scent of his pine soap, before exhaling.

"You made me a promise and you broke it, Dylan."

His face changed after that statement. His smile disappeared and he pulled his hand down, standing straight. "What are you talking about?"

"I know you're fucking my sister."

His face warped, and his eyes flashed with something I couldn't quite read, then he stepped back and said, "Let me get dressed."

He closed the door in my face and I grimaced, lis-tening to him shuffle around in the room. Several minutes later, he had basketball shorts and a T-shirt on. "Wanna come in?"

I stepped into his room, which I hadn't done since he'd moved in. It looked completely different. A single bed against the wall. A solo window next to it. The floors made of hardwood, a TV and an enter-tainment system across from the bed. There was a dresser and a clothing rack where his jeans and *button-downs hung. I wondered immediately how he afforded any of it. Had Roland paid for it? It had to have been Roland.*

"How did you find out? She tell you?" Dylan asked. I turned to look at him and he'd shut the door behind him.

"No. I saw you at her apartment."

"You saw me? You mean you followed me?"

"Yes, I followed you. She wasn't texting me back and you were leaving every night and I saw you touch her hand on Christmas night. You took her home, remember? Is that when it all started?"

Dylan fought a smile and shook his head. "Look, Mel, it's not even like that. We're just fucking and I told her that. She knows not to take what we have going on too seriously. I told her that out of respect for you."

"What? Do you hear yourself? You completely disrespected me by sleeping with her, Dylan! I specifically asked you not to get involved with her—to deny her!"

"Why are you getting so upset? Last I checked, Miley is a grown-ass woman who can make her own choices. She doesn't need you speaking for her."

"I told you about her! She has an addictive personality! You can't just fuck her and think that's all she'll want."

"So, she's like you," he said, looking me up and down, brows furrowing.

I stepped back. "What are you talking about?"

"She's like you. You have an addictive personality too. You're addicted to shutting your sister down."

"What the hell are you talking about?" I snapped again.

"Miley told me about you, Mel. She told me about your mom and how she used to have a bunch of boyfriends who always hit on you when they were around. She told me you even slept with some of them, and your mom used to get real mad about it. But she especially got mad about this one man— Calvin or something."

I panicked and glanced at the door. "Okay, I don't know what you're talking about or what Miley told you, but trying to spin this back on me isn't going to save you. I'm telling Roland that you broke my one rule and that I want you out ASAP."

"Calvin used to call you his slut. His nasty bitch. Am I getting that right? And you liked it? I mean, it probably fucked you up in the head a little bit, but you liked being that to him. You liked knowing he chose you over your own mother, didn't you? You carry that to this day, that's why you're so bothered about Miley."

I couldn't believe Miley had told him so much! That was between us! She promised not to bring it up again.

"Fuck you, Dylan!" I stormed around him but didn't make it to the door because he'd caught me by the elbow and spun me around. I gasped as he reeled me toward him and held me close.

"You don't like to see her happy," Dylan said with his face close to mine.

"Get off of me," I growled through clenched teeth, and this feeling was familiar, yet strange. I hated it. I loved it. Fuck. Dylan was right. I was so fucked up in the head.

"Whenever she is happy, you want to steal it all away so you can look like the better sister."

"Fuck you," I seethed.

"You want me," he mumbled, and his mouth was close to mine. *"I remind you of him, right?"* My heartbeat doubled in speed, the truth damn near swallowing me whole. I hated Calvin for what he did to me when I was fifteen, but I also couldn't say I didn't enjoy it. If it weren't for Calvin, I never would have slept with Isaac, one of the managers of the golf club I used to work at. And if it weren't for Isaac, I never would have been working the counter that brought Roland to me.

"You know that's all you had to say, right? That you want me to yourself?" Dylan went on.

I worked hard to swallow.

"Why else would you be following me around? Interrogating me? Gaslighting your sister? Just admit to me and to yourself that you want me—that you've wanted me since I first showed up."

"I don't want you."

"Well, I want you."

"Why?"

He shrugged. *"Makes me just as fucked up as you, right? Melanie, you look at me differently than you do Roland. Just admit it. You want to fuck me. I don't know why, when you've got so much going for you, but that's what excites you, right? Wanting what you know you shouldn't have?"*

I couldn't believe this.

"Miley told me so much about you," he said, fingering a strand of my hair. *"You get boyfriends and you get bored with them. Now you have a husband and you're bored with him and you're trying to make this about Miley, but you know damn well this isn't*

about her. Let me ask you this: Before I got here, were you having any issues with her?"

I blinked up at him, keeping my lips sealed.

"Were you even talking to her before she moved here?"

I stared at him.

"No, you weren't," he said. "Before she became such an addict to you, she told me you two were like peas in a pod. But then she tells you that she's attracted to me and you flip the fuck out and bring her addiction into it, despite the fact that she's doing much better for herself now. Why do you even care so much who she likes?"

"I told you why." My bottom lip quivered. "She's unstable. One wrong move and she could relapse."

"Maybe you're the one who's unstable. Maybe you're the one relapsing."

I realized he was still holding me so I snatched my arm out of his hands. "I want you out of here by tonight. I don't care what you have to tell Roland, but you need to be gone. And don't even think about going to stay with Miley because I own that apartment. She knows not to break any of my rules."

He grabbed me again. "You're gonna kick me out? Just like that? Because I'm right about who you are and who you've always been?"

I matched his stare. "You're not right about anything."

"You don't want Roland finding out about this part of you, do you?"

I clenched my jaw and my fingers twitched. I wanted to slap him, but the closer he got to me, the weaker my knees became, and the memories hit me *hard. Back when I was a teen. Back when Calvin would sneak into my room while my mother was asleep. He'd touch me in the dark, grope me, say things to me that made me feel special—like I was his and only his.*

Dylan smirked, took a step forward, and before my brain could register what was happening, his lips were on mine and he was kissing me.

CHAPTER FORTY

I heard a door shut and the laughter of men. Roland was back home and I didn't know what the fuck I had just read, but an instant fear paralyzed me and my heart was pounding.

A million questions raced through my mind. Did Dylan have something to do with Melanie driving over that cliff? Did he do something to her? Did Roland find out about them? No, Roland couldn't have known. He wouldn't have still been so chummy with Dylan if he knew that his closest cousin had kissed his wife.

That moment between Dylan and Melanie was intimate—the way he interrogated her, backed her into that corner. She didn't say it, but even I could feel her heart racing through the pages. And why was she worried about her sister telling him about this Calvin person? Whoever he was, he sounded horrible and had clearly taken advantage of her.

I heard footsteps and tucked the third journal under the cushion of the sofa to hide it. Then I got off the couch and walked to the door of the relaxation room. Dylan was coming up the stairs, his eyes tired, and a drunken smile on his face.

I broke out in goosebumps as he grinned at me. "'Sup, Samira."

"Wh-what are you doing up here?"

"Gotta pee," he said, then chortled. "Roland's in one of the downstairs bathrooms and Felipe is in the other."

He waltzed off, and when he rounded the corner, I left the room to go down the stairs. Roland was coming out of the bathroom as I walked down the hallway. He stumbled on his way out and I was sure he was drunk. I so badly wanted to ask him about all that I'd read, but I had to act normal.

"Are you okay?" I asked him.

He laughed. "Yeah. Just had too much to drink. Had to call an Uber."

I helped him toward the stairs and we took them up one by one. Dylan was coming down, smiling wide as he took each step.

"Yo—we have to do this again, bro!"

"We will!" Roland declared. "Real soon, man. Show Felipe out for me. I'm tired as hell. You can crash in one of the rooms if you want."

"Cool." Dylan kept going down and when I made it up, I looked over the banister. Dylan looked up at me and said, "G'night, *Samira*."

I didn't say it back. I looked away and pretended not to hear him. I didn't like how he'd said my name, or the way he looked at me, like he knew something I didn't.

Then I remembered something Melanie said in her journal. Dylan didn't drink. So why the hell was he drunk now? Was he pretending to be? Or had something caused him to turn to drinking?

I hurried to the bedroom with my husband hanging halfway off of me, making it to our bed and sitting him down. He flopped flat on his back and closed his eyes with a groan.

"So drunk," he groaned again.

I watched him, how his chest rose and fell, in sync with his deep breaths. How a smile lingered on his lips, like he'd had the best night of his life.

"Roland?" I called.

"Hmm?"

I sat beside him, looked down at him. "Does Dylan drink often?"

"Not often."

"Did he drink tonight?"

"Uh-huh."

"A lot?"

"No. Not much. He doesn't like to drink like that. Daddy was a drunk. Used to beat him for no reason sometimes. Mine did too. Probably why we grew up to be so close." Roland burped, then sighed. "His momma used to send him to buy her drugs. I think that's why my momma kept telling me not to send them money before his mom died. Even now, she tells me to make Dylan work for it because she just doesn't trust that side of the family."

I blinked in surprise. Wow. I had no idea. I knew Roland's mother wasn't close to her sister, but I didn't think it ran that deep. And about Dylan—he had to be pretending to be drunk if he didn't drink much. Why? Why pretend the night I mentioned Melanie? Over dinner he was acting a little off, staring at the walls, avoiding Roland's eyes.

I scooted closer to Roland. "Babe, I need to ask you something, and please be honest with me."

"You can ask me anything, Samira."

I felt bad taking advantage of Roland in his drunken, vulnerable state. But I also didn't want him to remember me asking any of the questions I had when he was sober again. This felt like the perfect chance to ask him about Melanie.

"Do you know who Melanie had an affair with?"

Roland was quiet for so long I thought he'd fallen asleep. His eyes didn't move behind his eyelids for a while, but then they popped open several seconds later and a full frown had taken over his face.

He sat up, pushed off the bed, and said two words that I never thought I'd hear him say.

"Fuck Melanie."

Then he hurried to the toilet to vomit.

Roland had fallen asleep shortly after his vulgar words and heavy vomiting. I made sure he was okay before going back to the relaxation room and shutting the door behind me quietly.

But as I turned around, I noticed one of the back cushions of the sofa was tilted. My heart dropped and my mind screamed three little words: *Someone was here.*

I rushed toward the sofa, picking up the bottom cushion. The journal was still in the same spot and I drew in a relieved sigh. I took a thorough look around the room to see if anything else was out of place, but all seemed fine.

Nothing else had been moved. My phone was still on the table next to the sofa.

Even so, I wasn't mistaken. Someone else had been in this room.

I stood back up and locked the door. I retrieved the journal, sat down and, despite my pulse pounding in my ears, picked back up where I'd left off.

CHAPTER FORTY-ONE

I liked the kiss, and maybe that made me a terrible, disgusting human being, but I liked it. I liked it so much that I ended up making out with Dylan on his bed, all while my husband was just a short walk away, practicing on his private course.

I hated myself in that moment, and I'm ashamed to admit that I also felt victorious. And with that victory, there was power in it, so I used that power to get more of what I wanted.

"Promise me you won't go to her apartment again," I breathed as Dylan kissed my throat.

"I promise."

"No. Really promise it this time."

He paused and looked at me. "What do I get out of it?"

I clasped his face in my hands. "Me."

"But you're not mine. You're Roland's."

"Don't worry about Roland."

"That's fucked up."

"So why are you kissing me?"

His throat bobbed as he looked down at me, then

he brought his head down again and kissed me, rocking his erection between my legs, groaning as I sucked on his plump bottom lip.

"Promise me," I breathed again.

"I promise. I mean it."

And Dylan did mean it.

I had to stop the kiss—I couldn't do this while Roland was so close to home. Guilt swallowed me whole as I left the room and bustled down the stairs. I went into my bedroom and took a shower, feeling dirtier than ever before, and when I got out, Roland was in the bedroom, taking off his practice attire.

"Mel," he said, side-eyeing me as he sat on the edge of the bed. "Come here."

Still wrapped in only a towel, I walked to my husband, my heart beating a mile a minute. I worried instantly if Dylan had played me—if he'd told Roland that I kissed him back just so he wouldn't be kicked out because of Miley.

Roland looked at me in the towel, then he grabbed the front of it and undid it. I stood naked before him and he smiled, holding me by the waist and bringing me closer.

"Lift your leg," he commanded. And I brought my foot up to the bed. He kissed the inside of my thigh and I shuddered. "When's the last time I did this to you?"

"I don't know," I breathed as he moved higher and higher, closer to an area that he hadn't touched in days. Roland was weird about sex now. Most nights, I wanted it. I wanted to please him and do things for him, but he would have rather read a book or read an article than fuck me. We had sex less often since getting married and I worried for us.

"Be still," he ordered. And my husband plea-

sured me with his tongue, and I hadn't expected it at all, but I was still turned on from kissing Dylan in the attic, so I accepted it, reveled in it.

I felt victorious, and maybe a little guilty too.

But I should have known that all of my selfish victory wouldn't last for much longer.

Roland had a trip to Washington two weeks after Dylan and I first kissed. In between that time, Miley was texting me again, asking to visit me. I always made an excuse so she couldn't. Dylan spent more time around the house, cutting his eyes at me and giving me looks. Whenever Roland wasn't in plain sight, Dylan would grab my ass or whisper something dirty in my ear.

We were trouble, but I couldn't help myself and I couldn't stop. I liked the flirting, the buildup, the risk. And as each night passed and these feelings built up, I'd ride my husband and pretend his body was Dylan's.

Then the moment arrived when Roland had to go, and it was only going to be the two of us in the mansion. Yadira had left dinner for me, so I set up two plates in the dining room and sent Dylan a text, telling him to join me. He came to the table in a white T-shirt and jeans, sat across from me, but we didn't eat.

I couldn't eat. For two weeks straight all I kept thinking about was fucking his brains out. Riding him until he orgasmed. Making him want me over and over again. Sometimes it was embarrassing that my mind would wander to such toxic, filthy thoughts.

But maybe Dylan was right about me. I was like Miley in a way. I did have an addictive personality too, only mine wasn't to drugs or alcohol. It was an *addiction to sex and attention. I could never get enough of it, and once someone showed any interest in me, I sucked it dry until I got bored with it. He was right. So, so right.*

Instead of eating, we went up to the attic and fucked.

And then fucked again.

We fucked every single day until my husband returned—in the kitchen, in the den, in the relaxation room, in mine and Roland's bedroom, and even in our shower, and when my husband returned home, I fucked him too, and I was purposely loud. It made Dylan jealous, and when Roland was at his golf course again the next day, Dylan took the first opportunity he could to grab me by the arm and drag me into the nearest closet, wrapping a hand around my throat and fucking me like he owned me.

This was sinful, deceitful, and completely ridiculous . . . but I couldn't stop. Because for the first time since being married, I truly felt like I was living. But then everything changed four months later.

Roland got into a car wreck.

CHAPTER FORTY-TWO

*R*oland was alive and I was so happy about that, but his injuries were severe and doctors had already warned that it would take him months to heal.

At first, it was nice having Roland home more often. He'd broken his arm and fractured his shinbone, which meant I had to be his limbs and help him. I didn't mind doing for him. In fact, I enjoyed being the one he called when he needed assistance. He requested Dylan here and there, but not as much as he did me. I guess he didn't want to look weak in front of Dylan—some kind of pride issue. I never questioned it.

But I noticed that as the days passed and shifted into weeks, Roland was changing. He was becoming bitter, in a sense. He'd gotten injured right before a huge championship game. He felt he could've won, and I knew he would have, but the trophy didn't go to him because he was forced to miss it. And as it always is with business, companies canceled contracts for endorsements with him, to jump on the new golf champion.

Before long, Roland was pissed about everything.

Pissed at his arm for being broken.

Pissed at the driver who'd hit his car and injured him.

Pissed that I didn't make his soup hot enough.

Pissed about how I prepared his alcoholic drinks.

He even got mad once about the way I sucked him off.

"Just get off me," he grumbled one night, pushing my head away.

"Oh my God. What is wrong with you, Roland?" I snapped, wiping my mouth with the back of my arm.

"I'm just not in the mood."

"You're never in the mood anymore."

"I have a broken arm and leg, Melanie. Only so much I can do right now," he grumbled, pulling his boxers up.

"Okay. Sure. Whatever."

I turned over with my back to him and shut the lamp off. Roland shut his off too and, several minutes later, I heard him snoring.

I looked back at my sleeping husband, then I climbed out of bed and tiptoed up the stairs.

I gave Dylan's door a knock. Then I heard quick footsteps and some giggling. I frowned at the door, grimacing deeper when he swung it open, shirtless, standing in only his briefs.

"Mel!" Dylan smiled at me.

I peered over his shoulder and noticed a woman with thick, curly black hair sitting on the middle of his bed in only a pink bra and panties. She waved. I snatched my gaze away, putting my focus on him again.

"What the hell is going on?" I demanded.

"Oh—this is my guest, Willa. Met her at the bar. She's staying the night with me."

All I could do was stare at him.

"What?" he asked, cocking his head. "You said promise not to sleep with Miley. You didn't say anything about hooking up with other people."

I shook my head, giving him an incredulous stare before turning my back to him and storming back down the stairs.

Roland had been home for weeks, which meant I spent less time with Dylan. And he'd put his attention elsewhere—on another woman—and she was in my house stealing that away from me.

I didn't go back to bed with Roland. I went to the relaxation room and stewed about the whole night, from my husband's rejection to Dylan's arrogance.

And then I realized that Dylan was just like all the guys from before. They'd sleep with me. Beg for me. Then they'd pretend I meant nothing to them after they'd had enough of me.

Every single guy was like this, even my own husband.

So that night I decided I was going to do something bad—something I knew would make Dylan want to leave the mansion. Because there was no way in hell he was going to have random women prancing around my house. Hell was going to have to freeze before I ever let that happen.

CHAPTER FORTY-THREE

I had a plan. No, I hadn't thought it all the way through, but it didn't matter. It would cause a rift, and a rift was what I needed right now.

I made my way up the driveway of the mansion, smiling as Miley followed me to the front door.

"I'm surprised you want me to move in," she said as we made our way up the stairs inside.

"Don't be silly. I talked to Roland and he said it didn't make sense to keep paying for an apartment when you can just stay in one of the rooms here."

"I mean, I thought it was stupid too, but it was your money, so . . ." She shrugged, dropping her bags in the middle of the floor once we were inside her designated room. "Damn." She sighed, taking in every detail of the room. There wasn't much in it yet, just a queen-sized bed in the middle of the room, a dresser with two nightstands to match. The room wasn't even painted, and the bathroom in this room was probably the smallest, but to Miley it was everything, I was sure. "This is way better than the apartment."

"Really?" I asked as she flopped down on the bed. "How so?"

"I don't know. I guess it feels homier here." She spread her arms on the bed, making angel wings like she was in the snow. "I get to see you every day, we can eat breakfast together. Tell each other stories. Girl, I've got hella stories for you."

I smiled but felt a pang of guilt after she'd said that. Her naivety made me feel like a vampire, ready to suck all of that naivety dry. Truthfully, even if I hadn't had my issues with Dylan, I wouldn't have minded Miley staying with me for a little while, now that I saw she was serious about getting better.

At first, I thought it would cause issues having her around, but it had been months and she was doing great for herself. Maybe traveling to another state was all she needed—a fresh start. A new perspective on life.

But I hadn't moved her in just to be sisterly. I'd moved her in to have her under the same roof as Dylan. If he wanted to have women flouncing around, he wouldn't do it here. Miley damn sure wouldn't have allowed it, and she'd aggravate him by being here, constantly able to watch him, see him, touch him. Maybe she wouldn't annoy him at first, but she would eventually, because Miley aggravated everyone. She was just one of those people who could get under your skin for no reason. I loved her to death, but one did have to have a high tolerance and an immense amount of patience while dealing with her.

I hadn't told Roland that Miley was moving in. I was still upset with him after the night he'd pushed me away like I was useless, and since he'd brought Dylan in without even giving me a heads-up, I figured it was okay for me to do the same. We had plenty of room, after all. It's what he always said about Dylan. Dylan never took up too much space. Never ate food that wasn't his. Never drank the last bit of coffee in the pot. He never did anything wrong according to Roland, but that was a fucking lie.

"You aren't this happy to be around me," I said to Miley as I sat on the edge of the bed.

"What do you mean?" she asked

"I mean . . . well, with Dylan here. You're under the same roof as him."

"Oh." She grinned and practically sank into her green turtleneck. "Yeah. That is true, but I don't know. I don't think he's as interested in me as I thought."

"Why do you say that?"

"I don't know. He stopped coming to see me so abruptly. I mean, he told me in advance that we were just going to sleep together and nothing more, but I think he found someone else to sleep with." She shrugged, like the thought of it didn't hurt, but I was sure it did. The smallest things always hurt her.

"Well, I think being here will give you the perfect opportunity to ask him what's up, don't you?"

She looked me in the eyes and when I saw that sadness seep away and the spark light her irises like stars, I felt a sense of accomplishment. I wanted Dylan to leave, and my plan would work.

My plan didn't work at first, but that was to be expected. Miley sought Dylan out as soon as possible and Dylan had free pussy under the same roof as him, so of course he was going to take advantage of that, the same way he'd taken advantage of me.

But it only took a month for him to get tired of that

too. *That was the thing with Dylan. He got bored very easily, and I suppose he and I were alike in that way. Isn't it so strange that the people we damn near hate are exactly like us?*

Spring had rolled around and Roland's arm was getting better. Still weak, but better. He conditioned in the home gym with a trainer and sometimes with Dylan, and they bonded even more, became even closer, and a couple weeks after that, Dylan started caddying for Roland on the practice turf again, preparing him for his first game back after his accident, which would be the first day of summer.

In between that time, Miley tried ridiculously hard to get Dylan's attention, to no avail. She'd walk around in skimpy clothing, laugh loudly, and drop things on the floor while he was around just to bend over in front of him. None of it worked.

"Why doesn't he want me?" Miley asked one night. *We were in my new shed. Roland bought it for me without question when I'd asked him, I suppose to work his way to my good side again. It worked. We had sex the night it arrived and for the first time in a long time he didn't complain. His therapy wasn't just healing him physically, but mentally as well.*

"I don't know," I said, sliding books onto the bookshelf. *"Sex is only good for so long. Eventually people get bored, Miley."*

"Yeah, but I mean . . . why doesn't he want more from me?"

I avoided her eyes, picking up the next stack of books. "I don't know."

"Do you think Roland finds it weird that we're sleeping together? You know, since in a way we're all kinda related."

"*Technically, you're not related to him, and neither am I.*" *I slid a few more books onto the shelf. "I don't think Roland cares. Probably because he knows Dylan isn't taking it seriously.*"

"*Dylan said that about us?*" *I remember her tone coming across as shocked and a little angry.*

Once again, the guilt was gnawing at me, but I couldn't stop. I was toxic that way. Always wanting to be better. Always ready to dampen someone else's mood so that I felt higher on my pedestal. I don't know why I was this way. I wanted to be better—do better—but I had no idea where to start then. In this moment, I realized I really needed mental help, but that didn't stop me from carrying on the conversation.

"*I've heard Roland say it,*" *I murmured.*

Miley was quiet for a while—so quiet I had to look back. And when I did, she was staring down at the floor with tears on her cheeks.

I sighed, placing the books down on my desk and walking over to sit with her. "Look, Miley . . . maybe he just needs to get to know the real you."

"*Yeah, but how? If he's telling Roland that it's not serious then obviously it isn't, so there's no point.*"

"*Wait a minute.*" *I looked her over, from her eyes to her chin, then back up again. "Are you really falling in love with him?*" *I asked, and my heart froze when I saw another tear skid down her cheek.*

She nodded and sobbed and the center of my chest felt cracked open. I had to rethink everything in that moment. I could be selfish, but not selfish to the point that it wrecked my sister like this. Not again. And if Dylan hadn't moved out yet, he was never going to. It was up to me to get him out now. Not Miley. I'd clearly used her enough.

I brought my sister in for a hug, feeling her tears drip on my shoulder. "You deserve better than him, Miley. So much better." And she deserved better than me too—a sister who put her through such hurt, even whilst knowing she'd fall deeper, and for what? To annoy Dylan? To make him start an argument with me? It'd been nearly three months now and he hadn't done any of that yet, which proved he never would.

All of this, I realized, had been for nothing.

CHAPTER FORTY-FOUR

I didn't know what else to do other than let things go with Dylan. He wasn't leaving. Miley was realizing he was no good and I was working on building her confidence back up so she didn't spiral, by putting her focus on other things like work and shopping; and, frankly, I was sick of playing this stupid game with him.

He brought more women over and escorted them out in the mornings in broad daylight. One time he did it while Miley and I were eating breakfast. He'd made himself and his one-night stand a cup of coffee, they laughed in the den as they drank it, and then she was gone five minutes later. All the while, Miley was sitting right across from me, avoiding my eyes, her head turned slightly to the side so she could hear their conversation, but it was all muffled, minus the laughter. I didn't miss the tears building up in her eyes and that made my heart ache for her because I didn't know what else to do. I could have given her another apartment, but I worried that if she was alone again, she'd do something terrible. I had to keep an eye on her as much as possible because this was all my fault. Her pain was because of me. It'd always been because of me.

Shortly after getting my shed, Roland wanted to surprise me by taking me to Hawaii. It was a quick vacation. He was going to meet his agent and publicity rep to discuss making his return a big one, and after their meeting was finalized over drinks and expensive dinners, we had five days to ourselves before we had to go back home.

But during those five days, something didn't feel right between us. There was a disconnect that I hadn't felt before, but while we vacationed it was both potent and devastating. We went out, had dinners, walked the beach, bathed in the sun, and swam in the ocean and the pools, but during it all, Roland no longer felt like my husband, and I didn't know why. It was a strange feeling. I watched him the entire time, spent all this alone time with him, and he felt like a stranger to me. He was still Roland, and I was still Melanie . . . but our connection had changed. Or maybe I had changed.

It hit me one night while we were lying in a bed that I was sure thousands of other people had lain on, that I was no longer in love with Roland.

I thought I still was, and that I would want him every day for the rest of my life—but as I looked at him, watched him sleep, watched him stir and snore, I came to the conclusion that I was absolutely wrong.

He was just a man lying next to me, one I didn't know anymore and one I didn't want to learn about again. Our marriage felt so empty lately, our arguments masked with gifts and surprise trips. Roland *wasn't good at clearing up an argument or making things better. He just buried it with money, and I was sure he'd gotten that from his mother. I'd met her once. Cathy Lewis. Lewis was her maiden name. She wasn't a pleasant woman. She was rude and she despised me, but she tolerated my existence for Roland because he was her only son.*

To Cathy, no one was good enough for her son. But I noticed Cathy always wanted to buy things for him. Or she wanted Roland to buy things for her. She'd send him gifts, like new golf clubs or tees or shirts. But in her notes to him, never did she say that she loved him. Her love was shown differently, through material things. Little knickknacks during her travels that would prove she'd been thinking of him when she bought it.

Roland's love was empty. Our love was empty. But I couldn't play a victim in this. I'd married him, knowing he showed his love this way—with gifts and material things. I'd married him, knowing damn well we probably wouldn't last. Not because of anything he'd done, but because of who I am as a woman. Always unsatisfied. Always wanting more. Always wanting attention from anyone who will give it to me. Always wanting to be touched, even though Roland wasn't much of a touchy person. Always wanting to talk, even though Roland wasn't much of a talker.

I went into this marriage knowing it would fail.

And the sad thing is, we could have tried to salvage it. I could have told him that I wanted to work on falling in love again, restoring what we had. But I'd cheated, and not with just any man—with his own fucking cousin. His favorite, most trusted cousin, of all people. I was worthless, and he deserved better. He really did.

"Roland?" I called. It was still dark, but the moon was shining through the double doors across the room that led out to a wide balcony. "Roland?"

"Hmm?" He turned over, sighing. "Yeah?" One of his eyes peeled opened before slowly closing again.

"I think . . ." I swallowed hard, the words suddenly lodging in my throat.

This time, both his eyes opened and he blinked several times at me before picking his head up. "What? What's wrong?"

"I think . . . we should get a divorce."

Roland stared at me for a long, long time, then he sat up completely and reached over to turn the nightstand lamp on. "What?"

I didn't want to repeat it. I had no idea if I was making a mistake by saying those words out loud. I would lose so much—not financially, but emotionally, mentally, and physically. But in my heart, I knew it was the best thing for us to do. For his sake, at least.

"Why do you want a divorce?" he asked, confused. "What did I do wrong?"

"You didn't do anything wrong," I countered quickly.

"So then why do you want a divorce? Look—I know I wasn't the best person to be around when I got injured. I—I bottled things up and I took it out on you and I'm sorry, Mel," he pleaded. "I was just upset about the wreck and my injury and—"

"It's not that, Roland." Tears fell down my cheeks as I reached for his hands. "I just . . . there are things about me that aren't good. And if I don't take action now, I never will and it will only make you miserable later."

He narrowed his eyes. "I don't understand."

"I cheated on you, Roland."

I didn't think it was possible for a man his size to flinch as if I'd slapped him, but he did. "You what?"

"I-it was a mistake!" I cried but he snatched his hands away and climbed off the bed. "I didn't even care about it, Roland! I swear! I don't even know why I did it!"

He paced the area at the bottom of the bed, fists clenched, shoulders hunched.

"I'm sorry," I whimpered. I climbed off the bed, cautiously making my way to him. Roland kept pacing, and I hated the pacing, so I grabbed his arm and turned him toward me. "Roland, say something," I pleaded. But he wouldn't look at me and I hated when people didn't look at me, so I grabbed his face next, tried to force his gaze on mine.

And he looked, but his hand shot up also. He clutched my face between his fingers, gripping hard, his upper lip curling back and his nostrils flaring.

"You have the audacity to try and divorce me, only to take my money and run off with someone else, after you fucking cheated on me?"

I struggled to pull myself out of his grip, but he only held on tighter, and it was hurting. "Roland," I struggled to say, clawing at his hand.

He backed me up until the back of my legs hit the edge of the bed, then he shoved me down. "I could kill you, Mel. Right here. Right now. I could fucking kill you, I swear to God."

Tears blinded me and he wasted no time grabbing my face again, forcing me to look at him. "I *don't care about your tears or your fucking sob story. You cheated on me when I was good to you. I gave you everything, and you let someone else take what belonged to me. And now you think you can just walk away, like it's that simple—like I'm just going to accept it? Fuck that and fuck you," he snarled. "You walk away, and you won't have shit, Mel, and I mean it. If you ever try to leave me after what you just did to me—to us—I promise you, I will make your life a living hell."*

CHAPTER FORTY-FIVE

I closed and dropped the journal, my heart rapidly thumping in my chest. I stared around the relaxation room, feeling anything but relaxed. Then I collected the journal and hurried out of the room, shuddering breaths, hands shaking, legs feeling like jelly.

I went downstairs to the mudroom, stepping into my boots and coat, but before I could open the door, someone behind me cleared their throat.

I froze when the person asked, "This again, Samira?"

It was Roland.

I worked hard to swallow and slowly turned to face my husband. He walked toward me, shoulders broader than I'd remembered, and his jaw set. "Why do you keep sneaking out?" He stood only a few steps away from me, slashes of moonlight on one half of his face. The other half was dark, unreadable.

"I—I'm not sneaking out," I said. My coat was still open and I started to slide the journal into it to tuck it under my arm, but he saw and his eyes narrowed.

"What is that?" He took a step forward.

"It's nothing—just a book."

Another step forward. "Are you lying to me?"

My heart beat harder, my stomach twisting into knots. "I'm not lying."

"So let me see it."

"No—Roland, you wouldn't care for it. It's just a silly romance novel." I tried to lighten the situation, but he wasn't having it.

"Let. Me. *See*. It."

I swallowed again, but my throat was now dry, and the saliva hurt going down. My fingers trembled around the book. I held it tighter, not wanting it to fall. What other choice did I have other than to show it to him?

After what I'd read, it was clear Roland had developed trust issues after what Melanie told him. And it was also clear to me that I didn't know Roland at all. The way he grabbed Melanie—the way he spoke to her in the journal. I couldn't see him doing that, and yet, as I looked at him, wary of his large hands, staring into his angry eyes, I realized that perhaps there was a side to him that had been buried deep, deep down and hidden. A side that may have possibly had something to do with her death.

I pulled the journal back out of my coat and he shot his hand out, reaching for it and catching me completely off guard. I flinched and backed away from him with the book and he squared his shoulders, frowning deeper. Was he going to hit me?

"Samira," he bellowed.

"Roland . . ." I shuddered a breath, clutching the journal tighter and as he took another step closer, my phone rang and scared the shit out of me. The song "Gold Digger" by Kanye West played and I'd never in my life been so relieved to receive a call from my brother. I pulled my phone out and showed the screen to Roland, hoping to distract him with it so he'd forget about the journal.

"It's Kell," I said, trying to keep my hands from shaking. "I should take this."

Roland frowned, then did a nod and stepped back. I tucked the book under my armpit again and turned away to answer the call.

"Kell! Hey!" I cried into the phone.

"Samira!" he shouted into the phone.

"What? What's wrong?"

"Why the fuck didn't you tell me?" he snapped, and for a split second I had no idea what he could have possibly been talking about—too preoccupied with thoughts of my husband strangling me.

"What are you talking about?"

"Your fucking *marriage*, Samira! Is this why you've been avoiding my calls? You went and *married* that crazy mother-fucker when I told you to stay away from his ass!"

I turned sideways and looked at Roland. He was still watching me.

"I'm gonna take this outside."

I didn't wait for him to answer. I opened one of the back doors and walked out, shutting it behind me and then hustling far enough away from the door so Roland couldn't hear.

"Samira?" Kell demanded.

"Yeah—I'm here. Kell, it's two in the morning. Why are you calling so late?"

"No, you don't get to ask me questions. I'm in my office right now and one of my coworkers sent me an email. In that email, I see an article about Roland Graham secretly getting married and honeymooning at a ski resort. And with who? A woman named Samira Wilder!"

I closed my eyes and drew in a cold breath. "I was going to tell you, Kell."

"I should have been the first to know about this, Mira!"

"Well, I didn't want to tell you right away! I knew you wouldn't support it!"

"Why, Mira?" he groaned. He was probably doing that thing where he pinched the bridge of his nose with his eyes closed. "Why the hell would you marry that man after all I told you?"

"Because I don't believe the rumors, okay?" Or at least I didn't. Now, I wasn't so sure.

"He had something to do with his wife dying. I know it," said Kell.

"You don't know anything, okay? No one knows anything but Melanie, and she killed herself."

"Are those the lies he's been feeding you?"

I shook my head, staring down at the snow on the ground. "I . . . trust him."

"You shouldn't. And where the hell are you? I'm coming to see you. I need to know you're okay."

"Kell, I'm fine. Seriously." I heard the door creak open and Roland was stepping out in boots and a coat. My heart started beating fast again as he approached.

"Everything okay?" Roland asked.

I nodded, then turned away. "Listen, I'll call you in a couple hours, after I've gotten some sleep, okay?"

"No—Samira. I need to know you're okay! I need the address—"

"Goodnight. I love you." I hung up before he could say anything else, then turned to look at Roland. He was giving me a sideways glance.

"Are we okay?" he asked, facing me fully.

"Roland, we're fine," I said.

"Then why does it feel like you're hiding something from me?"

"I'm not hiding anything." I stepped back, which I shouldn't have done, because he frowned.

"Come back to bed, please."

"I will. I just need to check the shed—"

"Fuck the shed, Samira! Come back to bed *now*!" he

barked. I flinched and took several steps away, my eyes stretching wide.

"I—I mean . . ." He sighed and closed his eyes, then lifted his hands in the air and focused on me, as if trying to calm a frightened animal. "Please just come back to bed, Samira. I don't care about the book. I don't care that you're staying up late, I just . . . I want you with me. You, my wife."

I nodded, trying desperately hard to keep my breaths steady, and as he offered a hand, I took it. My hands trembled as we made our way toward the mansion, and he probably assumed it was from the cold, but it wasn't.

I was terrified.

When we reached the bedroom, I put the journal in the bottom drawer of my nightstand and placed my phone on the top of it. And as we lay down and he wrapped his arms around me, holding me close—holding me to him as if I were his prisoner and could never leave—I came to the realization that my brother had every right to be worried about me.

This was the side of Roland that Melanie had mentioned. The possessive, territorial, hostile side. A side I didn't feel safe with at all. I waited until Roland fell asleep again and, with his arms still wrapped around my waist, I slowly reached over to my nightstand, picked up my phone, and sent Kell the address to the mansion, along with one little word he would understand without me having to spell it out.

Hurry.

CHAPTER FORTY-SIX

To my utter surprise, I fell asleep right next to Roland, even with all that was on my mind. But when I woke up, his arms weren't wrapped around me. His side of the bed was vacant and when I ran my hand over it, it was cool to the touch, which meant he'd been gone for quite some time.

I reached for my phone and there were three unread text messages from Kell, along with at least a dozen missed calls.

What's going on, Samira?

I'm worried as fuck. Why aren't you answering me?

I'm coming there right now.

His last message gave me relief. But not for long. As I sat up, I noticed someone sitting in the upholstered chair in the corner of the room.

"Oh my God!" I screamed. "Roland? What the hell?"

Alarmed, Roland stood and held his hands up in the air. "Sorry! I didn't mean to scare you."

"It's fine," I breathed, clutching my chest. "Why are you sitting there? What's going on?"

"Oh, I uh . . . I had breakfast made for you. I saw you moving around when I came back to check on you and kind of just . . . waited for you to wake up after getting the food.

Weird, I know. I just didn't want you to think I was avoiding you today." He turned to his left and picked up a tray with food and a drink on it, then walked up to me with his head slightly bowed, placing the tray down on my nightstand. On the tray was French toast, scrambled eggs, and a fruit cup, along with a cup of apple juice.

"What's all this?" I asked, sitting up with my back against the headboard.

"I had Yadira make it for you." He smiled, then shifted his weight from foot to foot. "I, um . . . I owe you an apology for my behavior last night." He stood several steps away from me, scratching his head awkwardly. "I didn't mean to snap at you the way I did."

"Oh." I pressed my lips, unsure what to say. I wasn't going to tell him that it was okay because it wasn't. It was far from okay to snap the way he did and it made me wonder how often he did it with people when he didn't get his way, or how close he was to grabbing me the same way he did Melanie when they were in Hawaii.

Stepping closer, he dropped to his knees on the floor while reaching for my hand. I let him take it and cradle it in his hands.

"There are things about me, Samira, that I know I need to control. I have a temper problem and I know that. I bottle things up, hide my emotions, and then I blow up when it all feels like too much. I'm working on that about myself, though. I want to be more patient. More understanding. I know you need your space and you probably feel solace in that shed, which is fine, but . . . it's just that when you run off in the middle of the night like that, it reminds me of when Melanie used to do it. She would go there to avoid me and I never knew how to handle it."

"How does that remind you of her?" I asked, even though I knew the answer. After reading her journals I felt like I had a clearer understanding of what went on inside Roland's head.

"She always used to run off in the middle of the night. Sometimes during the day too. Closer to when she passed, she spent a lot of time in the shed and I never really knew what she was doing in there, but I also never questioned it." He sighed, squeezing my hand. "I want to be a better husband with you, Samira. I made a lot of mistakes with Melanie that I don't want to make again, and a lot of it stemmed from a lack of communication. I want us to be clear with each other at all times."

It was funny he'd brought up the topic of communication because I instantly wanted to ask him what the journals were about. A part of me wanted to show him what I'd read, ask him if he knew about Melanie and Dylan, and if he did, why he'd allowed Dylan to stick around, but as I looked into his hazel eyes, it registered to me that he couldn't have known. There was no way he would have still had the journals, the shed, or even Dylan around if he knew the truth.

I came to the conclusion that Roland had no clue what was written in Melanie's journals. He'd never set foot in the shed since she'd passed, I was sure, because if he'd spent at least five minutes in there alone, he would have discovered the journals, the same way I had.

I squeezed his hand back and sighed. I was weak for him. I still trusted him, and a part of me still believed he couldn't have had anything to do with Melanie's passing—that it was all a big coincidence and I was overthinking a lot of it.

"How do you feel about golfing with me?" he asked.

"What?" I laughed.

"I bought you some clubs as a surprise." He grinned, and I couldn't help smiling right back at him.

"I have never golfed in my life, Roland."

"That's why I'm here. I can teach you."

I huffed a laugh and watched as he brought the back of my fingers up to his lips. He folded them over his hand and kissed my knuckles and I melted. How was it possible to love him so much, yet also feel like some of my trust in him was dwindling? Was he innocent? Was he *not*? Was he hiding something and not telling me? I needed to know . . . but for now, I needed him to give me the mental space to figure it out, and if golfing with him would do the trick, then so be it.

"Okay, fine." I turned to grab my breakfast tray. "You can teach me, but don't be surprised if I end up breaking one of the clubs."

We'd spent an hour on the course. Spring was looming, but the air was still cold. The skies were gray and the snow had mostly melted, some white piles still lingering in shadowy places the sun couldn't reach.

Beyond the many acres of green turf and flapping flags were towering pine trees that ran for miles. There was nothing out here—no one to see, and no one who could see us. We may as well have been in the middle of nowhere.

As Roland took a swing at his golf ball, I stared ahead at the trees, feeling a breeze pass by me. I pictured a woman running toward the pines, her dark hair flapping in the wind, and a white scarf around her neck. She turned to look back, and her skin was chalky, blood dripping from the top of her head, running over her forehead and nose, and eventually spilling over her full lips.

I gasped and blinked.

"You okay?" Roland asked, getting into a perfect stance with the handle of his club in hand.

"Yeah." I tried blinking the image away and lowered my head, closing my eyes briefly before opening them again, but when I looked up, I still saw her, only she was running between a line of trees now, fading into the darkness. Then she was gone.

Melanie.

Roland took a swing and the club collided with the ball, causing a loud crack. I startled and whipped my head over to watch the ball soar before landing with a soft bounce and steady roll into a sand bunker.

"You're up," he said, smiling.

"Right." I nodded and he handed me one of my clubs, then placed a ball on a tee.

"What was the book you were reading last night anyway?" Roland asked, placing his hands on my hips to fix my posture. I had my arms out, clutching the handle of the golf club.

"Oh, it was just some romance book. I finished it and wanted to get the sequel from the shed. There are a lot of books in there."

"She read often," he noted, stepping away. "When do you think you'll get her stuff cleared out so you can make use of it for yourself?"

"Really soon. I already organized it. Just have to take pictures of some of the stuff that's in good condition to sell online and I'll donate the rest."

"Good."

It was quiet so I took the opportunity to bring the club back and swing at the ball. The club hit the ball, but the ball didn't go very far. Not nearly as far as Roland's.

"That was a shitty swing," I said, huffing a laugh. "Maybe I need a professional's guidance." When I looked at him, he wasn't smiling or laughing with me. His face was serious as he watched me.

"Did you find anything in there?" he asked. His voice was different. Not light and easygoing like it was seconds ago. It was deeper. Huskier.

"Anything like what?" I gripped the handle of the club tighter, feeling a drop in my belly.

"I don't know. Something you think I should know about."

"No," I said quickly. "It's just clothes and books and jewelry. Not much."

His face remained the same. Somber. Unsmiling. Then he turned toward the golf cart and climbed behind the wheel. "Riding with me to the next hole?"

"Yep."

I climbed into the cart, but as we drove I heard someone shouting my name. With a frown, I looked over my shoulder and spotted someone walking onto the golf course from the direction of the mansion.

Roland stopped driving and looked back too. "Who the hell is that?"

The person got closer. Closer. And I gasped when I realized who he was.

CHAPTER FORTY-SEVEN

"Shit! That's Kell!"

My brother was storming onto the green, his brows furrowed and his jaw tight. He had on jeans and a wrinkled T-shirt, as if he hadn't changed clothes in days.

"Kell?" Roland asked. "Your brother? But how did he find you?"

I wanted to answer, but my tongue was stuck in my mouth, heavy and swollen. Roland glanced at me before climbing off the cart, turning to face my brother, ready to greet him.

But Kell wasn't having it. As soon as my brother was close enough, Kell brought his arm back and punched Roland square in the face, and Roland's head went flying backwards, his eyes wide with shock.

"Kell!" I screamed, climbing out of the golf cart.

"What are you doing to my sister, huh? You think you're gonna hurt her too and get away with it?" Kell shoved Roland against the chest, and though Kell had always seemed pretty strong to me, his strength was nothing in comparison to Roland's. Roland was broad in the chest and shoulders, while Kell was lean in those areas. Plus Roland was several inches taller.

"What the hell are you talking about?" Roland snapped, his eyes nearly bulging out of his head as he looked between Kell and me.

I didn't even know what to say. All I could do was watch, tongue still swollen like a dead fish.

"Did he hurt you?" Kell demanded.

"No, Kell! He didn't hurt me!" I finally shouted. "Why would you hit him?"

"You told me to hurry, Samira! I got on the first flight I could and I'm here now!"

"You told him to *hurry*?" Roland countered. "What the hell is that supposed to mean?"

I looked at him and his bottom lip was bleeding.

"No, Roland, I—it's not like that. I just told him to hurry and come see me. I really wanted to talk to him in person."

"Really?" Roland swiped a thumb over his bleeding bottom lip. "So your brother punching me on sight doesn't have anything to do with you telling him to hurry?"

"Roland, I—"

"No—you know what? Don't bother. I get it. I see now you're just like everyone else." He stepped away. "I mean, *fuck*, Samira. If you don't trust me, why the hell did you marry me? Why the hell did you let me bring you all the way here to be with me if you thought for even a second we'd end up where we are now?"

Roland stared at me and there was anguish in his eyes, so raw it pained me too. My heart ached for him and I wanted to cry, especially when I noticed tears lining the rims of his eyes, but he wouldn't cry in front of me or Kell. Roland didn't seem like much of a crier, and if he ever did, I was sure he did it in private. Never with an audience.

"I'll be at the house icing my lip," Roland grumbled, then he walked away. Not once did he look back and he didn't even bother taking his clubs with him. That's how I knew he was pissed and hurt. He loved those clubs. They were custom made for him and he cleaned them almost every other night.

I faced my brother and threw my hands in the air. "Kell, what the hell, man? When I text you to *hurry*, it doesn't mean hurry to punch him in the face!"

"Well it's not like he didn't deserve it!" Kell snapped.

I dropped my hands to my hips. "How the hell did he deserve that? You don't even know him!"

"I know he killed his last wife," he shot back.

"No, you asshole, you don't know that! You don't know shit and neither do I, all right? So just relax." I sighed, stepping away and placing a hand on my forehead. "This is a fucking shitshow. And where are your things? Did you even sleep?"

"How the hell am I supposed to sleep when I think my sister is about to get murdered? He's lucky I didn't call the fucking cops on his ass."

"Oh my God, can you please stop using words like *cops* and *murder*? Look, last night I got a little paranoid, okay? But things are better today and he explained himself, so I shouldn't have jumped the gun and sent you those texts."

"The fact that you even had to send that message says enough, Samira." He peered over his shoulder. I looked with him and we could still see Roland marching toward the house, his shoulders hiked and his head down as he held his lip. "How the hell could you marry him? I told you to stay away from that man!"

"I know you did, but I also heard him out and I don't believe he's responsible for what happened with his first wife."

"Wow," he scoffed. "He must really have you dick-whipped. Or attached to his money. Is this some kind of retaliation for me having to cut you off? Because if it is, then we can fix that—"

"No—it's not about any of that." I glanced over again. Roland was farther away now, passing Melanie's shed.

"Look, I found something, okay?" I told him in a lower voice. "Something personal from *her*."

Kell's eyes narrowed. "Something like what?"

"She used to write in these journals . . ."

Kell cocked his head, confused. "Okay?"

"Her journals tell a lot about what was happening while she was with Roland—before she died. I haven't finished reading them yet, but I think there's something in there that might explain what led her to drive over that cliff."

"That's a stretch, Mira." He scratched his head. Then he rubbed his arms. "Fuck, it's cold."

"Let's ride back to the house." I collected my clubs and Roland's and placed them in the back, then climbed behind the wheel of the golf cart, heading back to the station.

"She cheated on Roland with his cousin," I said.

"*What?*" Kell spat. "She wrote that in her journals?"

"Yes. Apparently, she was seeing a therapist and he told her to write down where she thought her marriage went wrong. She goes deep. You wouldn't believe some of the things I've read so far. She had a sister who lived here for a while too."

"Seriously?"

"Yes. And supposedly she didn't show up to Melanie's funeral. Roland told me he hasn't seen her since Melanie died and he finds it strange since they were close."

"Maybe she was in denial about her death. Happens more often than we think."

"No, Kell, I'm telling you. Something isn't adding up with this. I want to take this as just one big coincidence, but knowing Melanie cheated on Roland with his cousin and that her sister didn't show at the funeral is really fucking weird. The way she describes her sister is like you and me, as far as our bond goes. Well, in a way. If one of us died, we'd show up at the other's funeral, no matter what we have going on."

I parked the cart and focused on Kell. "That's why I need you to do me a favor."

"What kind of favor?" he asked, rubbing his arms with chattering teeth.

"I need you to find out where her sister is."

"What? How the hell am I supposed to do that?"

"I don't know! You have resources with the agency, right? You guys can dig deep to get rid of the bad stuff—you tell me about it all the time. Have whoever does the digging to look for you. I've tried googling her but can't find anything. She's not on social media, but she has to be out there somewhere and if she is, I feel like she knows something."

"Fine, I'll see what I can do, but I'll be honest. Sounds like you're trying too hard to prove your new husband is innocent. What if it turns out he isn't?" Kell asked as we made our way toward the mansion. "What if you find out something you don't want to know?"

I didn't know how to answer that, so I didn't. Instead, I said, "You have to apologize to him."

"Apologize?" He balked. "For what?"

"You punched him on his property, Kell. You embarrassed him."

Kell rolled his eyes and I stopped walking.

"If you don't, I'll leave your ass out here in the cold. This is my fault, okay? I feel bad. You have to apologize."

"Fine, Samira! Damn!" He rubbed his arms again. "I don't even know why you moved all the way out here to Cold-As-Balls Land anyway. Get me next to a fire. I'm freezing."

I stifled a laugh as he moved past me and he smirked.

"Let me go get my bags from the driveway."

Kell apologized to Roland, but not with much enthusiasm. Honestly, I don't think it helped much of anything. Roland was clearly still disappointed and hurt by me. He accepted Kell's apology and they shook hands over hot coffee in the kitchen, but he could hardly look at me. After Kell's apology, Roland said he was going out for a while, went to the mudroom for his coat and shoes, and was out the door in a matter of seconds.

I felt horrible, both for how I made Roland feel, and for having Kell panic like that and fly all the way out here. I admit, the night before, I'd panicked, and I sent my brother that text without thinking about the consequences. I could have responded, but deep down I wanted Kell to show up, I just thought he'd arrive subtly.

I realized I could use Kell being around to my advantage. His resources were good. His job dug up dirt all the time, and if one of his clients had skeletons in their closet, their agency made magic happen and often made it disappear with settlements and nondisclosure.

His people could find Miley if no one else could.

"Despite all of this, I did want to see you in person," I said as we sat in the den. A fire was going and Kell was on his second cup of coffee.

"Well, you should've just said that, not have me thinking the worst and spending money to fly all the way out here."

I fought a smile. "How's Ana?"

"Pregnant as hell and driving me fucking crazy," he muttered, then sipped.

"And you really don't want to know the gender early?"

"I do, but she's dead set on finding out when the baby is born." He shrugged.

"What are you hoping for?"

"A boy. As you can see, girls have way too much drama for me to keep up with." He eyed me and laughed.

"Ha. Ha." I laughed with him while waving my middle finger in the air.

He placed his coffee mug on the table as his phone vibrated in his hoodie pocket.

"Oh, shit," he said after a while.

"What?" I asked.

"You remember Lola Maxwell?"

"Yeah, of course. I did a gig for one of her parties once and I went to her gala with Roland when we were only dating—a few weeks before we decided to get married and all. He didn't want to go because we were trying to hide, but he also didn't want to miss such a huge event, so we went. We purposely avoided taking pictures, but it was fun."

"Yeah, well TMZ just reported that she and her husband were found dead in their home." He picked his head up, looking me in the eye. "They think it was a homicide."

"What?" I gasped, sitting upright. "Who would do that?"

"I don't know. Doesn't say who yet, but it says they already have a suspect in custody. I'm sure they'll release that information soon." Kell shook his head and rubbed his face. "See, I come across news like this and I think the world is too damn evil for a baby to be in. Lola Maxwell was a good person and this is way too close to home." He shook his head again. "Always some crazy shit happening in Miami, man."

"Aw, Kellan," I cooed.

"Don't use my whole name on me, *Samira*." He pressed his lips, shutting the screen of his phone off and sliding it back into the pocket of his hoodie.

"You know . . . you can't prevent the evil that happens outside your home, but you can make a difference by raising your baby to be good. You're good, and even though Ana gets on my last fucking nerve, she's good too." I laughed as he battled a grin. "Your baby will be okay."

"I know, I know. Just nervous about becoming a father." He collected his coffee mug and took a long sip, taking a look around the den. "Anyway, this isn't weird to you?"

"What?"

"His first wife—Melanie, or whatever—she used to live here, right?"

"Yeah . . ."

"You don't feel weird about that? Living where she used to? Same bed, probably the same furniture. Same floors, even. Hell, some of her hair is probably still in the crevices of this place"

I took a look around and I hadn't noticed it before, but the den did have a hint of a woman's touch. I could tell Roland tried to cover it up with masculine furniture and rugs and portraits, but there were little things that screamed a woman had been here before, like the roman numerals clock on the wall, the glass ornaments on the bookshelves, and even the window nook with its green and white cushions and pillows. Green was her favorite color. How had I not realized it before? I supposed I only realized now because of the damn journals. Prior to reading them, I didn't pay any attention to that stuff. Now it was all in my face, glaring at me, taunting me.

I dropped my eyes to my jean-clad thighs. "I try not to think about it."

"You're better than me. What else did the journals say?"

"There's so much, Kell." I rubbed my forehead. "Honestly, half of it doesn't even seem real." I sat forward, placing my coffee down on the table too. "She was very promiscuous. Like, she admits that she loved sex, loved to feel in control with men. It almost came as no surprise to me that she cheated with Roland's cousin after explaining how she was, in the journals."

"Does Roland know about her and the cousin?"

"No. I don't think he does. He still hangs around—the cousin."

"What?" Kell's mouth hung open.

"Yeah, I know."

"Wait . . . you don't think he might've had something to do with it too, do you?"

"I don't know. All I know is Melanie cheated with the cousin and that Roland clearly doesn't know about it because they're still really close. You name me one guy who would still be close to a family member who had an affair with his wife."

"Not one," Kell murmured, then sighed.

"Exactly."

"Shit." He sat forward, placing his elbows on his knees. "What if this is some big, elaborate scheme?"

"What do you mean?"

"I mean—and maybe I'm thinking too much like a publicity rep—but what if *both* of them have something to do with it? Or what if the cousin knows something and Roland keeps him around so he doesn't say anything?"

"I don't know. I thought that for a while too . . . but then I think about Melanie's sister. The way she just disappeared after Melanie died. She also slept with Dylan—Roland's cousin—and Melanie tried to split those two apart a lot, just to have all of Dylan's attention."

"What?" Kell frowned, confused. "What kind of shit is that?"

"I have no idea."

"Damn." He sat back. "This is fucked up, sis."

"I know."

"And you really don't think Roland is involved at all?"

I released a shallow breath and sat back against the leather of the sofa too. "I want to believe he isn't. He promised me he isn't."

"Dudes lie all the time. They'll promise anything, especially men like Roland who are famous. Trying to make a fresh start and a new name for himself. To me, it looks like he's trying to rebrand himself and make people forget about that whole scandal—show that he's moved on from it and that the world should too."

I didn't want to think that was the case. I loved Roland so

much and I wanted him to be good, but what if it was true? What if Roland had only married me to make people forget? To make the world realize there were still women like me out there who believed his innocence?

If he was invited to Lola Maxwell's mansion party and even her gala months ago, he was purposely putting himself in the public eye. He knew there would be important people around and that, more than likely, people would speak to him, despite what'd happened. Innocent people don't hide and he was proving his innocence. He was gaining respect again. What if all of that was just for show?

Kell's phone rang and he dug into the pocket of his hoodie to take it out, then he groaned and turned the screen toward me. There was an image of Ana kissing him on the cheek, her blond hair curtaining the side of her face and her name at the top of the screen.

"Let me take this," he said, then he stood and left the den, rounding the corner to get to the kitchen.

I picked my coffee back up and as I sipped, I heard a door shut. Down the hallway, I spotted Dylan shrugging out of his coat, and I froze. The sight of him walking in here, using the key Roland had given him, made me uneasy and made every hair on the back of my neck stand up.

I didn't like the thought of him having a key—not after finding out how involved he was with Melanie—but what was I going to do about it? I couldn't exactly bring up what I'd read in the journals right now, and if I told Roland that I wasn't comfortable with Dylan around, I would've needed a reason, and I couldn't tell him what I'd discovered yet. I was certain at this point he had no idea Dylan slept with Melanie, and something told me Dylan wanted to keep it that way.

He came down the hallway and into the den with a smile. "What's up, Samira?"

"Not much." I pressed my lips, looking at him more intently than before. His long-sleeved shirt was rumpled, and he had on a pair of jeans with black marks on them that looked like grease marks from a car.

"Where's Roland?"

"He went out." I didn't really want to talk to him so I kept it brief.

"Oh, okay."

"Why are you here?" I asked, trying to keep the edge out of my voice. And better yet, why the fuck did he still have a key?

"Oh, I was just switching out a part in my car. Roland told me I could borrow some of his tools from the garage." Dylan looked at me oddly. "Is everything okay?"

"Everything's fine."

Kell stepped around the corner then and noticed Dylan. His shoulders squared and he tipped his chin as Dylan looked back.

"Oh. Who's this?" Dylan asked, smiling again.

"This is my brother, Kell," I said. "Kell, this is *Dylan*."

Kell kept a straight face—I loved that about him. He could hold a mean poker face, always knowing when and when not to react.

"Dylan, nice to meet you." Kell stuck his hand out and Dylan shook it.

"Likewise, man." They shook a few seconds longer than a usual handshake and I noticed Dylan trying to pull his hand away but Kell was clinging to it while holding his gaze.

I cleared my throat and Kell finally released his hand. Dylan reeled his hand back and ran his palms down the sides of his jeans. "Well, don't let me hold you two up. Didn't realize you were having company, so apologies for interrupting."

"Don't worry. It's fine," I murmured.

"Okay." Dylan looked between us. "Let me go find those tools." He smiled on his way out of the den and Kell didn't sit until he knew he was gone and out of earshot.

And when he sat, he said, "Nah. There's no way that guy had anything to do with the first wife's death. Did you see how nervous he was when I shook his hand? Doesn't seem like he has the balls." Kell unlocked the screen of his phone again. "We've got some digging to do, but first I need rest, so I need to find a hotel."

"You could stay here?" I offered, grinning sheepishly.

"Yeah, fucking right." He laughed, already on his phone, searching for hotels.

I took Kell to a hotel in town and before he got out, he asked, "You gonna be okay in that house by yourself? You know you can stay with me, right? Two beds."

"I'll be fine, and I should be back whenever Roland returns. Just come by tomorrow for breakfast."

"All right. I'll stop by."

"'Kay."

"Text me if you need me sooner."

"I will."

He walked to the trunk, took out his bags, then knocked on the trunk to let me know he was square. I watched him enter the hotel, and when I could no longer see him, I drove back to the mansion, but not without a million and one thoughts running through my mind, the main one being whether Roland was already back at home or not.

CHAPTER FORTY-EIGHT

Roland wasn't home and the mansion was quiet and empty. It felt strange. As I roamed the halls, making my way to the staircase, all I kept seeing was the woman in white in the corner of my eye. Sometimes she smiled. Sometimes she laughed. Sometimes she just stared at me, haunting me. I knew what she wanted. She wanted me to figure out what the hell had *really* happened to her, but now I was anxious. Diving deeper meant discovering even more things about Roland that I wasn't sure I wanted to know. I liked what we had before, but I realized that was all surface level.

Maybe I *needed* to dive deeper, figure out whether to stay and fight or run and never look back, while I could. As tempted as I was to go to the shed and read more, I didn't right away. Instead, I ran some bath water in the clawfoot tub and sat in there a while, trying to soak the worries away, but the silence of the mansion was deafening and made it nearly impossible to clear my mind. All I kept thinking about was Melanie in this tub, doing the same thing I was doing— ridding herself of her worries. Or in the shower, her tears blending with the stream as she thought about the way Roland hurt her.

I moved my feet and forced the water to swish but it wasn't enough, so I sank beneath the water with my eyes closed and held my breath.

I listened to my thudding heartbeat, felt the warmth of the lavender-scented water on my face. But with my eyes closed, I could picture her even more clearly.

Red lipstick.

White clothes. Red splatters.

Her mouth stretched wide-open, crying for help.

Running. Running. Driving. The engine of a car growling, tipping over the edge of a cliff.

I emerged and drew in a deep breath, resting my elbows on the edge of the porcelain tub. When I opened my eyes, I noticed someone leaning against the counter only mere steps away and drew in a sharp gasp.

Startled by my reaction, Roland's eyes stretched wide and he lifted his hands in the air. "Whoa—hey, it's just me."

"Yeah, I see that now," I said, panting. That was the second time he'd snuck up on me within the last twenty-four hours. "What are you doing? Why are you standing there?"

"I was checking on you," he said, frowning a little.

I wiped my face some more, then sank deeper into the water to hide my chest and shoulders. All that was out was my damp head.

"Samira," he called.

I avoided his eyes, focusing on the bubbles that weren't as foamy as they were minutes ago. I wasn't very good at confrontation either. I suppose I got that from my mother. Instead of finding my father and cursing him the fuck out, she stewed about it all over the house, bottled it up. She never gave him the raging words he deserved.

"I want us to talk about earlier," said Roland.

"Okay." I finally looked at him. His arms were folded, head angled.

"What was that about? You didn't tell me your brother was visiting."

"I didn't think I had to."

"I mean, no, you didn't have to, but it would have been nice to know so I could've prepared, especially for that blow he gave me."

I dropped my gaze. "I'm sorry about that. And for telling him to hurry."

"Why, though?" he asked, taking a step forward. "I—I feel like I've been as open as I possibly can with you. I know I scared you last night and I sincerely apologize for that, but what other reason than that have I given you for you not to trust me?"

None. He'd given me none. It was just those damn journals. I saw her point of view and was viewing him through her lens, and I couldn't help doing it. Yadira warned me not to believe everything I'd read, but I didn't listen. Now I was torn.

"Samira." I looked up and he was clearly at war with his words, his eyes glistening again. "I want you to trust me. I want you to believe me."

"I do believe you."

"So then why did you tell your brother to hurry here? What did he need to hurry for? That's pretty urgent to send to someone who you know already doesn't trust me being with you."

I sat up and stood, the bubbles and water dripping off me, and reached for a towel on the rack. I stepped out of the tub and onto the dry mat, looking into my husband's eyes.

"You want to know what this is about?" I asked.

"Yes! I've been wanting to know for days, Samira!"

"It's about your relationship with her! It's like you married me to try and save your own ass—to try and make the world forget about her death. It's about me feeling used."

"What? Are you serious?" He pressed his hands to his chest, stunned. "Samira, the last thing I ever wanted to do was get married again! But I fell for you! I fucking *love you* and I wanted you, and for once since Melanie died, I thought some-one was finally seeing me for who I really am! Not like how the rest of the world had labeled me, but for me. The *real* me."

I watched his hazel eyes, how they reddened, glistened. He blinked and the wetness was gone, but they were still red. I felt awful because in a way, just like Melanie, I was the one tearing my marriage apart. Sneaking around. Lying to him. Distrusting him. *Fearing* him. I was just like her, and that alone scared the hell out of me.

"I . . . I really don't even know what to tell you, Samira. I don't know what else to say about this. If you feel that way—like you can't trust me or be with me—then we might as well cut this marriage off where it is, because I refuse to go through this again. I refuse to stay with someone who doesn't love me."

But I did love him, and I wanted to scream that truth, but I also didn't want to look weak or pathetic in this moment. Not while I was naked and slippery and vulnerable. I hated this was happening too, but I didn't know what the hell to be-lieve anymore and I probably wasn't going to know until I finished those journals.

He needed to know about Dylan, that was a fact, but I also needed to see if Melanie had ever brought her affair *with* Dylan up to him in the first place, before I dragged that to the table like a cat with a dead bird. Roland could have known about her having an affair, but it didn't mean she'd told him who the affair was with. But if Roland did know about Dylan and Melanie, it was going to change the trajectory of *every-thing*.

When I didn't say anything, Roland left the bathroom with his head down, and after I'd changed, I went to the bed-room, but he wasn't there. I peered out in the hallway and one of the guest bedroom doors was halfway open, the light on.

With a frustrated sigh, I turned back for the bed and climbed beneath the comforter, and for the first time since moving into the mansion, I cried.

I wanted the truth. I also wanted us to go back to the way things were, but a part of me knew we never would. Not when there was a possibility I could have been wrong about Roland and he may have been lying to me this whole time.

I needed answers, and perhaps I was becoming obsessed with the whole idea of him and Melanie, despite the fact they'd been over for years, but I couldn't help myself.

For all I knew, my life could have been in danger and if it was, I wasn't going down without shedding some light on the truth for the whole world to see.

At five in the morning, the day after having breakfast with Kell, I got dressed and went to the shed. Kell had left three hours after breakfast to catch a flight back to Florida and told me he'd dig for information on Miley right away. Roland was avoiding me as much as possible and I had no words for him, so we stayed apart, sleeping in separate rooms and eating separate meals. I couldn't live like this for much longer, so that left only one thing for me to do.

I had to finish reading her journals. And this time, no matter how much Roland knocked on the shed or how obsessed I felt, I wasn't leaving until I got to the very last page of the very last journal.

CHAPTER FORTY-NINE

*R*oland never did ask who I'd cheated on him with and after what'd happened, I didn't have it in me to tell him it was Dylan. I'd hurt him enough.

Months went by, and eventually I transitioned from the master bedroom to the room Miley used to stay in. Miley had been bumped up weeks ago to a manager's position in a department store and had moved out. She'd found her own place and was able to pay for it with her job. I was proud of her, but I also missed her.

I slept alone in her room every night, and every morning that I woke up, I thought about the night in Hawaii. The rage in Roland's eyes was terrifying. I'd never seen him like that before and a part of me feared he really would have killed me if he could. Now, when he was around, I practically walked on eggshells around the mansion, all while he and Dylan boasted and laughed and were the best of friends.

I hated everything about it. If Roland knew it was

his own cousin who'd fucked me, he wouldn't have been so friendly with him. I wanted to tell him, just to get it over with—and to give Roland every reason to get rid of me and let our marriage go—but hadn't I been selfish enough? First in my marriage, and then with my sister, and now I wanted to sabotage Roland and Dylan's bond because it wasn't fair to me.

But I'd made this bed and perhaps I deserved it. Instead of kissing Dylan back, I should have pushed him away and told Roland what'd happened right away so he could kick Dylan out right on his ass. But I kept going back for more.

I couldn't stand to look at myself in the mirror anymore. I began losing weight from my lack of eating. I was hardly sleeping, so I'd spend time in the shed, glued to a computer screen, making designs people probably wouldn't buy because that was better than sitting in a room in the mansion, being ignored.

Who would buy from me anyway? I wasn't popular. I didn't keep up with my Instagram account, mostly because I didn't care for posting a ton of images of myself, even though the public expected that of me.

I didn't want to be the basic athlete's wife who took pictures of herself, waiting for likes, flaunting my athletic husband and all the money he had that I got to spend. I didn't want to be the wife who people assumed had only started her clothing line because she was married to a famous person and wanted to profit off the status.

I wanted them to know this was my idea—that I'd built this myself without Roland's help. I'd used his money to kick-start it, yes, but all the ideas, all the designs, all the paperwork and business licenses—I did it myself, without his help.

I once had this vision of starting my own clothing line and selling a ton of items, but even when it came to that, I was losing my passion for it. That night in Hawaii with Roland had completely drained me of any creativity, any love, any desire. I needed help but I wasn't going to get it from anyone inside the mansion.

Miley was doing great. I was happy for her, but also jealous of the fact she could escape this place so easily, no looking back and no worries about her future.

I'd considered purchasing my own apartment to hide out in but knew Roland would come looking for me, demanding me to get rid of it and come back to the house. Right after Hawaii, he took me off as a primary account holder with his bank and changed all of his card numbers so I couldn't go on shopping sprees whenever I wanted, like before. If I wanted something, I had to ask him . . . and after what'd happened, I never wanted to talk to him again, so that left me with nothing.

I could've stayed with Miley, but I didn't want her questioning why I wanted to be away from home. If she were to ask, I was sure I would've spilled everything and I didn't want that. She'd fallen in love with Dylan and I had betrayed her. I had enough truths out in the open to face. I didn't need to lose my sister too. She was all I had left and this wouldn't have been the first time I'd thrown her under the bus. I couldn't keep bringing her into my problems again. So, there I was. Feeling stuck. Hopeless. Feeling like I deserved to be exactly where I was.

"*Are you okay, Mrs. Graham?*" Yadira asked me one day, placing my breakfast in front of me.

I blinked, not even realizing I'd been staring through the glass of one of the double doors, at the pergola.

I looked down at my plate of eggs, avocado, and strawberries, then up at Yadira, who was giving me a concerned stare. "*No, Yadira. I'm not.*"

Yadira studied my face carefully, then pulled out the seat to my left and sat. "*I couldn't help noticing you and Mr. Graham don't have dinner together anymore when he's home.*"

"*Yeah.*" I picked up the fork and shuffled the eggs around.

"*Is everything okay?*"

"*It's not . . . but it doesn't matter.*" I forced a smile and looked her in the eye.

"*Of course it matters. You don't look well.*"

I didn't know what to say to that, so I said nothing at all.

Yadira pushed out of her chair and went around the corner to the mudroom. When she returned, she sat in the chair again and placed a white card down on the table. I read the words, **Walden Counseling.**

"*You should go and see Dr. Walden,*" said Yadira. "*He's a nice man. Very understanding. He listens and gives great advice.*" She placed a hand on my shoulder. "*Please, Mrs. Graham. Go and visit him. He saved my life. Maybe he can save yours too.*"

"*Saved your life?*" I asked. "*How?*"

"*Before this job, I was in a really bad depression. I'd lost my mother and after her death, I felt like my life was going nowhere. I lost weight, just as you have. I stopped socializing, just as you have. I just* wanted to curl up into a ball under a blanket and never come out of it."

I pulled my gaze away. That was exactly how I felt, but I didn't think anyone had noticed. Not only that, but I didn't think I was depressed. Just in a rut. I also felt lonely. Anxious. Scared. But when I researched, sure enough, it all linked to depression and I didn't know what to think of that. None of my family had ever believed in depression. We were always told we'd get over it, move past it—that we'd be okay. The way it went was if we kept moving forward or blocking the feelings and pretending the trauma never happened, then we'd be fine. But would we be? What if the trauma became too much to bear? What if the trauma was actually ruining everything good in your life?

I picked up the card, holding it between my forefinger and thumb.

"Think about it," she murmured, standing again with a gentle smile gracing her lips. Then she went back to the stove to finish dinner for the night.

CHAPTER FIFTY

It felt strange sitting in the waiting room in front of Dr. Walden's office. I had my Chanel bag in the middle of my lap and my cell phone in hand. I checked the time on my phone and it was seven minutes past my appointed time. I wanted to get up and leave right away—forget all about coming there.

I wasn't crazy. Seeing a therapist was crazy. I remembered my mother always saying therapy was for the weak—that Black people and especially Black women didn't need a therapist because we were strong.

According to my mother, Black women carried generations of burdens on our backs and were powerful for it. Fighting our tears. Fighting others' battles. Having others step on our backs just so they can climb to the top. But why was it that in this moment, I felt weak? I felt broken down and like I couldn't go on anymore, and if anyone were to step on my back again, I would break in half.

Clearly, my mother was wrong.

I hated my own face and skin. I hated my negative thoughts and the tears that dripped down my cheeks every night in the shed. I hated everything and felt no reason to live anymore. I wanted to die.

Mama was wrong about therapy, and I accepted that for a fact as soon as Dr. Walden opened his door and smiled at me. He was an older man—most likely in his sixties. But there was a warmth to him as he stood in his turtleneck sweater and khakis, smiling and revealing wrinkles in his brown face. His smile was big and wide and genuine and I felt this urge to jump up and hug him and that said a lot because I didn't even know him yet.

And when he said my name, "Melanie Raine," I sobbed because for the first time in a long time I felt seen. I had given him my maiden name and he'd used it, and it'd been a very long time since I'd heard the name Raine. My name. The name I was born with—the name that belongs to me and makes me the woman I am.

(P.S. I know you're reading this, Dr. Walden, but I'm following your advice and telling my story the way I remember it.)

"Please come in," Dr. Walden said, and I felt foolish with my bottom lip trembling, my eyes thick with hot tears.

I walked past him into his office and sat on the cozy gray sofa against the wall. His office wasn't very big—a room inside a building that collided with other random independent practices, but with the gray-blue paint on the walls, the bookshelves, and even his cluttered desk, it felt welcoming and homey in a way.

I placed my bag beside me and as he sat down in a chair across from me, he eyed it. "An expensive bag you got there," he said, picking up a notepad and pen. "Was it a gift?"

"Oh—uh, no. I bought it for myself a couple months ago." I glanced at the creamy chevron purse, then back at him.

"You bought it for yourself," he noted. "Where do you work?"

"I don't work. I get money from my husband—well, I used to. We used to share an account."

"Really?" He wrote something on his pad. "How do you feel about that? Spending your husband's money?"

I shrugged. "I don't know. I guess . . . fine?"

"Fine?"

"Yes. When I was spending it, I liked shopping. He used to tell me I could buy whatever I wanted and never complained when I did."

"He never gave you a shopping limit?"

"No."

"Why do you not share an account now?"

"He . . . cut me off."

"Why?"

"That's why I'm here. To talk about that."

"Right." Dr. Walden finished jotting down a note, then placed his pen and paper down on the table beside him. "Melanie, in our emails, you told me you wanted to talk about your marriage. You also mentioned your past as well, but your marriage was what you spoke of most. So, tell me . . . what is it about your marriage that has been troubling you?"

I stared into his wise brown eyes, then down at my bare fingernails. "I want a divorce from him."

"So why don't you get one?"

"Because he won't let me."

"He won't let you? What do you mean by that?"

"I mean, I told him I wanted one a few weeks ago, and he told me if I go anywhere he'll make my life a living hell." I glanced up and Dr. Walden had his notepad and pen again. He scribbled something quickly.

"Tell me more about your husband," he said.

"What do you want to know?"

"What does he do? What's his profession? What's his personality like?"

"Um . . . well, he's a pro golfer," I said.

"Ah. Explains the purse," said Walden, smirking.

I huffed a laugh. "Yeah. He's been golfing since he was a teenager, went superstar mode right around the time we met."

"Which was when?"

"About five years ago."

"Okay. So what about his personality?"

"Well, he can be nice. Giving. Funny in a dry kind of way. He's a great lover and really smart."

"These are all positive things," Walden noted. "So why do you want to divorce him?"

"Because I cheated on him."

Walden set his pen down on the notepad and tilted his head, but he didn't frown, didn't narrow his eyes or look at me with judgment in them. Instead, he appeared confused and mildly stunned by my honesty.

"Normally it's the other way around. By that, I mean when someone wants a divorce, it's because the other person cheated and was caught, but you cheated and now you want to divorce him?"

I shrugged.

"Is it because you've fallen in love with another man?"

"Not exactly."

"But he wants you to stay in the marriage? Make it work?"

"Yes, he wants me to stay, but he doesn't care about making it work anymore. I think he just wants to make me miserable." I brought a hand up and touched my cheek. "When I told him that I wanted a divorce, he, um . . . he grabbed my face really hard. We were on vacation and it hit me that he deserved better and that I wasn't happy in our marriage anymore, so I thought I would spare his time, walk away . . ."

"Was that his first time being aggressive with you?"

I sniffled and wanted to answer, but my throat was thick with emotion. Walden reached for the bamboo box of tissues on the table between us and offered one to me. "It's okay. Take your time."

I grabbed a couple and dabbed at my cheeks. "I'm a bad wife," I said through tears. "I never should have agreed to marry him."

"Why do you call yourself a bad wife?"

"Because I married Roland knowing we wouldn't make it. And I cheated on him with someone he cares about a lot—someone very close to him."

Walden was quiet a moment and I didn't dare look at him, so I kept wiping my tears away, but they wouldn't stop falling.

"Does he know that?"

"Know what?"

"That you had an affair with someone close to him?"

"No. He hasn't asked who I had an affair with. I don't think he wants to know. Or maybe he doesn't care to know."

"Sometimes the unknown can make certain events feel like they've never happened. He's suppressing his emotions and shielding himself from the *truth. Perhaps he knows it was with someone close and refuses to acknowledge that to protect himself."*

"I guess so."

Walden shifted in his seat. "Melanie, I want to go back to my question before. Was that his first time getting aggressive with you?"

"Yes, it was. He's usually calm. Never that quick to anger, but I think my confession really hurt him that night and he just kind of blew up. I'd never seen him get like that before."

"Do you think he will hurt you again?"

I looked into his gentle eyes and they were full of concern. "I . . . I don't know, honestly. I think if he ever finds out who I had an affair with, that he might hurt one of us."

With a nod, Walden wrote another note, and while he did, he asked, "When do you think things changed between you and Roland?"

I had to give his question some thought. I tried to think it through, but couldn't think clearly at the time, so muddled with emotion and also relief that I could finally talk to someone without the weight of judgment, so I just shrugged.

"I want you to try a coping technique that has helped some of my other clients tremendously. What you do is you buy a journal, and with that journal I want you to sit and think about when you felt your marriage unraveling. Take your time with it. If you have to, write every event down from the moment you met him to now, sitting here, talking to me. Perhaps then, it'll be clear to you why you feel the way you do. And I think, as you do, you'll find the answers to your problems, and then we'll discuss it further and work on finding the best solutions."

I nodded. "Okay."

"*Do you like to write?*" he asked.

"*Sort of.*"

"*I've noticed with a few of my clients that they like to write their traumas and experiences as memoirs. What they discover can cut deep and they're hard realizations, but they learn so much about themselves and even begin to remember things they'd purposely blocked out so they wouldn't have to remember the trauma. Perhaps you can try that?*" he offered. "*It may help you delve deeper into what really shifted things in your life and your marriage and why you really want the divorce from your husband.*"

I nodded again. "*I can try that.*" And this was the moment I started asking myself, when did things go so wrong with me and Roland? It hadn't started that night in Hawaii. Things had begun unraveling way before that—before we were even married—and I wanted to blame Miley, blame Dylan—hell, I even wanted to blame Roland's mother for her lack of parenting and not showing him real love, but our problems didn't stem from any of them.

It stemmed from the night before we got married.

He didn't have a bachelor party and I didn't have a bachelorette party. We saw each other the night before, though it would have been considered bad luck to do so.

I was in a hotel penthouse and he came to visit me. But he hadn't come alone. There was someone with him.

CHAPTER FIFTY-ONE

"*Hi baby!*" *I squealed, throwing my arms around Roland's neck after opening the door. Chuckling, he hugged me tight and kissed me on the cheek.*

"*Hey, baby.*" *He placed me back on my feet, and when he moved to the side, I noticed the person behind him. He appeared to be around our age, a Latino male with fair skin, wavy brown hair, and light brown eyes. He waved and I waved back cautiously.*

"*Who's this?*" *I asked, keeping a smile in place as I looked between Roland and the other man.*

"*Mel, this is Felipe. You haven't met him before, but he's a good friend of mine. Takes pictures for some of my games sometimes.*"

I had to admit, it felt a little odd, him bringing a friend to my hotel room, but at the time I didn't think to question it. I invited them both in with a smile.

"*Felipe is a great photographer,*" *Roland said after fixing me a glass of wine.*

"*Is that true?*" *I asked Felipe, accepting the drink.*

"*I am,*" *said Felipe with a grin.*

"Yes, and as you can see, he has his camera."

"I see that," I said with a laugh.

"I brought him here so he can take pictures of us." Roland looked me in the eyes and I looked back, confused for a moment, but then it hit me.

"What kind of pictures?"

"Keepsakes," he said. "I want him to capture us and how we feel the night before we get married. Excited. Primal. Feral."

"You mean you want him to take pictures of us . . . naked?" I blushed and sipped my wine and Roland nodded and revealed all his teeth as he smiled.

"Is that crazy?"

"Only if you think it is," I giggled, then I glanced at Felipe. He turned his head, peering out of the window, pretending he wasn't listening to our conversation. "You won't feel weird that your friend is shooting us?" I whispered to him.

"Nah. I trust him. Plus he already signed an NDA."

I sighed, sipped my wine, and then said, "Okay. If this is what you want." That was the thing about me. I was so head over heels for Roland at the time that I wanted to do whatever to please him and make him happy. It didn't matter that he'd already had Felipe sign the NDA without my consent, or that he'd brought him to my private suite. Whatever Roland wanted from me, I gave to him.

Roland told me he had something for me in the car and went to get it. While he did, Felipe took off his camera bag and then began fiddling with the lens of his camera.

When my fiancé returned, he had a white bag with a black ribbon for a handle and inside it was green lingerie.

"My favorite color," I cooed.

"Try it on," he insisted, and I skipped off to the bathroom, putting on the matching set. The bra was lace and see-through, and I felt silly looking at myself in the mirror. I'd had my fair share of nights in lingerie, but not like this. Not with another pair of eyes around. My soon-to-be husband was out there waiting and his friend had a camera, ready to snap private photos of us. Though I was nervous, I was also excited about it. I loved when Roland revealed his spontaneous side. I didn't see it often, but when I did, I never forgot those moments.

I tipped my chin confidently, then walked back out of the bathroom.

I took several pictures with Roland, who had taken his shirt off to get in on the fun with me. Felipe gave us instructions to enhance the photos and it was entertaining at first. But then we kept drinking and Roland insisted that I take pictures alone. I posed on the bed, half naked, in front the lens of a man I didn't even know, while Roland sat in a chair in the corner of the room and watched.

And then Roland told me to take off my bra, so I did. He told me to be myself, so I did. I climbed off the bed, went to my makeup bag and pulled out a red tube of lipstick. I rubbed it on my lips, then walked over to Roland and kissed him on the cheek. He laughed.

I went to the patio doors to open them, throwing my arms up in the Vegas heat, drunk and unafraid. I was exhilarated that night. I was getting married to the love of my life in a matter of hours. I had no worries, no fears. Nothing to fret about.

I turned and cupped my breasts and Roland groaned and smiled.

"Do you like that?" I asked him, and Felipe kept

shooting. I bit my bottom lip and climbed back on the bed.

"You realize that after tonight, you won't be able to have sex with another man ever again, right?" Roland asked.

"Then maybe we should all just have a three-some!" I exclaimed, breaking out in a laugh right after.

Felipe stopped taking pictures. Roland glanced at him, and then back at me, his jaw flexing.

"I'm kidding, babe. Relax," I said.

"No, you're not." Roland sipped from his wine-glass.

Felipe lowered his camera nervously, slowly, side-eying Roland. Before long, Roland stood and picked up his shirt off the edge of the bed.

"Where are you going?" I asked.

"I'm going to get some ice," he said, heading for the door.

"Roland. I was just kidding," I hurried to say.

"While I'm gone, I don't care what you do. Don't care how you do it. But I want you to know it'll be the last time another man ever touches you again."

My eyes swung over to Felipe and then back at my fiancé. "Roland. You can't be serious. I don't even know him."

"Does that matter to you right now? Only seconds ago you wanted a threesome with him."

I clamped my mouth shut, taken aback by his blunt response.

Roland opened the door and peered back at Felipe, who was standing in the middle of the room, clinging to his camera. "I'll be back with that ice soon."

The door closed behind him, and I had no idea

what the hell to make of what'd just happened. Was he fucking around? Was he serious? Was he testing the both of us?

My head was spinning, my mouth tacky and tongue thick. I climbed off the bed and went for the wine bottle, pouring myself another and guzzling it down.

"Roland is crazy." Felipe huffed a laugh, sitting in the chair Roland was in only seconds ago. "We'll just wait for him to come back. He's had too much to drink. He's not thinking straight."

"He won't come back," I stated, pouring myself another glass.

Felipe placed his camera down on the table next to him. "Is this a trap or something?"

"Let's just keep taking pictures," I instructed, turning with my wineglass. "Come on. Stand. Pick up your camera."

Felipe stood, but not without a frown. He was in a sticky situation and I had no idea why Roland was allowing this, but he had a point. I wasn't fully kidding about the threesome. In fact, I would have worshipped Roland for the rest of my life if he'd said yes to it in that moment. Having sex with a man I loved and a complete stranger at the same time. It was a fantasy of mine that I'd told him about often, one he said would probably never be fulfilled because he never wanted to see another man touch me.

I wasn't ever going to be with another man again. It was only going to be Roland for the rest of my life and that haunted me in a way.

Roland forever.

Only. Roland.

The words from my childhood rattled in my head: You dirty fucking slut. You nasty bitch.

I shook the thoughts away, throwing my arms up and posing for more pictures. Felipe kept shooting. I kept drinking and drinking, drowning myself in alcohol, trying hard not to think of the past—of what this moment really reminded me of—until my actions weren't my own.

Before it could register to me, I was pushing Felipe down in the chair in the corner again, taking his camera out of his hand, and placing it down on the table beside us. I wanted to own this moment— prove that it was mine and mine alone. That I was in charge. That this was my decision, not Roland's or anyone else's.

I kissed him, and kissing him felt good—reminded me of the past, back when I could kiss whoever the hell I wanted, whenever I wanted, no commitments. Back when my sexuality had peaked, and when I'd prided myself in the number of men I could make weak in the knees.

Felipe didn't resist my kisses, and he damn sure didn't resist when I dropped to my knees and told him to lower his pants. When we both climbed on the bed, lip-locked, gripping and grasping each other's hair, he finally caved in to the moment.

Roland didn't come back at all that night. I didn't see him again until the next day, when I was walking up to the altar in the private ballroom of the hotel. Roland's mother was there, and Dylan, who I didn't really know so well at the time, and his agent. Felipe was there with his camera, snapping photos, but I pretended he didn't exist because this was a new day, and I'd had my fill of him, and now I belonged to Roland. Only Roland.

Forever.

"Why did you let that happen last night?" I asked

when we shared a dance beneath the stars, gliding on the marble balcony of an expensive hotel.

"Because now you can't say I didn't give you a night to do whatever you wanted with no regrets. Now you can only want me."

"What did you do last night?"

"I went to my room and tried my hardest not to think about it, which was impossible, might I add."

"Roland . . . you should have asked me first before bringing him there." I stopped dancing to look up at him.

"It's what you wanted, Melanie. You've always wanted an extra man around. You've been talking about threesomes since I met you. I wanted you to get whatever you needed out of last night and be done with it. And I can trust Felipe not to say a thing. Plus, we're in Vegas and whatever happens here . . . well, you know the rest."

"Why would you marry me if you feel like that?"

"Like what?"

"Like you aren't enough for me."

"Because I love you, and I'm going to work toward being more than enough for a woman like you."

I blinked up at him, then looked away, over my shoulder. My eyes connected with Felipe's and all I could feel was guilt, shame. Roland's words were kind and sweet and I wished in that very moment he would always be enough for me, but even that night, I knew he wouldn't be.

I was not a monogamous woman. I wanted what I wanted when I wanted it. I owned my sexuality, carried it like a shield and a weapon if need be. I should have walked away that night, given Roland the chance for something better before the ink dried, but I didn't because there was hope in his eyes and

I wanted to cling to that hope. I wanted to be the right woman for him, and I wanted him to be the only man for me. I wanted to change and accept my new life.

But the truth is, I never stopped thinking about Felipe. Every time he came around or popped up for a visit, I felt this tug in my gut, this burning heat between my thighs, a yearning for him that Roland had created without even realizing it, and I tried so hard to ignore it. I tried to forget about the night with him before my wedding—forget about the way he pulled my hair, spanked my ass, kissed me between my thighs. But it was impossible to stop thinking about it. Still, I didn't cave or fall into temptation. I remained loyal . . . until Dylan moved in.

And damn, was Dylan a surprise. I suppose I had so much bottled up in me that when I saw him, I was ready to pounce. I got possessive and hungry and needy and Felipe wasn't around as much, but this other man was. And he looked at me. He saw me. He wanted me too, and damn if I didn't want to own that, claim it. And eventually I did.

I went back to Felipe after seeing you, Dr. Walden—after realizing that the night with him in the hotel was the root of what was wrong with me and Roland. I'd had issues before and Roland knew that, but he didn't care. He wanted me against all the odds . . . but I stopped wanting him. And therein lay the problem.

I hate admitting this, but after the Hawaii stint and months after therapy, I met Felipe in a hotel again and let him fuck me. For hours I let him have me, and we even spoke about living together if I left Roland. It was a good night, but then it ended and he had to go. I drove back home, eager to walk into the mansion with my suitcase to prove to Roland that I'd been out, most likely with someone else, and he did see me. He was coming down the stairs as I was coming up with the suitcase. He stopped on the steps, glanced down at it, looked me in the eye for a brief moment, then kept going down, but I didn't miss the tick in his jaw, or the flame that'd started in his eyes.

He didn't care then and he doesn't care now. Whether he knew I was with another man or not, it clearly didn't faze him anymore. The damage had already been done a long time ago, and neither of us was willing to own up to it, so instead we dealt with each other's bullshit and stomped around the house in fits and rages.

My husband no longer wants me, so why the fuck won't he just let me go? Why does he keep me around? What does he expect to get out of this other than more affairs and bitterness? Is it his pride? Does he think I'll shout about my affairs to the rooftops? Write about it in a book to make him look bad? Because I damn sure am not going to sabotage myself that way. Writing to you is already too much for me.

So, where do we go from here, Dr. Walden?

CHAPTER FIFTY-TWO

She'd gone back to Felipe? But . . . we'd just had dinner with him. How could Roland allow him to be around after that? He was there that night—he gave her permission to do things with his friend. It was just like the situation with Dylan, except I didn't think Roland knew about Melanie and Dylan . . . but now I was starting to second-guess that too.

Something bumped against the shed and a sharp gasp broke out of me, the journal falling out of my hands and thudding on the floor. Then I heard footsteps pounding into the ground. I rushed to the window to look out of it, heart pounding, and my pulse in my ears, but didn't see anyone out there.

I drew the blinds on the windows and sat back down in the chair. Someone was out there. Was it Roland? Was he watching me now? He had to have been on to me after the situation with Kell. I needed to talk to him about it in full, yes, but at the moment, my heart was racing way too fast and my hands were shaking. What if I did bring it up and he killed me too?

I picked up my phone and sent Kell a text message.
Check in with me every hour, okay?

Kell responded right away: **What's going on? Do I need to call the cops? You trapped?**

No. Just a little anxious right now.

Should I fly back out? I can, just say the word.

No. it's okay, Kell. I'm okay. Just check in with me. I'll be okay.

Fuck. Okay, Mira. But I swear if I don't hear from you every hour I'm calling the police and then flying out there to finish beating his ass.

I huffed a laugh and turned my phone face down.

I fell asleep in the shed. When I woke up, the sun had risen, golden rays peeking through the gaps of the white blinds. I checked my phone and there were text messages from Kell. He was worried because I hadn't responded overnight.

I sent him a text back and told him I was fine, then I stood and made my way to the door to crack it open. The coast was clear, so I hurried out, shutting the door behind me and marching across the lawn to get to the back door of the mansion. Once inside, I checked mine and Roland's bedroom and then the room he had been sleeping in, but he wasn't in either of them. I trotted down the stairs to check the garage, and his SUV was gone. He wasn't home. So who did I hear the night before?

I rushed through the hallways, passing the portraits on the wall and the elongated windows until I was in front of Roland's office door. I pressed the pads of my fingers against the wood and looked inside. Vacant. I had to do this now if I planned on not getting caught.

I'd noticed before, when we first moved in, that there was a book of contacts on his desk. I found it in the top drawer and placed it on top of the desk with shaky breaths. And when I opened it, I went to the letter F. Felipe's name was second on the list. His number was written on the line below his name.

Maybe he had something to do with Melanie going over that cliff. If they were as close as she said they were toward the end, and were sleeping around unbeknownst to Roland, he had to know *something*.

I typed the number into the keypad of my phone and my thumb hovered over the button. I looked up at the window, and was certain it was my hysteria and lack of sleep getting to me, but *she* was out there, standing in middle of the yard. *Melanie.* The blood was dripping from her head much faster now, soiling her entire outfit and scarf. Her face warped, like she was in so much pain.

I pressed the call button, then paced the office with the phone pressed to my ear, ignoring the window.

"'Ello?" Felipe answered. His accent was familiar, and I was relieved that it was actually him.

"Hi—Felipe? This is Samira."

"Oh, Samira! Hi! What is going on? I am surprised to be getting a call from you."

"Yeah, well, I have a few questions for you." There was no point in stalling. Melanie was still outside the window, in the yard. She was stepping closer to the house. My hands trembled. So much for ignoring her.

"Okay? What's up?"

"I'm going to cut straight to the point. I know about your night with Melanie—the night before she and Roland got married."

The line was quiet, and for a moment I thought he'd hung up. Then he said. "Did he tell you about this? He had me sign a nondisclosure that night. I thought we weren't supposed to talk about it ever again?"

"So he did have you sign one?" She wasn't lying about that.

"Yes. We'd been drinking the night before his wedding and it came up in conversation and I told him I wouldn't be opposed to helping him out. He'd already had the contract printed—like he had been thinking about it way before that night. I don't know. He did say he knew it was a mistake going in, but that he thought it would make her happy, show her that he cared about her needs."

I swallowed hard and glanced at the window again. Melanie was getting closer. I turned away from the window.

"Okay . . . well, I need you to talk to me about your relationship with her. I found these journals she used to write in. She talks a lot about her affair with you around the time she died."

"Affair?" He sounded completely confused. "What do you mean?"

"You weren't still sleeping around with Melanie closer to when she passed away?"

He cleared his throat. "We were um . . . well, yes. We were sleeping together. But it only happened twice, and I regret it deeply. Roland doesn't know about those two times."

"Were you planning on being with her at all if she were to leave Roland?"

"Absolutely not!" he exclaimed. "Listen, I sorely regret what I did to Roland, especially when I found out that she died. I was eaten alive by guilt, but I never would have done that to him—be with her after she left him. Never. I got caught up in the moment with her again and she told me they were about to get a divorce and that she wouldn't tell him we were sleeping around, so I did it. But I stopped it right away. She got angry with me because I wanted to end things, called me a coward, but I never spoke to her again after that. Please, Samira. Do not tell Roland. He is a great friend of mine and—and I care about him very much. I made a mistake and I shouldn't have. Please, I'm begging you. I have a fiancée now. I can't have her finding out about this either."

I closed my eyes. I could hear the panic in his voice. And as much as I could have assumed that he did have something to do with it—or perhaps even corroborated—something in my gut told me he had nothing to do with Melanie and that cliff—that he was just a man in the middle of their mucky marriage. I believed him. He had nothing to gain by doing something to Melanie. Roland and Dylan, however, had a lot to lose. It all circled back to them.

"I won't say anything, Felipe." I turned to face the window. Melanie was right outside of it, staring at me, the blood dripping faster. My heart raced, and I closed my eyes. *She's not real. She's not there.*

"Thank you," he sighed, relieved. "Why do you ask all of this anyway?"

"Just curious," I said. I wasn't going to tell him that I didn't trust Roland—or that I thought he had something to do with Melanie's passing.

"Okay." He paused. "Even if I had taken such a risk to be with her, I don't think it would have lasted. She was too hardcore for me," said Felipe.

"Hardcore? What do you mean by that?"

"I just mean . . . well, while we did things, she liked to be called dirty names. I'm not sure why . . . but I didn't like to say them. I'm more a lover, you see. So . . . her fetishes just weren't for me."

"I get it."

"Okay. I have to go, but you won't say anything about this?"

"I won't, Felipe. You have my word."

He sighed, relieved, we said goodbye, and then I hung up. When I looked at the window again, Melanie was gone.

I closed the contact book and left the office, going back to the shed and picking up where I left off.

CHAPTER FIFTY-THREE

It's been a year and six months since the night in Hawaii. Roland is hardly ever home. Dylan moved the fuck out, thank God. I said it before, but I'm really thinking about buying an apartment and putting some distance between me and this place. I'll miss my shed. My happy place. My escape.

If I leave, will Roland tear the shed down? I bet he would, just to spite me. Today I found the golf clubs I bought him for his birthday, broken in half in the garage. He broke them in a rage, I'm sure. I told him he deserved better. He has the choice to accept the fate of our marriage and let it go. Why does he allow himself to suffer like this?

It's been five months since I've been seeing Dr. Walden. I feel better. Refreshed. Renewed. I don't feel the need to write in here as much anymore. I've taken his advice into account. Roland won't walk away from this marriage, and neither will I. He won't acknowledge me and I've accepted that. It's fine. Whatever. But he can't get mad at me when I end up doing what I want.

I want to run off, fall in love with another man—someone who will cater to my every desire and give me everything I want. Someone who won't hurt me or get angry with me when I express how I feel. Someone who will understand that I am the way I am and don't really want to change it.

I have been thinking, maybe if I find someone else to be with, will he let this go? Let me run off with my mystery man to do what I please and forget about me? Divorce me so I'm not the bad guy here and the public doesn't attack me? I don't care about his money. I don't need any of it. I just want to leave and not have any bad blood between us.

Dr. Walden says he thinks Roland is keeping me around to help me. He thinks Roland knows exactly how I am and that he's accepted it, and that a part of him still wants to work out our marriage. I don't believe that though, and I think it's too late to try and work things out now.

I could walk away.

Start from scratch and even change my identity—everything there is to know about me.

I don't know where I'd go, or how I'd get money, but I could do it.

I just need to figure out where to start.

CHAPTER FIFTY-FOUR

It's been a while since I've written here. But I have to document my discovery because this is seriously fucked up.

I got a call today. It was from our accountant, Jeff. Roland wasn't answering the phone and Jeff wanted to speak to me right away, despite me not being on Roland's accounts anymore. We were good friends—in fact, Roland met Jeff through me. He informed me that some of Roland's numbers aren't adding up and that he found several wire transfers going to a bank called Mountain Capital Banking in Denver. He was curious if I'd created the account without Roland's knowledge and if he should have kept it off record.

I don't bank there and neither does Roland, so I called the bank to ask about the account and was told the money was going into the account of a charity called Designer Hearts and that my name was listed as the account holder. And not my nuptial Melanie Graham. Melanie Raine.

"*That must be a mistake,*" I said to the bank's customer service rep. "*I don't give to a charity by that name. I've never even heard of them.*"

"*Well, Mrs. Graham, it says right here on the account that you authorized the wire transfers from your husband's account to this one when you opened it. You also opened up a secondary account for an Yvette Dennis on August eleventh and gave her access to the account for her use as well.*"

"*What?*" I shrieked. "*I don't even know an Yvette Dennis! This has to be someone pretending to be me and using my information!*" I put my phone on speaker as the woman started talking again.

"*Okay. Mrs. Raine, if you believe that is the case, we will have to look into this, but I'll have to forward your call to our fraud department. Do you mind being put on a brief hold?*"

"*No. It's fine. I'll wait,*" I muttered because this was ridiculous. While I waited, I went to the browser on my phone, thinking this had to be some kind of scam. I searched for the name Yvette Dennis and several hits popped up. There was a website called renovateforya.com and an Instagram page with the same title.

I clicked on a Facebook link with the name and it took me to a profile of a woman who had red faux locs in her profile picture. Her eyelashes were full and fake too, and she was posing with a hammer in her hand and a dusty worker's belt around her waist, standing in the kitchen of a home that appeared to be in the middle of a big renovation.

I scrolled through her profile. She was married to a man named Rodney Dennis. There were images of her and her husband as I scrolled, but then I came *across one where she was with someone familiar and a gasp shot out of me.*

I cupped my mouth, staring at the photo of her and Dylan. They were seated on an expensive leather couch, both wearing burgundy shirts with the words We Renovate For Ya.

Dylan?

My mind was reeling. But then I remembered something—a detail he'd spilled once before. When we ate brunch together, Dylan told me he had a sister named Yvette. But how the hell could she have had access to my account? I didn't open this account—I never would have done it. In August, I despised Dylan, and had despised him for months before that.

And it hit me. Like a swift punch to the gut, it hit me and I realized in that moment that Dylan had been in our house so many times, around our personal files, in and out of Roland's office, and passing my shed. He had access to every fucking thing we owned and we trusted him—well, Roland did.

I hung up the phone and called Jeff back.

"Do you think Roland would authorize this?" Jeff asked as soon as he answered. "He never mentioned any type of payments to a designing charity that you supported. I'm going through my notes now and don't see it listed."

"No," I murmured. "I don't think he would have."

"Should I call him to clarify?"

"No—don't worry about it, Jeff. I'll ask him when he's home and let you know what to do after I talk to him."

"Okay."

I hung up, still staring out of the window across

from me, and I didn't know how, or why, but it became clear to me that Dylan was stealing from Roland right under his nose, and that motherfucker was using my name to do it!

Roland was prompt about his taxes. No, he didn't check his bank statements every day—he had too much money to bother—but that's what he had Jeff for, and Jeff reported everything to us, never missed a beat. If Jeff didn't know something or there were items in his statements that were questionable, it meant Roland hadn't authorized it—that someone had hacked into his accounts or that Jeff made a mistake, and Jeff never called about his mistakes. He always corrected them first before informing us. And if it involved me, he often asked me first because I could be spontaneous with his money—when I had free access to it, anyway. I liked to spend and had even donated to a couple of popular charities for Roland before . . . and Dylan knew that.

Dylan had moved in and accessed all of my and Roland's personal belongings, our files, bank account numbers, social security numbers, passwords—everything. Roland kept all of his documents in his office, stored and locked in the bottom drawer of his filing cabinet, but the key to that cabinet was in a cup on a shelf in his office. And I was sure Dylan had seen Roland use it on more than one occasion. I stored my financial records in our bedroom closet or locked them in my shed—but it was just a shed. It could still be accessed pretty easily.

On the outside, it appeared I had authorized this. Simple charity payments made every other month, wedged between basic withdrawals, bill payments, grocery bills, and golf retreats.

But that wasn't the case here. Roland's own cousin had been stealing from him, and what was worse is that he used me to do it. Me, of all people!

I should have been devastated, but instead, I smiled. I'd been waiting so long to find a way to make Roland hate Dylan without bringing up the fact that we'd slept together.

I'd waited so long to get rid of him and have him out of our lives for good. I wanted him to lose Roland's trust. Lose his money. Lose his love. The same way I had.

After all, Dylan was the one who kissed me first. It was time to get rid of him for good.

CHAPTER FIFTY-FIVE

Things didn't go as planned with Dylan. I fucked it up, just like I always fuck everything up. I don't know what to do anymore. I've been thinking about leaving—disappearing like a fucking ghost.

I probably shouldn't even be writing this, but I found someone in Sageburg who makes fake IDs. I'll move to California, get a desk or retail job and find a roommate who will be willing. I'll change my hair, my style, everything.

I can't pack any bags—Roland will see and get suspicious—and I can't book flights with any of the cards or he'll figure out where I'm going.

I could ask Miley to do it for me though. I'll reach out to her and see if she'll do me this favor. She has to. I've done so much for her. It's her turn to help me now.

CHAPTER FIFTY-SIX

I got a text from Miley and I've been finding it really hard to process. All she had to say was one name and I knew exactly what was happening. Why does this have to happen now, when everything was going so smoothly for me to leave?! Oh my God . . .

My whole life is catching up to me and I know no matter how fast I run, it will continue biting me in my ass. If I don't leave now, I'll never be able to escape this horrid life. And I'm so scared. I'm fucking shaking. I can barely write.

I have to go now, before it's too late.

CHAPTER FIFTY-SEVEN

I flipped to the next page of the journal, after the last entry, but there were no more words. The sun was higher in the sky now, gilded rays sweeping over brown boxes and tan walls.

"What? No." I read the last entry again. The words looked like she'd scribbled them down quickly, and there was a wrinkle on the page, as if it'd gotten wet. I ran the pad of my finger over it, wondering if she was crying while writing it.

I placed the journal down and stood, going to the book-case, scanning it to see if there were any more journals, or books I may have missed that could've been journals, but there were none. This was the last one.

Turning to face the door, I blew out a breath. What the hell had happened between the time she found out about Dylan, to that final entry? Why was she afraid? Seriously. What the hell was going on?

I walked to the window and peered out. The grass was bright and shimmered with dew from the glowing sun. I checked my phone and it was four minutes to one.

Several yards away, I saw Roland standing in his practice attire and Dylan was at his side, toting his golf clubs for him. Dylan was talking and Roland was nodding, and then, as if they'd both sensed someone was watching them, they turned their heads and looked directly at the shed.

I backed up, hitting the edge of the desk. They looked away, and after Roland brought his stiff arms up and whacked the golf ball off the tee, they walked the green. As soon as they were out of sight, I collected all of the journals, placed them in the bottom of one of the boxes, covered them with some of Melanie's clothes and scarves, and then left the shed to get back to the mansion.

After finishing all the journals, I needed to act normal. Instead of selling anything, I was going to pack up all of Melanie's things in the car and drive it to town to donate all of it. I didn't have time for taking pictures and posting it to sell. I just needed to make a move.

I didn't want him to catch on to anything I was doing in there while her personal belongings were still around, because if he had anything to do with what'd happened to her, I needed to collect as much proof as possible.

But first, I needed to find Miley.

CHAPTER FIFTY-EIGHT

I cleared out the shed in two days and got rid of everything but the journals. I kept those stored in a small box and put them next to the bin of photos that I now realized were most likely taken by Felipe.

Roland had a meeting with his agent in California, and when he flew out, I was relieved. I had the mansion to myself, other than a quick visit from Yadira, who had made me dinner. When she was gone, I locked every door, then went to Roland's office to get on one of the laptops.

I read more articles that had deeper details of Melanie's death. There was one website with images of Roland and Melanie together in Hawaii and it was reportedly the last time they were seen together—a whole year before she passed away. The person who'd written the article claimed it was suspicious that they'd stopped going out together, stopped going on trips and being seen in public. Another reason to blame Roland for her death.

I sighed and sat back against the leather seat, and my phone rang, "Gold Digger" playing.

"Kell?" I answered.

"I've got bad news for you, sis."

"No, please don't tell me that," I groaned.

"I had one of my guys do a deep search and I mean *deep*. Like you said, Miley isn't on social media. Melanie never posted a photo with her sister on her socials, which I found odd since she was her only sibling. Nothing came up for Miley Raine other than an apartment connection, but I called the landlord and he said her apartment was cleared out two days after Melanie was reported deceased, and that a man turned her keys in for her. I asked him if he knew who the man was and he said he couldn't remember, but that he was in a rush to go. That was a dead end, so I had my guy search deeper into Melanie and he found an old newspaper clipping on a website that mentioned her and Miley's name in the comments."

"Okay." My back straightened. "What was it about?"

"I'll send you the link. But, Samira . . . I have to tell you, none of this feels right. All of it feels shady as hell and I don't think it's safe for you to be there. You need to come back to Miami. You can stay with me and Ana for as long as you need to. I just don't want you in that house anymore."

My heart was beating harder, faster, but I was in too deep to leave right now. "Send me the link."

After a little griping, Kell hung up and sent the link to my email and as soon as it appeared in my inbox, I clicked it. It took me to a website for a local newspaper based in Raleigh, North Carolina.

I scrolled down to the header.

Man Sentenced to Prison for Raping Fifteen-Year-Old Girl and Molesting Sister

There was an image of a man below the header. He was Black with dark brown skin and steely, empty eyes. He had an afro, scraggly beard, and his brows were deeply furrowed. I could feel the anger radiating off him from that image alone.

I had to collect my thoughts and breathe before reading the article.

> A man named Calvin Thompson has been sentenced to prison after reportedly raping a fifteen-year-old girl. Sources tell us that the teen girl was the daughter of Calvin's girlfriend, and that he had been repeatedly raping her teenage daughter for three months. During that time, Thompson was also sexually abusing his girlfriend's other daughter.
>
> Thompson pleaded not guilty in his court hearing, but according to the police report, the victim who was raped went into the police station to report the crime and police found his DNA on her, along with dark bruises around her neck.
>
> Thompson was found guilty of statutory rape and battery of a minor and will serve twenty-five years in prison.

I scrolled down and there was a string of comments.

I know those girls, poor things. They'll have to live with this forever.

This is about the Raine sisters, right? I knew them in school. I always thought something bad was going on in their house. Miley was always sad and skipping school and Melanie was always smiling and in everyone's face. Always seemed like she was hiding something and pretending to be happy. Guess this was it.

How the hell didn't the mother know this was happening to them under her own roof?!?

This guy can rot in hell. What a bastard.

Calvin Thompson. I knew that name. Melanie wrote it in her journals. Dylan was taunting her about it. Who the hell was this Calvin guy? He'd raped Melanie and molested Miley? So this was why she'd panicked and why Miley had been in and out of rehab. This man had assaulted them.

I thought about the words she wrote: *You dirty fucking slut. You nasty bitch.* She'd thought about them while with Felipe. Dylan said them when she'd confronted him about sleeping with Miley. Calvin must have said them to her when he'd raped her and she'd been living with that—had been tormented by those words for years. The only person who knew about the abuse, outside of Miley, was Dylan, and he'd thrown it in Melanie's face like it meant nothing to him.

My mind was spinning now and my eyes hurt from the brightness of the screen, so I closed the lid of the laptop and stood a moment. After a few deep breaths, I sat down in the cushioned recliner and closed my eyes. This went way deeper than I thought. *Way* deeper. I don't even know why I cared so much to find answers. Melanie was gone now and my marriage was crumbling to pieces over unanswered questions about her death. I could've just forgotten about this whole thing and let it go, like I did with everything else that stressed me out. But, in this particular case, I couldn't. The truth was out there and I felt too close to it to give up now.

My eyes popped open again when an idea hit me. I went to the web browser on my phone to search for Calvin Thompson.

Several things showed up. Mostly news articles from North Carolina about his conviction over a decade ago. There were several Facebook pages listed and I clicked through each of them, because surely, one of the profiles had to be his. One of the links opened up a page where the profile image was a dog, and it said the person was from Raleigh, North Carolina. I scrolled the page, but there wasn't much but reshared memes,

Black Lives Matter articles, and some political pieces. I was scrolling so fast that I almost missed an image.

I went back up and shuddered a breath, my thumb hovering over the image. There he was. Calvin Thompson standing with the handle of a leash in his hand, a dog on the other end of it. The same dog in his profile photo. It hadn't been twenty-five years yet. When the hell did he get out?

My thumb tapped against the side of my phone. Everything in me was telling me to just drop this, run away from this whole thing and focus on my life again, my crumbling marriage.

But I couldn't.

I *wouldn't*.

Because images of a bleeding Melanie still haunted me and I still had no idea where Miley was, but something in my gut told me this Calvin guy had an idea.

For the first time in my life, I felt like I had a purpose. I wanted to prove Roland was good—that he was a great husband who'd made a few mistakes—and I was going to do that. For once in my life, I was going to finish something I'd started and find out what really happened to Melanie.

CHAPTER FIFTY-NINE

I was a fool.

It was two in the morning and I was looking up flights to Raleigh. I needed to speak to Calvin, and maybe that made me crazy considering his reputation and what he'd done to Melanie, but I had my pocketknife and pepper spray kit from Kell, and I wasn't dumb enough to go alone.

I had called Shelia and she agreed to meet me with Ben if I flew her out. I was lucky she was off work for the week, using some of her vacation hours. I didn't feed her all the details, but I braced myself for all the questions she'd throw at me as soon as she saw me.

Seeing as Calvin was a sex offender, his address was easy to find. Nothing about him was private anymore. All of it was public knowledge, so I used that to my advantage. I booked the tickets, sent the hotel info to Shelia, and left the mansion.

After the plane landed, I met Shelia and Ben at a Holiday Inn twelve miles out from Calvin's address. I parked the rental car and spotted them standing near the entrance, deep in conversation.

Drawing in a long breath, I collected my tote bag and keys

and climbed out. Shelia noticed me first and smiled as I made my way toward them.

"Samira! Girl, I've missed you!" she cried, wrapping her arms around me and hugging me tight.

I smiled over her shoulder and hugged her back. "I missed you too."

"So you went and married a golfer," she said, quirking a brow, grinning.

"A crazy-ass golfer," Ben quipped, and I turned toward him to play punch him. "Hey, Ben."

"Don't *hey Ben* me. You dragged us all the way to another state for what? See, Shelia might fall for that 'don't ask any questions, just do' stuff, but I'm not Shelia. I've got a lot of questions."

"I know. And I'll answer them, but let's go inside first."

I checked us in, making sure to book two rooms with my own credit card and not the one Roland gave me. Shelia and Ben dropped their bags off and later met me in my room.

"Is this about him? Your husband?" Shelia asked, eyeing me worriedly.

"Sort of," I said.

"We need more than that, Mira," she murmured.

I sighed, then pressed my back against the wooden head-board of the bed. "It's about Roland in a way, but it's really more so about what happened to his first wife."

They looked at each other, then back at me. "Wasn't it ruled an accident or suicide or something?" asked Ben.

"It was at the time, but the police brought Roland in as a suspect because they found bruises on her body and suspected homicide. They couldn't prove anything on Roland's end, but the case is still open."

"I knew it!" Ben exclaimed. "And you think he killed her, don't you?"

"No, I don't!"

"So then why are we here?" Shelia asked.

"I found these journals from Melanie, Roland's first wife. She wrote about this guy named Calvin. Well, Kell found an article from years ago that explained exactly who Calvin was to her. He raped her and her sister when they were fifteen, and went to prison for a couple years. He was sentenced to twenty-five years, but I just found out that he got out early."

"She had a sister?" Shelia asked.

"Yes. They were pretty close."

"So where is the sister now?"

"That's the thing, I have no idea. No one knows. Roland said he didn't hear from her after Melanie died. Said she just disappeared."

"And you think this Calvin guy might know something about where she is?" Ben asked.

"I do."

"This sounds dangerous, Samira." Shelia fidgeted on the bed. "If you don't think Roland had anything to do with it, what if this man did? You can't just show up to his place and confront him with something as serious as this. We're talking *murder* here."

"She's right." Ben's head shook from side to side. "He sounds like a loose cannon. And he's a fucking rapist. There's no way in hell I'm letting Shelia or you around someone like him."

"Trust me, I understand that, but I really need to know what he knows. Something about all of this isn't adding up and I don't know what to believe anymore. My marriage is already falling apart and I feel myself going crazy over this."

"Why don't you just leave Roland? Forget about all of this? It's not your burden to carry. You're still young, Samira. I—I didn't realize you'd jump at the chance to marry him after I told you Ben was moving in. If I'd known, I wouldn't have said a thing about you going—"

"No—Shelia. Stop." I sat forward and grabbed her hand.

"Don't try and pin my actions on yourself. I agreed to marry him knowing there could have been some drama along the way. I just didn't think it went *this* deep. And when he told me he had nothing to do with her passing, I believed him."

"But you don't anymore."

I bit into my bottom lip and shrugged, fighting tears as Shelia watched me. All of this was a mess. I was digging myself into a cavernous hole and had no idea how the hell I was going to get out. "None of what I'm doing makes any sense to me anymore," I mumbled. "But there's something about all of this that is *screaming* at me. I—I feel it breathing down my neck. Like it's attached to me. Even if I walked away from Roland, I wouldn't let this go. It would haunt me forever." And it would. Images of Melanie haunted my dreams at this point, pulling me out of the little bit of sleep I managed to get.

Shelia squeezed my hand and Ben gave me a sympathetic look. "Well, we're here now. And you need us. If you really feel like you have to talk to this Calvin guy, so be it." She glanced at Ben. "There'll be three against one. You ask your questions, and then we leave."

"Fine," Ben said. "But you don't tell him who you really are. Lie—make something up. Say you were a friend of Melanie's in high school or something. Doesn't matter, just don't reveal who you really are."

"Right." I nodded, then smiled weakly. "Thank you guys. Seriously. I owe you."

"Slide us a couple grand from that golfer of yours and we'll be straight," Ben said, laughing.

"Ben!" Shelia shouted, picking up a pillow and throwing it at him. I laughed with him and then we went out for a quick bite to eat. When we got back and went our separate ways to our rooms to try to get some rest, I took out my phone and there was a text from Roland.

Coming home early. Can't concentrate.

We really need to talk about where we stand.

Shit. Why was he coming home early? He was going to notice I was gone and I had no idea how I was going to explain any of this when I got back.

If I got any information from Calvin that was useful or proved he may have had something to do with Melanie and Miley, I was going to have to tell Roland about the journals and about the article I found about him.

But not right now.

Right now, I needed to focus on bringing my A-game.

CHAPTER SIXTY

My heart was pounding on the ride to Calvin Thompson's house. Ben was driving, Shelia in the passenger seat. I was seated in the back, my mind going a hundred miles per hour, thinking of all the ways this could go wrong.

Before I knew it, Ben was parking along the curb of a one-story brick home. The red bricks looked grimy and there were oil stains on the cement driveway. No cars were there, and I had no idea if Calvin had a car.

Ben looked back at me. "You sure about this?"

I nodded and unclipped my seat belt. "Yeah. I'm sure." Before I got out, I picked up my tote bag and felt around inside it for my knife and pepper spray, then I slid the handle of the bag onto my shoulder. Ben walked up the driveway first to get to the door. The stoop was small, so only Ben stood on it while Shelia and I waited on the sidewalk behind him.

He gave the doorbell a ring and a dog started barking. I held on to my tote bag tighter as Ben took a step back, side-eyeing me before focusing on the door again.

"Hush, Cannon!" a deep voice snapped on the other side

of the door. My heart was beating like a bongo drum now, the blood rushing to my ears when I heard the lock click. The door opened halfway, brown fingers wrapping around the edge of it. I could only see half of the man's face, but I knew right away it was Calvin from the pictures online.

"Can I help you?" he asked, narrowing the eye we could see. He had a heavy Southern accent.

I stepped forward. "Hi. Are you Calvin Thompson?"

"Who's asking?"

"I'm Wendy. I was a classmate of someone you knew."

"I don't know a lot of people," he grumbled, and I could tell he was ready to shut the door in my face.

"Melanie Raine," I hurried to say before he could close it. When I said her name, his eyes went wide and he snatched the door open completely. "Why are you asking me about her?" he snapped. His dog stepped outside, sniffing at us, grunting.

"Well, I'm a journalist, and I'm writing a piece on her case for the papers, since she was local." I glanced at Ben, who was glaring at Calvin, daring him to try something. "We did a little digging and found out that you were once in a relationship with her mother."

"Who told you that?" he retorted.

"We have sources." I smiled, but my hands were shaking. I slid them into the pockets of my jacket to hide them.

"Yeah, I dated Pauline for a while. So what? What's that got to do with anything?"

"Calvin, I have reason to believe you didn't rape Melanie and that your plea to the judge on the case was honest. After doing a little research on her, we learned some things about her." I stared into his eyes and kept my composure, hoping he'd believe me about his innocence.

Calvin tipped his chin and looked me up and down. He was lowering his guard. Good.

"May we come in?"

He looked at all three of us, as if memorizing our faces, then he nodded once and turned, going back into the house.

I looked back at Ben and Shelia and they gave me a wary look before looking at each other. With slow headshakes and sighs, they followed me into the house anyway.

CHAPTER SIXTY-ONE

Calvin didn't have much in his home, but he kept it tidy and clean, which I could appreciate. Shelia, Ben, and I sat bunched together on his only sofa and he brought a chair over from his dining area to sit on, then looked at us as he lifted his leg and placed his ankle on top of his knee.

"So you say you went to school with Melanie?" he asked.

"I did," I murmured.

"Were you good friends with her?"

"No. Not really. She never really noticed me."

He scoffed. "She never cared to notice anyone but herself . . . that is, unless you had something she wanted."

"What did she want from you, Mr. Thompson?"

"Wasn't about what she wanted. It was about what she couldn't have."

"What do you mean by that?"

"I mean she lied on me." He frowned then and looked at my empty hands. "Shouldn't you be recording this or somethin'?"

"Yes, right. Sorry." I whipped out my phone and went to the voice recording app. "Please continue."

"I never raped that girl," he stated. "She wanted me and she came on to me. In the beginning, I always turned her down. Told her she was naïve, crazy. But one night, I got too drunk around her, and her mama had gone off to work, and she led me into her room. One thing led to another and then it all went to shit after that."

"So, the whole time, it was consensual with Melanie? You never took advantage of her?" I asked, stunned. I don't even know why I was stunned. After reading her confessions, this seemed exactly like something she would have done, but still—she was a minor when it'd happened. He was older and knew better and had taken full advantage of the situation.

"No. Never."

"So, what about her sister? Miley?"

He dropped his leg and sat up straight. "Never did anything to her either. That was a full-blown lie, but Miley went along with it, of course, to save her sister's ass. Them two were like peas in a pod. Melanie always plottin' and destroyin' everything she touched and Miley always tryin' to fix it." He sighed and bent down to rub his dog on the top of the head.

"Why would Melanie lie about something like that?"

"She got mad because I told her it wasn't right what we were doin'. I told her I couldn't even look at Pauline no more and that I was leavin'. She tried gettin' me to stay, told me she'd do anything. I'm assuming when I told her no, that hurt her or somethin' but she didn't reveal that hurt to me. Instead she started groping me, asking me for one more time. So I gave it to her, but that was my mistake. After we finished, she told me if I didn't stay, she'd tell the cops I raped her. I told her she was full of shit and that I was leaving anyway, but that was my mistake. Never should've underestimated that girl. She ran off to the police station that same night, lied on me, had me in prison for nine years 'til I got out on parole. Prison got overcrowded and I had good behavior, so it was pretty much like a second chance for me. My life has never been the same since then, though."

"I'm sorry to hear that." I looked at his dog. I couldn't tell what breed he was—he looked like a mix of a boxer and a Labrador.

"Mr. Thompson—"

"Just call me Calvin."

"Right. Calvin. Did you ever see Melanie again after getting out?"

"No. Didn't want shit to do with that girl ever again."

"What about Miley?"

"Her either."

"Do you know she died? Melanie?"

"Yeah, I know."

"Oh?"

He stopped petting his dog to give me his attention. "Just 'cause I never saw her again, doesn't mean I didn't look her up to see whose life she was currently wrecking. She married some golfer, right?"

I tensed at the thought of Roland, who was now *my* golfer. "She did."

"Rolled off a cliff." Calvin huffed a laugh and I glanced at Shelia, whose face was warped with confusion.

"Probably sucked the man dry. Same way she did me, her mama, and even her sister. I don't even think she's the one who went over that cliff."

I frowned and cocked my head. "What do you mean?"

He folded his arms, and I could tell my time with him was coming to an end. "I mean Miley was the druggie, not Melanie. She did drugs all through high school from what I remember. Drugs always made Melanie cringe. I know because I tried to get her to smoke weed with me once and she refused."

"So what are you saying?"

"Do you not understand what I'm getting at?" he
snapped.

I shook my head.

"Melanie and Miley were *twins*. They shared the same
damn DNA."

I blinked, stunned again. How the hell didn't I know this?
Roland *never* mentioned that they were twins. Why didn't he?
The journal never mentioned they were either.

"But fingerprints...the cops would've pieced that together," I said.

"Not if the body was severely bloated when they found
it," Ben said. I glanced at him at the same time Shelia did. He
shrugged. "Just saying. I've watched a lot of crime shows. If
her body was found in the water, it was probably hard for
them to get a proper fingerprint analysis. Maybe all they had
to go off of was the DNA."

"True. And I think Miley is the one who drove off that
damn cliff, not Melanie. Miley could be suicidal sometimes. I
think Melanie used her sister as a scapegoat and bailed on her
own life. When I saw they were suddenly accusin' her husband and rulin' it a homicide, I figured she had somethin' to
do with it—that she'd run off to start over somewhere and
caused a shitstorm just to ruin his life, same way she did mine.
I don't know how, but she's good like that. Good at creatin'
lies." He rubbed behind his dog's ears. "He must've done
somethin' to really piss her off. Cryin' rape is one thing, but
murder? Now that's fucked up." He chuckled. "Bet you she's
on a private island somewhere, soakin' up the sun and livin'
her best damn life while he suffers."

"Wait—what? So you really think Melanie is still out
there somewhere?"

"Oh, I *know* she's still out there somewhere. She's gotta
be. She's a lotta things, but she was never suicidal. That was
more Miley's lane. No telling where she is, and it's been years.

Doubt anybody'll find her or even believe my word for it."
He dropped his arms and stood up, his dog rising with him.
"But as badly as I'd love to see her get caught in whatever shit
she's caused, I'm aimin' for a better life and don't want shit to
do with any of hers, so I need y'all to leave now."

I stood and Ben and Shelia did the same. "I understand.
Thank you for your time." Ben and Shelia headed for the
door, but I stopped and turned to look back at him. "Oh—
before I go, do you think you can get me in touch with
Pauline?" If there was someone who knew where Melanie
was, it was her mother. She had to know. Who else would she
have turned to when there was no one left?

"Yeah," he grumbled, lumbering toward the narrow hallway. "Hopefully it's still the same. Wait right here."

His dog watched me a brief moment before following his
owner. When they were gone, I looked back at Shelia and
Ben, who were both staring at me with dubious eyes.

"It'll be quick," I whispered.

I noticed a desk in the corner and walked toward it. It was
neat, like the rest of the home, notebooks stacked properly
and his pens and pencils in a single plastic cup. I heard Calvin
rifling around so I took the opportunity to open one of the
drawers. There was nothing inside it but more pens and sticky
notes. I opened the other drawer and saw paper clips, a mag-
net, and Sharpies.

"What the hell are you doing?" Ben hissed.

I glared back at him. "Shh."

Seconds later, Calvin returned and had a notebook in
hand. He went to the desk and took out one of the pads of
sticky notes, used a pen from the cup to write down the number, and then handed it to me. "Hopefully you can get ahold
of her."

"Thank you." I tucked the paper in my tote bag, but my
eye caught the necklace around his neck. It was a gold chain,
and on the end of it was a dangling dove.

A dove that looked exactly like the earring I found in the bathroom drawer in the mansion.

Oh. Shit.

As if he noticed where my gaze had gone, he looked down at the necklace too, then lifted it to tuck it beneath the collar of his T-shirt.

"That all?" He stared harder at me.

"Yes. Thank you again for your time." I rapidly turned away, passing Shelia and Ben at the door and scurrying down the driveway.

When we were all inside the car, I pressed my back against the leather seat, damn near hyperventilating.

"Samira? Samira! What's wrong?" Shelia wailed, turning in her seat to look at me.

"I—he had on—"

"Breathe, Mira! Breathe!"

I pressed a hand to my chest, then looked toward the house. The corner of one of the blinds on his windows was tilted upward, but it dropped quickly when I noticed. He was watching us.

"We have to go. *Now.*"

"Don't have to tell me twice. That man was weird as fuck." Ben had the car started and peeled off in seconds.

I looked through the window, back at the house, then down at my shaking hands.

"Mira, what did he have on?" Shelia asked, still looking back at me.

"His chain. There was a—a dove on the end of it."

"Okay? And?"

"And Melanie had the same kind of dove jewelry. It was her logo for the clothing line she was going to start."

"Aw, shit!" Ben shouted. "Are you saying what I think you're saying?"

"I think he *did* see Melanie after he got out."

"And you think he did it?"

"I—I don't know. I don't know." I pressed my hands to the sides of my head. "I need to think. I—mean there could be so many reasons they could have met. Maybe she heard he was out and wanted to apologize for what she'd done? In her journals she said that she was going to get a fake ID and leave. She also said Miley mentioned a name in a text, and I think it was his. I think he wanted to see them, but Melanie refused and bailed, and he got to the sister."

"Or, maybe he actually found her and fucking killed her ass before she could flee and the sister got spooked and ran away," Ben shouted.

"But he said Miley was her twin. It would make sense that her body was found with heroin in her system. Also my brother said someone turned Miley's keys in for her. A man. What if it was him? I don't know how it all comes together with Calvin, but I do know Melanie was shady as hell and she wanted to get away from Roland. She hated her life. She even talked about starting over—running off to California and making a new identity. Melanie was desperate to get away and Miley was an addict. Maybe it's all just a cover-up."

"That is a wild fucking theory," Ben said.

"I know." I sighed. "None of this is making any sense, but it's hard to know what to believe at this point. He had the dove on his chain. He was around her before she died. I know it. I just don't know what his part in this is." I pressed my forehead to the back of Shelia's headrest. "I have to ask Roland about this. I don't think I have a choice anymore. If there is a possibility that Melanie is still out there and that she faked all of this, we have to find her. And if there is a chance Calvin knows something or did something, it will help us. It'll prove that Roland is innocent after all and that she purposely set out to destroy his life as payback or something."

"Right," Shelia said. "But that doesn't answer the question about her twin. If Melanie is out there somewhere, and if that was her sister's body in the car that went over the cliff and into the water, how the hell could she have made her drive over that cliff at the exact time she needed it to happen?"

"I have no idea," I mumbled, then shivered. "I really don't know."

I looked out of the window, watching as the cars passed by and the green trees blended together. "There has to be a reason for all of this."

CHAPTER SIXTY-TWO

I couldn't stay in the hotel another night. Roland was on his way home and I wanted to beat him there, so I caught the first flight I could and flew back, but not without thanking Shelia and Ben and sending them back home too.

During my flight back, I was anxious. I didn't know what I was going to find out by talking to Roland, but after seeing that dove on the end of Calvin's chain, I was almost positive Roland was innocent. If Calvin was right and Miley was the body they'd found, it meant Melanie was behind all of this. But what I couldn't figure out was why Calvin would even tell us that if he was a part of it too? There were holes in this tragedy and I needed to plug them.

And there I was feeling sorry for Melanie for weeks, having bloody visions of her in my head, wanting so desperately to uncover her truth and find out what'd happened to her. All of that, and there could've been a possibility none of it was real—that she'd faked it all just to escape the shitty life she'd created.

There was no way she killed her sister though. No, if they found drugs in the body and it was Miley's, that meant Miley must have relapsed, based off what I'd read and how vulnerable Miley was. But like Shelia said, that didn't explain how Miley got into Melanie's car. Did Melanie make her drive over that cliff? Was it even Miley behind the wheel? For all I knew, Melanie could have spiraled too and tried drugs like Miley did to numb her pain, especially if she was at her wits' end. She never said she was against drugs in the journals, but Calvin did mention she wasn't a fan of them when she was younger.

It was a stretch, yes, but I didn't know what else to believe at this point. I had all these theories running through my mind, and I was sure the answer was right at home, waiting for me. All I had to do was ask.

CHAPTER SIXTY-THREE

W hen I drove up to the mansion, Roland's car was in front of one of the garages. He'd been home and had been there for a while now. I could tell because the hood of his car was cool to the touch.

I collected all of my thoughts, drew in a long, deep breath, and then went inside. The house was darker than usual, nothing on but a light in the den and in the kitchen.

"Roland?" I called, but no one answered.

I wasn't sure where he was, but I needed to talk to him, so before finding him I went back out the door and around the house to get to the shed so I could retrieve the journals. But as I neared the door, I noticed it was cracked open and a light was on inside.

I hurried toward it and pushed the door open, and there he was. My husband. Standing in the middle of the shed, his head bowed as he read the journal in his hands.

He didn't look at me right away, but I was certain he'd heard me come in. He kept reading, his jaw ticking, his eyes hard on the pages.

"Roland," I called.

"How long?" His voice was raspy, gruff.

My pulse was pounding in my ears. "How long what?"

He picked his head up, grimacing at me. "How long have you known about these?"

I wrung my fingers together. "A couple weeks now. I found them when I started cleaning the shed."

"And you didn't think to tell me about it?" He closed the journal and lifted it in the air. "Is this why you've been sneaking around? Acting so jumpy around me?"

"Yes," I confessed, and he sucked his teeth and shook his head.

"Wow, Samira. *Wow*." He tossed the journal onto the desk, making the pages flap.

"How much did you read?"

"Oh, I read enough. Trust me."

I stepped into the shed, easing the door shut behind me. "Roland, I know you're upset right now, but I need to ask you something very important."

"What, Samira?"

"Do you promise me you had nothing to do with Melanie's death? Like nothing at all?"

"I've promised this to you so many times. I don't know how much more I can." He glanced back at the journals stacked on the desk. "I know from what you've read that it probably looks like I did something, but I didn't, Samira. She was a liar. All she ever did was fucking lie."

I nodded, tucking my cold fingers into my jacket pocket. "Did you get to the part . . . about her affair with Dylan?"

"Yes." He dropped his head, staring down at the floor. "I always suspected it, but . . ."

"Did you ever talk to him about it?"

"No. By the time I figured it out, it was too late. Our marriage had already gone to shit and she still wanted a divorce."

"So why keep Dylan around if you knew what they'd been doing behind your back?"

"Because I knew how Melanie is. And I didn't keep him around. I told him he had to leave—find somewhere else to stay. I didn't tell him I suspected anything about the affair. I just blamed it on my marriage—said we needed some space as a couple to work through some things. I love him like a brother, and in my heart, I forgave him, but I couldn't cope with him being in the same house as us anymore, so I made up an excuse to get him to leave."

"So, you forgave him, but not Melanie?"

He whipped his gaze up, locking eyes on me. "Samira, you don't fucking understand. You may think Melanie was this nice, endearing girl, but you're only seeing one side of this. There were so many times when she *attacked* me because I wouldn't even look at her."

"Attacked you?"

"Yes! Prior to her telling me she'd cheated, she tried so hard to get a reaction out of me. But I was still recovering from my injury and I was fucking depressed about it, and I just didn't care about anything else at the time. And I hate admitting it, but it's the truth. I was angry about my life and where my career was headed, and Melanie didn't give a fuck. All she cared about was herself. When we went to Hawaii, she told me she'd cheated, and I didn't react. I didn't know how to react. Instead, I was ready to walk away, give the entire situation some space so we could both collect our thoughts. Hell, I was even willing to forgive her and to make it work, but she didn't like that I was going to leave the room without saying anything, so she *slapped* me. And that night she just kept hitting me, demanding me to react, demanding me to show her how I felt, and I just—I *snapped*. I . . . I grabbed her a little too roughly on the face and I know that scared her, but she brought it out of me. She kept hitting and shouting at me, calling me a pussy and a coward and saying how I didn't deserve her and that she was going to cheat again, and I lost it. You can only poke a sleeping bear so much, Samira."

My heart was in my throat. "Oh—Roland, I'm sorry. I didn't know."

"No, you didn't know, Samira, because you never asked. You just assumed that everything written in those journals was the truth without considering my side of things. You did exactly what everyone else did and jumped to your own conclusions, ready to blame me without hearing me out first."

"No—don't say that." I walked toward him as he turned his head. "Roland, I don't blame you, okay? I—I understand. I just . . . I got a little scared, I admit it. I was worried after reading about that night you grabbed her. I didn't know what to believe."

"All you had to do was ask me about it. I would have told you everything. You can't hide stuff like this from me, Samira. I told you I wanted us to be honest—to communicate—and you promised to give me that," he pleaded.

"I know, I know." I shook my head and grabbed his hands. "And I'm so sorry. I feel terrible for making you feel so alone, Roland. She clearly wasn't good to you. She's hurt you so much and I don't want to do the same. I'm sorry."

He let out a breath, then cupped a hand around the nape of my neck, kissing my forehead. "Where did you go?" he asked after a brief pause.

"I flew out . . . to North Carolina."

He released me and looked down at me with a frown. "For what?"

"Did you get to the part in the journals about Dylan mentioning a guy named Calvin?"

"I think so . . ."

"Did she ever tell you about him?"

"No—not that I recall."

"Well, that's because she accused Calvin of rape when she was fifteen."

"What?" His eyes widened, jaw going slack.

"Yes. I have the article. And it's why I went to North Carolina. I wanted to ask this Calvin guy about Melanie but . . . Roland, I—I saw something on him that changes the trajectory of this entire situation."

"What did you see?"

"He was wearing a chain with a dove on the end of it. When I first moved in, I found that same dove on an earring in one of the bathroom drawers. I think it was Melanie's."

Roland narrowed his eyes. "What are you saying, Samira?"

"I'm saying that I think Calvin knows a lot more about what happened with Melanie than he admitted to me, and that Melanie is probably still out there."

CHAPTER SIXTY-FOUR

Roland stepped away from me, giving me a disgusted scowl. "What? How the hell can you even say that? I saw her body, Samira! It was her!"

"But she had a sister, right? And they were identical twins, Roland! Why didn't you ever tell me that?"

"I—I didn't think it mattered."

"It definitely matters. Think about it! Same DNA. Same looks. It might not have been her!"

He blinked. "No—even though they were twins, I could tell them apart. Miley was rugged. Melanie was more proper. That body looked like Melanie's."

"Are you sure? Because after finding out what I know about Melanie, and how she's so quick to sabotage people's lives, it would all make sense. Maybe something happened to Miley that she couldn't control and Melanie used Miley's body as a scapegoat. She wanted out of her own life."

Roland shook his head. "There's no fucking way."

"Think about it, Roland. Melanie wanted to get away from you and erase all that'd happened. I don't know if you got to this part, but in her journals she said she was going to create a fake identity and go to California."

"No." His head shook repeatedly and he squeezed his eyes shut, turning his back to me. "If she did that, it means she *wanted* this to happen to me. She wanted people to think that body had something to do with me."

"Does this sound like something she'd do?"

"It sounds extreme, Samira." He faced me again. "And yes, she was fucked up and could be selfish, but that crosses a line. I mean that body looked just like her. It was bloated from the water, but her clothes, her shoes—she was even in her car. It had to be Melanie."

"So then why can't anyone find Miley?"

He shrugged. "I don't know! Miley has always been hard to keep up with and I wasn't that close to her! She's probably out there hiding somewhere after all this, still grieving or something!"

"Roland, you can't just pretend this isn't a realistic option, despite how fucked up it is. Miley was the one with the drug issues, not Melanie. Why would Melanie suddenly do heroin? I'm sure you would have known that she'd developed a drug habit, no matter how much you avoided her at the end."

He slumped his large body down in the rolling chair and dropped his face in his hands. I went toward him, lowering to my knees between his legs. "She might still be out there, Roland. And I think that Calvin guy knows more than he told me. What if she went back to him for something?"

"Why would she do that? If he raped her, why?"

"I think he's helping her hide, probably in exchange for money. He got out of prison a few months before Melanie died. They could have found their way back to each other again around that time, made some kind of plan."

I grabbed his hands and forced him to look at me. "You have to figure this out, Roland. If she did this to you, you have to find her and prove to the world that you're innocent."

"How the hell am I gonna do that? If she is out there, I'm sure she made it to where I'll never get to her, and if she did go back to that Calvin guy and you went there asking questions, he's probably told her by now and they're both going off the grid. Why would you even go there alone?"

"I didn't go alone. Shelia and Ben met me."

He inhaled and sat back against the seat. "This is fucked up."

"We have resources, Roland. I can have one of Kell's guys look deeper. He can help us."

"Kell knows about this too?" He groaned.

"They only want to help us, babe. Right now, everyone is rooting for you. I've always been rooting for you and I want to figure this out. Not only for you, but for both of us, so we can move the hell on from this."

"And what if we don't find her? What if it turns out it was her body and not Miley's?"

"If that was Melanie's body then the only way we'll know is if we find Miley. I'm sure Melanie contacted her about leaving. They were close. The answer is out there somewhere, and it's time for you to find it, Roland. You can't live like this anymore—not when none of this is your fault."

As if my words had triggered him, he sat forward and clasped my face in his hands gently. "You really think she's out there?"

"I do."

He studied my eyes, his hazel irises focused and intense. "Okay." He released me and stood, bringing me up with him. "Where do we start?"

CHAPTER SIXTY-FIVE

The first thing we did was find out more about Calvin. I called Kell and he shouted at me about going to see Calvin in person, but after he'd calmed down, he took my instructions and went straight to work to find out more about him.

While he did, Roland and I did our own work. There was a room in the house that he said Miley stayed in, and she'd left some of her things behind.

We looked in the closet, past some of Roland's extra coats and shoes, and came across a small jewelry box. I opened it and there were studs inside that looked like they were for a nose piercing, some earrings, and a necklace. I pulled the necklace out. It was made of gold and had the word *Sister* on it.

Was this the necklace Melanie spoke about in the journal—the one she said Miley had sold for drugs? I studied it. There were scratches on it, like it'd been around for a long time. She said Miley sold both of them. Had she lied about that too?

I reached farther back and found a burgundy box with a lid. I glanced over my shoulder at Roland, who was watching

me. Taking the lid off and setting it aside, I dug into the box
and there were photos inside.

"Oh my God."

"What's that?" Roland asked, stepping closer.

"They're pictures." I flipped through them. They were
Polaroids of Melanie and Miley. They appeared to be teen-
agers here, wearing bright pink shirts and glittery eyeshadow.
I kept flipping through them but came to a sudden halt when
I got to one of the last pictures.

I felt a drop in the pit of my stomach and stood, walking
to Roland to show him the picture.

"That's him?" he asked.

"Yes. That's him."

I looked down at the picture again. One of the twins was
sitting on Calvin's lap, smiling at him with her arms locked
around his shoulders. He had his nose buried in the crook of
her neck. I couldn't make out which twin it was. Throughout
the photos they looked exactly the same, both of their hair
natural, in wild black puffs. This twin in the current photo,
whichever one she was, had on a black T-shirt with a green
butterfly on it. I didn't know the twins personally, but after
reading the journals and getting an idea of Melanie's tastes in
fashion from the items in the shed, the outfit in the picture
didn't seem like something Melanie would've selected as a
teenager.

"I think this is Miley sitting on his lap."

"Miley?" Roland took a harder look at the picture. "I—I
don't know. I can't tell."

"If that is Miley, does that mean she was also with
Calvin?"

I went back for the rest of the pictures and there were
more of them. Miley walking hand in hand with Calvin.
Miley kissing Calvin on the cheek. Miley holding the camera
in the air and smiling as Calvin lay beside her, asleep.

"What the hell is this?" I muttered. "None of this is making any sense."

"You're telling me. You think Melanie was the one taking some of these pictures?"

"Yeah—she had to be."

"So why would she say he raped her? All of this looks like some kind of dirty little secret."

"Maybe he was messing around with both of them and things got messy. He threatened to leave both of them, but Melanie took things too far. Same way she did with Miley and Dylan." I cupped my mouth. "She never mentioned this in her journals."

"Of course she didn't," Roland grumbled. "Melanie liked an audience. She wrote for herself and her therapist. I remember hearing her on calls with him, telling him how she had something she wanted him to read. He would read what she wrote and dissect it, whether it was lies or the truth. She was playing the victim. She always had to be the victim. That's what narcissists do."

I collected all the pictures and stuffed them back into the box. "I think we need to pay another visit to Calvin. If he's still home, then it proves he doesn't know much about anything and that I was wrong and maybe the chain is just a coincidence. But if he's gone . . . well, then we'll have our answer. Either he did something to both of them, and isn't saying it, or he's helping Melanie cover this all up so she can stay hidden."

"Still doesn't make sense why he would do that. He ruined that woman's life."

"Then she ruined yours, but you still loved her, right?"

Roland clamped his mouth shut and stared at me with wide eyes.

"Yeah. I thought so." I stuffed the box back into the closet and shut the door. "She has that kind of pull on men, I'm realizing. Ropes you in. Mesmerizes you, takes advantage, and then finds a way to fuck you over." I sighed and turned for the door. "We should go book flights."

We headed downstairs, and as we rounded the corner, I noticed a shadow at the front door. I paused as the doorknob jiggled. Roland swiftly grabbed my hand and forced me behind him, probably thinking the same thing I was. Someone was trying to break in.

The silhouette behind the opaque glass didn't look like anyone we knew. The doorknob jiggled again and then the door swung open.

CHAPTER SIXTY-SIX

"Dylan! What the hell, man?" Roland barked when he saw his cousin coming in. Dylan was wearing a blue hoodie with the hood over his head. He stared at us, confused, then reached into the hoodie, plucking out one of his AirPods. "What the hell are you doing, man?" Roland demanded.

"Yadira told me there were leftovers," he said, shutting the door and walking deeper into the house. He looked at me and Roland oddly. "Why the hell does it look like you two have seen a ghost?"

Roland glanced down at me, then back at Dylan.

Dylan shifted his weight on his feet. "What's going on?" he asked, his voice more hesitant.

"I know you're the one Melanie cheated on me with," Roland said.

Dylan's smile immediately evaporated. "Wh-what?"

"I've known for a while now, Dylan."

He stared at Roland, stupefied.

"Look, Roland, I—I didn't mean for that to happen. I took things too far with Melanie and I'm sorry but she—"

"I really should punch you in the face." Roland stepped

closer to Dylan, and I worried that he really was going to punch him.

Dylan threw his hands in the air. "Roland, I'm sorry, man."

Roland glared at Dylan for a long time, then he sighed and his shoulders sagged. "Trust me, I want to punch you . . . but I can't keep losing people, man."

Confused, Dylan looked back at me. I shrugged and pressed my lips.

"I forgave you a long time ago."

"You did? How long have you known?"

"I suspected it back when Melanie was still here. One minute you two were talking and friendly and the next you weren't. I figured she was upset that you went against your word about Miley. She told me she wanted you to stay away from her, but you didn't. And when she told me she cheated on me, it became clear to me after a while. I didn't want to think it was true but . . . now I know that feeling in my heart was real."

Dylan's eyes lowered regretfully.

"I don't want to hurt you, but I will tell you that we need your help and you can't say no."

"Okay." Dylan lifted his head again, his worry fading. "Help with what?"

"I'll tell you while we book the flights," Roland said, clapping his cousin's shoulder.

"Flights?" Dylan hollered, whipping his head back to look at me.

"Trust me. It's a long story," I muttered, following them to Roland's office.

CHAPTER SIXTY-SEVEN

When we touched down in North Carolina, a sense of dread swirled within me. The questions were screaming in my mind and I had a feeling the answers were closer than ever before, but that they would come with deadly truths.

Roland booked a rental and we drove straight to Calvin's house. He parked along the curb and then peered through the passenger window, studying the home. "This doesn't look like a place Melanie would have run to."

"Well, if she had nowhere else to go . . ." Dylan shrugged.

My phone rang in my bag and I dug it out. It was Kell.

I answered and put the phone on speaker. "Kell? What'd you find out?"

"So apparently this Calvin Thompson guy used to own a club. He filed for bankruptcy about two years before the whole rape scandal. Melanie's mother worked at the club and they met there."

"Really?"

"Yeah. We found out through a former employee of his. She told us everything. He started losing money and hooked up with Melanie's mother, Pauline, who had some money rolling in from her previous husband who died, and I don't think he was those girls' father. Then again, we aren't sure because the birth certificates don't have the father's name. Anyway, Calvin moved in with her for about a year, won a lottery from a scratch ticket for fifteen grand, then got convicted a couple weeks later."

"Wow. Calvin must've wanted to ditch them when he won the money. So where is her mom now?" I asked, glancing at Roland.

"Her mom died in 2012. Cancer." In 2012? I gave the timeframe some thought. That was the same year Melanie met Roland.

"What else did you find?"

"Not much else, honestly. After he was convicted it's radio silence for years. He eventually got out on parole, got a job, works second shift. Seems to me he kept his head down and avoided trouble when he got out. His parole only lasted a few months because it seems he was doing well for himself and creating a better life, and seeing as the sisters were no longer in Raleigh, I'm sure that made it much easier for his case too."

I looked at the house through the window. "Yeah, that sounds like a great comeback story, but I don't believe he's suddenly become some law-abiding citizen."

"There are some other things, not about him though. We found Melanie's birth records and saw she shares a birthday with Miley."

"Yeah, they're twins," I sighed. "Just found that out." I side-eyed Roland and he pressed his lips apologetically.

"Okay, that's good you know. The other thing is a drug rehabilitation record for Miley. It dates back to 2012, right around the time her mother passed. Apparently, she was checked in by a woman."

My heart dropped. "How do you know this?"

"My guy can hack into bookings, electronically filed papers, police records, and call logs. All I do is ask the questions and he finds the answers, but a lot of it isn't legal so I'd appreciate if you kept that between us. Anyway, there's footage of Miley being checked in."

"Send it to me."

"Okay." Kell hung up, and seconds later my phone pinged and there was a video attachment from him. I opened it and Roland leaned over the middle console to see while Dylan leaned forward.

The camera was at an angle, but it clearly showed two women entering a clinic. One of the women was helping the other stay on her feet, and then a security guard met them with a wheelchair.

"There." I pointed at the screen, at the girl being forced into the chair. "That has to be Miley, right?"

I couldn't make out the other woman. Her back was to the camera as she signed papers, spoke to a man behind the counter, then she turned and said something to Miley, pointing a stern finger.

Then she left the clinic, but not without looking back over her shoulder, and when she did, I saw her face as clear as day. It was Melanie. Her hair was straightened, and she wore a button-down blouse, a pencil skirt, and heels.

The video ended just as it framed her face.

She'd checked Miley in. "I think Miley was in and out of rehab around the time you two met. She ignored Miley for a while when you two got married. She never told you about any of this, right?" I asked Roland.

"No. Never."

"Miley must've relapsed because of her mother's death. But why would Melanie completely abandon her sister when she met you? She was ignoring her calls for days."

Roland shrugged. "I don't know, Samira."

"Melanie was jealous of Miley." I looked back and Dylan

was peering through the windshield. "She, um . . . well, when we were messing around, she would always ask me who I thought was better—her, or Miley. I would always say she was. It's what she wanted to hear, so I said it. I think it's because of the whole Calvin situation. I think he made them compete against each other to prove their worth to him."

"If so, that's really fucked up," I muttered.

I faced forward again and noticed Roland's grip had tightened around the steering wheel.

"I'm sorry, Ro," Dylan murmured.

"Don't. Let's just figure this shit out and be done with it. I'm tired of her fucking up everyone's lives."

Roland killed the engine and climbed out of the car. I got out too, Dylan followed suit, and Roland led the way up the driveway to get to the door. He didn't press the doorbell like a person with manners would have done. Instead, he banged on the door with one of his fists.

"Roland, calm down," I whispered.

He side-eyed me, shoulders hunched, slowly sliding his hands into the front pockets of his jeans.

We stood there a minute. When a few more seconds passed, Roland pressed the doorbell. "I don't think he's home," he said.

I walked around the house to one of the windows and looked through it. It was dark inside, the house vacant. I noticed a wired fence at the back of the house and went toward it.

"Samira!" Roland hissed. "What are you doing? He's not here!"

"Maybe we'll find something." I kept going to the fence and heard Roland groan and Dylan hiss the words "What the fuck?" but they followed me anyway.

I lifted the rusted latch and pushed the gate open, and as soon as I did, something growled and huffed.

"Oh shit!" Dylan howled.

Calvin's dog was running toward me, galloping like a horse. I gasped and wanted to run, but I couldn't. My legs locked, every instinct telling me to be still and remain calm.

The dog huffed, bringing its paws up and planting them on my thighs. He started sniffing me and then let out a small bark.

"Good boy," I said shakily. He remembered me. "Shh . . . good boy. Cannon, is it?" He whimpered then, and I rubbed the top of his head and stroked behind his ears like I saw Calvin do to him. He dropped to his paws again and immediately looked back at Roland and Dylan, snarling at them.

"No, it's okay." I bent down to rub his body. "They're with me. It's okay." I stood again, going to the fence and guiding Roland and Dylan ahead. Cannon rushed forward to sniff at them and then he snuffled and turned away, trotting back to the plastic doghouse. Calvin didn't have much in his backyard. There was a folding chair and a man-made fire pit, and just past the doghouse was a small storage shed.

My eyes swung over to the back door, and it was cracked open.

"Guys." I pointed at the door.

"No—Samira." Roland caught my hand just as I was about to grab the doorknob. "We are not about to get charged with breaking and entering."

"What if there's something in there that helps us?"

"I don't care, Samira. We'll wait for him to come back and get permission to go in. We can't just go into his house."

"He's right, Samira," Dylan said.

"Let's just go back to the car and wait," Roland insisted.

"What if he doesn't return? What if Melanie is in there hiding right now?"

Roland frowned, then stepped back with a sigh. "This is fucking crazy."

"I know." I reached for the doorknob again and pulled it open. The door creaked on its hinges and I walked inside.

"Samira!" Roland hissed again, but he didn't stop me this time. "*Fuck*."

I was in the kitchen. It was small. The countertops were green. It was clean but the faucet was leaky. The walls were white and bland, the floors black and green linoleum.

I went deeper into the house and found myself in the living room, where I'd been last time with Shelia and Ben. Not much was in here but the desk, and I'd already looked through that, so I turned toward the hallway. There were two doors across from each other at the end of the hall. I took the one on the right first. It was a bathroom. I opened the mirror cabinet and there wasn't much inside it. A razor, some aspirin, soap, shaving cream.

I checked the drawers, hoping to find something that may have screamed it was Melanie's and that she'd been around recently, but nothing was there. It was all his stuff.

I went across the hall to the other door. This was his bedroom. A single mattress was on top of a metal bed frame. A handmade-looking dresser was against the wall. A closet was across from the bed and I went to open it. There were gray uniforms inside with the name Calvin stitched on the chest. They looked like janitorial uniforms.

A white container was on the floor and I bent down to slide it out. Taking off the lid, I went through the box; it contained files in a file holder, documents, and even his birth certificate.

I dug deeper and came across a photo of Calvin standing with a middle-aged woman. Her features were similar to Melanie and Miley's. This had to have been their mother, Pauline. I examined the photo closer and there was a chain around Pauline's neck, a dove hanging on the end.

It was the same necklace Calvin was wearing.

"Shit." I knew what that meant.

I was wrong. That dove didn't belong to Melanie. It was her mother's and he must have been wearing it as a keepsake.

Maybe Melanie only used the dove for her branding. I put the photo back, closed the container, and put it back in place.

"Samira." Roland was standing by the bedroom door when I pushed to a stand. "We need to go."

"Yeah." I sighed. "I didn't find anything. No signs of Melanie."

Roland stuck his hand out and I took it. He guided me through the narrow hallway and back to the back door where Dylan was standing by the fence.

"If Pauline died in 2012, then why did Calvin give me her number? He had to have known she was dead, right? Certainly, he looked for her after he got out and discovered she was no longer alive."

"I don't know, Samira. None of this shit adds up." Roland sighed.

"But one of them is still out there—Miley or Melanie. I don't know which, but they have to be if one body was found and the other disappeared."

My eyes ventured over to the shed. That's when I noticed there was a lock on it. "Why would he lock a tool shed?"

"Samira," Roland groaned. "Let's just go. It's getting dark."

"Just let me check it really quick." I went up to the shed and there was a small window on the side of it. I looked inside, at the shelves on the wooden walls, and tools either stacked or hanging from them. My gaze lowered to a white object beneath one of the shelves. There was a green light flashing on it.

"What is that?"

I went around to the lock and yanked on it. It didn't budge.

"There's something in there."

"It's just a tool shed, Samira. Let's go," Roland hissed at me.

I shook my head and went back to the side of the shed. There was a stack of bricks and I picked one up, lifting my arm and smashing the window in.

"What the fuck!" Dylan shouted.

"Samira! What the hell are you doing?" Roland barked.

I didn't answer him. I brushed the rest of the glass away with the brick and then climbed on the edge of the shed to get inside. The window was wide enough for me, but neither Roland nor Dylan would fit, I was sure.

I lowered my upper half in after grabbing the closest shelf, doing my best to avoid the glass on the floor. When one of my feet made it through the window, I set it down on the ground and balanced myself enough to stand upright.

The shed was small and tight. Just like the inside of Calvin's house, it was neat and organized. I looked down and the blinking light was coming from what looked like deep freezer, but a shelf was on top of it. On the shelf was a black camera bag. I opened the bag to find a camcorder inside it. It looked old. I opened the screen, and the camera had battery, so I went to the images to flip through them. He had to have been hiding something. Why would he keep a camera locked in a shed? I kept flipping and there were hundreds of photos. There were some of him, some of hardware. But then the images transitioned. There were half-naked women on display, some in lingerie. Some not even aware they were being recorded. In one image, it looked as if he was in a store and was recording a woman wearing leggings, without her permission. A chill ran down my spine.

I kept clicking through, passing all the random women, until I came across an image that made my heart jump to my throat.

It was video of Melanie. I pressed play and she was in a car, the side of her head pressed to a window as the camera recorded her.

"You'll be back home in no time," a man said. That man was Calvin. I pushed rewind on the video and locked on her face. There was a bruise on her cheek. Her hair was frizzy. She appeared unconscious. Another chill struck me.

I clicked over and there was another video of her. The freeze frame had her mouth wide open, her eyes wide and in shock. My heart pumped rapidly as I pressed play.

"TELL EVERYONE THAT YOU FUCKING LIED!" Calvin's voice came through the camera like an alarm.

"I—I'm sorry!" Melanie's voice was high-pitched as he pointed the camera in her face. He panned out and moved the camera left, and there was someone sitting at a table. Her mouth was duct taped, her hands behind her back in the chair.

"I don't want your apologies, little Melanie. I want you to confess what you did. I want it on camera so I can show the world what a lyin' little bitch you are." He moved quickly toward the bound woman at the table; it was Miley. He put the focus on the table, at a needle and a silver spoon, and something in a foil packet. I gasped, my hands shaking as I clung to the camera.

"You confess for the whole world to see, or I'll pump your sister with so much heroin she'll be brain damaged."

Miley's voice was muffled as he pointed the camera at her. Tears were streaming down her cheeks. He reached forward and snatched the tape off her mouth. She screamed and he placed the camera down, but kept it angled at her. I could see him cupping her mouth, whispering something in her ear.

She nodded helplessly and he released her slowly. "Please," she begged.

"No, no. I don't want you to beg, Miley girl. See, I know how Melanie operates. She used you the same way she used me." He picked up the camera and turned it to Melanie again.

"I'm sorry, Calvin!" she cried. "Please! Just let us go!"

"Let you go? I served NINE YEARS in prison because of you, bitch!" His voice boomed and he was in her face again. "I was beaten and shanked and raped! *Actually* fuckin' raped, unlike *you*! So you tell the world what you did! Right now!"

She sobbed, unable to form a coherent sentence.

Calvin pointed the camera away, back at Miley. "Okay. Since you don't wanna fucking speak." He charged to Miley again, focused the camera down to face her, and there were ruffling noises in the background. Miley was pleading for him to stop and wait, but he didn't. He was in the camera frame too, and he used a knife to cut at what I assumed was tape behind her back. Then he gripped her wrist and slammed her left arm on the table.

"Calvin, please!" Melanie begged in the background.

But he didn't listen. He picked up the needle he had on the table and wasted no time injecting it into Miley's arm. Then he looked into the camera with a sneer and said, "One down, many more to go."

The video cut off then, and I flipped through it to see if there were more videos, but there was nothing else of Melanie and Miley. Just dog pictures and more random women being recorded.

Hands still shaking, I replaced the camera and then moved the shelf that was above the deep freezer. There was a lock on the freezer, which meant he was definitely hiding something.

I looked around and spotted a hammer, snatched it up, and then whacked at the lock. I heard Roland calling my name, but after that video, I couldn't stop. I was right to be suspicious of Calvin. He had been with both of them!

I didn't stop hitting it, not until the lock popped and broke off.

When it did, I pulled it off and opened the freezer.

There were frozen bags of vegetables inside as well as

frozen meat. I moved all of it aside, digging deep, ready to give up . . . but then I noticed something that didn't look like meat at all.

I pushed the bags over; it was dark inside the shed and I couldn't tell what the hell it was, but I pushed down and it was hard, yet soft in places. Taking my phone out, I turned on the flashlight and flashed it down.

And when I saw what it was, I screamed louder than I ever had in my entire life.

CHAPTER SIXTY-EIGHT

I stumbled backward, bumping into one of the shelves.

"Samira! Samira! What happened?" Roland shouted through the window.

I gripped my chest, my heart pumping rapidly, beating like a drum. *No . . . no. It couldn't be.*

I went toward the freezer again, flashed the light down. Beneath a plastic bag was a face. The eyes were wide open, the tip of the nose pressing against the bag. Dark hair and red lipstick smeared the bag from the inside. I recognized her face. I knew it very well, despite its frozen state.

It was Melanie. It had to be after what she did to ruin his life.

He brought her all the way back here. And he *killed* Miley. That was why they found heroin in the body. That was why there was trauma to her head. Calvin forced her to relapse and then killed her.

Something thudded outside the shed and a sharp gasp left my lungs. I rushed back to the window. Roland wasn't there anymore, and I couldn't see anything from the side.

"Roland!" I shouted. No answer. "Roland!" I screamed.

I heard what sounded like a gunshot and dropped my phone to clutch my chest. "Roland!" I screamed again.

There was a crack in the shed by the door and I bent down to look through it with shaky breaths. I heard feet shuffling through the grass. Saw Cannon pacing back and forth, in a frenzy. Then I saw someone walking toward the shed, dressed in all gray with dirty sneakers. And it wasn't Roland or Dylan.

I looked around, but there was nowhere to hide. The door rattled as he grabbed it, then the whole shed shook as he grunted and snatched at the lock.

"Fuck," I whimpered. I heard keys jingle and turned my gaze to the window. I hoisted myself up to the shelf and climbed up to get to the window again. My upper half was out, but I lost my footing and fell to the ground just as the lock on the shed clinked and the door was snatched open. As I fell, I felt something slice my palm, but I couldn't focus on the pain nor could I really feel it. I hopped up and saw blood dripping from my palm to my arm, and then I looked up, and Calvin was inside the shed, peering through the window and right at me with angry eyes.

"No." I glanced left. Dylan was sprawled out on the grass by the fence and I had no idea where Roland was and that terrified me even more.

Run.

I didn't know where the fuck I was going, or what direction to head in, but I ran. I turned toward the trees and ran for my life. It was darker now, only a sliver of sunlight over the horizon. I rushed between the trees, feeling naked branches slapping me in the face.

I panted raggedly, tripping over tree roots and stumbling, but I refused to fall. I looked over my shoulder and saw his silhouette. He was chasing after me. My belly felt heavy with dread, my blood pumping with adrenaline and fear.

I spotted an opening to my right and I took it, and as I ran there was a hill. Too busy looking over my shoulder, I tripped over another tree root and tumbled face forward in a bed of wet leaves.

My breaths were ragged, and I could hear his footsteps getting closer. I looked over and there was a log. I crawled toward it, moving to the other side and lying flat on my back, hiding behind it.

I winced, my hand stinging from the cut, and lifted it up just enough to give it a look. The slice was deep, blood gushing. I reached up and took the satin scarf off my head, wrapping it several times around the wound.

Then I lay still, and the footsteps were louder. He was close. I could hear him breathing, the twigs snapping beneath his weight.

In that moment, I felt the urge to pray. I couldn't remember the last time I'd prayed, but right now, I needed God to save me. Calvin had killed two women already and he could do it again.

I listened hard, my lips moving, begging God to help me. It sounded like he was moving ahead, passing the log. I didn't dare look up, for fear that he'd see me. I kept the back of my head pressed to the ground, wishing my whole body would sink into the earth so I could dig my way to safety.

"You should have minded your own fucking business!" Calvin roared.

I cupped the unbloody hand around my mouth to stop myself from making any noises. He sounded close. He was lurking now, trying to figure out where I was.

"I knew exactly who you were when you showed up at my door. Knew you weren't a damn journalist. You think I wouldn't keep tabs on what her husband was doing? I always thought he'd figure out what happened with me because of her, and that he'd come looking for me. But he never did. He moved on and married you."

My heart was beating so loud I could hardly hear him.

"Should have left it alone," he muttered. He was so close.

I heard his steps, the soggy leaves on the ground squishing as he stepped down on them.

"Had nothing to do with you. But now you know too much. All y'all know too much and I'm not going back to prison. Nah. Fuck that. I'd rather die than go back there."

I heard him step one more time, and then I saw his eyes. He was on the other side of the log, leaning over, looking right down at me.

I screamed to the top of my lungs and rolled over, shooting to a stand, and he immediately pointed a Glock 45 at me.

"There's nowhere else to run," he said. "Just stand there and take this bullet."

I threw my hands in the air. "Wait! I—I believe you! I know she lied about you! I know she ruined your life, okay?"

"Yeah. She did. But like I said, you know too damn much. You gotta go."

"Please," I begged as he wrapped his finger tighter around the trigger. "She—she wasn't fair to you, and I get that. She never should've done what she did to you. She never should have lied to try and keep you around!"

"But she did and I'm like this because of her!"

"D-did you kill Miley?"

He quirked a brow, as if the question didn't need asking. "Why?"

"Wasn't exactly the goal to kill her. Just wanted to fuck her up a little bit but I gave her too much. She overdosed. Not like Miley didn't deserve it too. She went along with Melanie's lies. Both of those girls were fuck-ups. So goddamn selfish and ruthless."

"But you have to know you won't win," I said.

"Won't win what?" he snapped.

"In the end. You have to know you won't win."

"What the fuck are you talking about—"

Before Calvin could finish his sentence, my husband charged forward and tackled him to the ground.

CHAPTER SIXTY-NINE

The gun went off as they both went down and I dropped to the ground, covering my head. I heard punches being thrown, bones crunching from the blows, both of them grunting.

I crawled away, pressing my back to the thick trunk of a tree. Roland was on top of Calvin, gripping the gun and turning it sideways so it wasn't pointing at him.

"Don't fuck with my wife!" Roland snarled.

"I already fucked one. Maybe I'll fuck another!" Calvin shot back.

That pissed Roland off. He freed one hand to punch Calvin in the face, but it was like Calvin had taken many punches to the face, and after being in prison, maybe he had. He hardly reacted to the blows. He ate them and didn't let go of the gun during it—not until someone else showed up.

Dylan rushed up to them, kicking Calvin square in the face. Calvin grunted and blood went flying out of his mouth and Roland got ahold of the gun and started to stand, but Calvin was back up again, tackling him back to the ground.

They both fell and I wailed for Roland. The gun flew across the ground and they both clambered over each other to get to it, punching and kicking and shoving their elbows into each other's faces, but before either of them could grab it, I picked up the gun and stood.

My hands were shaking as I pointed it down at Calvin. He and Roland peered up at me, then Roland moved away while Calvin pressed up weakly on one hand, raising the other one in the air.

"Samira," Roland called, stepping toward me. "Don't."

"Listen to him, Samira." Dylan was on the other side of me. "You do this, and you'll have to live with it for the rest of your life. It'll haunt you until the day you die."

"He was going to *kill* me!" I screamed hysterically. "He was going to kill all of us! He killed Melanie, Roland! He killed Miley too!"

Roland was quiet. "Samira. It's okay. I love you and I don't want you to live with this. Hand me the gun and I'll take care of it."

Calvin laughed after spitting blood. "Listen to your husband, Samira. Hand the pretty boy the gun."

My hands shook and Roland came closer to me. When he wrapped his hands around it, his eyes found mine, and there was safety in them—a safety I hadn't felt in a long, long time. His stare was both apologetic and sincere, as if he was saying he was sorry for everything—as if he'd put me through this, but he hadn't. I led us to Calvin. This was all my fault. We almost *died* because I was stupid and reckless and decided to confront a predator. But I did it for them. For the twins. For Roland. I finished something for once in my life, despite coming so close to death.

I released the gun and Roland took it, but as he did, I saw Calvin rise and leap forward with his hands out, shoving Roland facedown to the ground. I grunted and fell with him and saw the gun land at Dylan's feet. He picked it up, and just when Calvin flipped Roland over and brought his arm up, about to punch my husband yet again, Dylan raised the gun and it went off.

A bullet went into Calvin's back, the gunshot echoing through the woods.

Blood dripped from Calvin's lips and Roland shoved him away. Calvin landed on his back, eyes wide open, staring up at the sky, and I couldn't believe it, but he was smiling. His blood stained his teeth and he choked and gurgled on some of it, but he didn't stop smiling.

Roland crawled to me and pulled me into a tight embrace, bringing my face to his chest and forcing me to look away.

But I didn't have to look away to know Calvin was dead, and that all of this with Melanie, Miley, and the journals, was finally over.

CHAPTER SEVENTY

A lot happened after Calvin died.

We called the cops first thing and they showed up and found Melanie's body in the freezer. She was chopped to pieces, according to what one of the detectives told Roland. We went back home after three long days of being questioned, writing testimonies, and speaking to lawyers.

Of course it had leaked that Roland was involved, which created a whole other situation. When we got back home, we were bombarded by journalists camped out on the road of the mansion. Suddenly, Roland was this wounded and wronged man who everyone wanted to love. The media ate it up and some even apologized for thinking he murdered his own wife. A lot of them sought interviews, and his agent and publicist agreed it was a good idea for him to do some of them—that we both should appear in some of the interviews together, to look stronger. Publishers wanted him to write a book, and previous endorsers were blowing up his phone, begging him to come back to them to represent their brands. He wanted to do all of it, but not right away. First, he needed to digest everything that'd happened . . . and I did too.

The night we got back home, we both showered together

in silence, but it wasn't awkward. We were both deep in thought, glancing at each other every so often. He washed my back and I washed his and then we stood beneath the warm stream, holding each other until the water turned cold.

When we were out and dressed, Roland sat on his side of the bed with his back to me. His shoulders were hunched. He wasn't okay.

"Roland?"

"Yeah?"

I sat beside him and grabbed his hand. "You okay?"

"Honestly? No." He shook his head and gave me a humorless laugh.

"Wanna talk about it?"

He was quiet a moment, his gaze on the floor. "You know, all this time I thought Melanie's death was *my* fault."

"What do you mean?"

"I mean that for the past three years I thought she'd driven herself over that cliff because of me."

"Oh."

"I thought that—I mean, for *years* I thought I made her hate her life so much that she would have rather been *dead* than to be around me a second longer."

"Why didn't you just let her leave?"

"She could have left, Samira. She could have walked out that door anytime she wanted to and I wouldn't have stopped her. I'd said things out of anger, yes, but if she really wanted to go, she could have. But I was raised by a mother who didn't believe in divorce. Even when my father would beat the shit out of my mother, she still stayed. She didn't feel free until he died. And I was loyal. I still am."

I lowered my gaze.

"I think that's why I got so angry with her that night. She told me she'd cheated to make me angry. And that alone infuriated me because I wanted our marriage to work. I wanted us to be okay. Things like that happened all the time in marriages, but I witnessed people making it work. I wanted to make her happy. Even after she told me, I tried finding the words to mend us, but I never did. All I could think about was the way I grabbed her. I'd promised myself I would never do what my father did to my mother—to any woman—and I did it anyway. I put my hands on her when I shouldn't have."

"We all make mistakes, Roland."

"I know, and that's a big regret of mine. Because I was so angry and worried, I made her angry and worried and I thought she killed herself because she felt trapped. I thought *I* was the reason." His voice cracked and he squeezed my hand. "And the worst part is I wished she *would* leave. I wished she would just go away so my life would be easier . . . and when she actually did I just . . . I went numb. Everything in me went numb because I'd made a stupid wish and I immediately wanted her back. I could have helped her—saved her from that Calvin motherfucker if I hadn't been ignoring her. She had no one to turn to—no one to express herself with anymore. I'd taken that privilege away from her and I regret it so fucking much."

I rubbed his hand with the pad of my thumb. "Melanie wasn't good to you, Roland. I understand you're upset, and that you have regrets, and no, she didn't deserve to die like that—her or her sister—but she wasn't good to you. She tainted your marriage. She even said in her journals that she knew it wouldn't work out between you two."

He looked up at me. "So why did she agree to marry me then?"

"I don't know, babe." I rested my head on his shoulder. "But what I do know is that I don't want to be anything like her. I agreed to marry you because I truly do love you and you mean so much to me. I want our marriage to work."

"I love you too and I want the same thing."

We were quiet a moment.

"The journals . . ."

"I'll burn them," I stated.

"What did you tell the cops anyway? Didn't they ask you how you found out about Calvin?"

"I just told them I found an old newspaper clipping in her things and looked it up. Found out what happened to her and her sister and I investigated—became a sleuth."

Roland chuckled. "You almost got yourself killed, Samira." He tipped my chin. "I don't want you to do anything that crazy ever again."

"Well, unless you have another wife hiding out there somewhere that I don't know about, I doubt I'll have to."

He laughed, then kissed me on the lips.

There was no way I was going to tell the police about the journals. They revealed too much of that night between him and Melanie and would have stirred up even more shit for Roland. He was healing from that and working on himself, and I believed he was. He regretted his actions and was learning from them every day.

I wanted the journals gone for good and I wanted to protect him no matter what, so we agreed that we'd burn them on the weekend, turn them to ash and never bring them up again.

We were going to restart as a happily married couple, and Roland would take his wins after having so many losses because after everything Melanie put him through, even after her death, he deserved it. And no one was going to ruin him again. Not when he had me in his corner.

CHAPTER SEVENTY-ONE

"That's the last one, right?" Dylan asked. We stood in front of the firepit beneath the pergola, watching the journals burn, the ivory pages turning to dark embers.

"Yep. Last one." I sighed. "I'm glad to finally be rid of them."

"Me too." Dylan stepped sideways and looked back at the kitchen, where Roland was opening the fridge for a beer. "Thank you for not telling him about . . . you know."

"Yeah, well, after all that we've been through the past week, that's the last thing he needs to know about. But that's not happening anymore, is it? You're done stealing from him, right?"

"Oh, yeah. That's been done. I got spooked after Melanie confronted me about it, and cut it off. I regret doing it and not gonna lie, I really only did it to piss her off. It was fucked up of me and I'll tell him about it . . . just not right now. Maybe when things slow down. I don't want to throw too much at him at once after everything that happened in Raleigh."

"Right. That's wise," I said.

Dylan sat in one of the chairs and released a long sigh. I

studied the bandage beneath his eye, where he'd been hit with the butt of Calvin's gun. "I can understand why she wanted to leave," Dylan said. "She was a bad wife and she admitted it. Probably would have saved so much stress with Roland if she'd just taken off."

My head cocked, and I looked at Dylan more intensely. "What are you talking about?"

"Oh—well, I mean, she always said how she was going to get a place of her own and go."

"No, I mean about the bad wife thing. You said she admitted it. When did she admit that?"

"Roland told me she was saying stuff like that to him."

I frowned. "When?"

"Shortly after the whole Calvin thing." He laughed nervously, revealing all his teeth.

"Roland and I have been stuck together like glue since the whole Calvin thing happened. I don't remember him saying that to you."

Another nervous laugh. "Well, then Melanie must have said it to me before or something. I don't know. It was so long ago I can't even remember. All of it is a blur." Dylan blew out an exaggerated breath and pretended to shake off something invisible.

I was quiet a moment, watching Dylan. He dragged a palm down his face, tapped his foot on the ground and caused his leg to bounce.

"I just think it's strange you say that, because from what I read in those journals, Melanie hated you, Dylan. Up until her end, she literally hated you. I read all about it. That doesn't seem like something she would have shared with you—running away and all."

"Look, you didn't know, Melanie, a'ight? She always said stuff to me or Roland to try and hurt us, get under our skin, but it never worked." His eyes shifted over to the double doors of the house and I looked with him. Roland was on the phone now, most likely talking to his agent. He'd been receiving a lot of calls from his agent for bookings.

"Did you read her journals?" I asked, snapping my gaze back on Dylan.

"Why would I read her journals? I told you I didn't know anything about those until a few days ago, when you were talking about them on the flight to North Carolina."

"They were in her shed, out in the open. If I found them, I'm sure someone else came across them too. I always suspected someone had. They were too visible and way too easy to find. And one night I heard someone outside the shed. It was you, wasn't it?"

Dylan's Adam's apple bobbed, and as the fire kept roaring, turning the pages to ashes, a shadow seemed to pass over his face. No longer was he smiling. His features stiffened and his eyes locked right on mine.

"Enough with the questions, Samira." His voice was different. Deeper. "Melanie is gone. Calvin is dead. The journals are burning. Just let it go."

My heart sank. "Dylan . . . did you have something to do with what happened to Melanie?"

He tossed his head back and drew in a deep breath, then lowered his head with a slow exhale. "You and Roland are happy now, right? Your husband is innocent and you've proved it. He's about to make millions off of this crazy-as-hell comeback story, and you can sleep peacefully knowing that. Isn't that all that matters? Why backtrack?"

"You're still stealing from him, aren't you?"

Dylan was quiet, but his jaw was set and his left eye was twitching.

"What did you do?" I asked, nearly breathless. I could hardly hear my own voice, my heart was beating so loudly.

"I didn't do shit."

I closed my eyes briefly and shook my head. "You know,

this whole time I've been racking my brain trying to figure how the hell Calvin could have even found Miley. I mean, me and my brother searched her name high and low and not much came up for her. And I kept asking, how did Calvin even figure out where to find them? After finding out what they did to him, I know for a fact they wouldn't have reached out to him. He was deranged as fuck."

Dylan's eyes were glistening now. He looked down at the fire, but I clapped my hands, forcing his attention back on me. "Nah-uh! You tell me now, or I swear to God I'll tell Roland you stole from him—that you're probably still stealing from him, you shady *motherfucker*!"

He shot to a stand and walked around the firepit, bending low to get in my face. "It's not about what I did, okay?" he hissed through gritted teeth. "It's about Melanie always trying to ruin everyone's lives for her own personal gain. She was a selfish fucking bitch and she needed to go away, and I remembered Miley telling me about this Calvin guy all the time and how she felt bad for what they did to him. She told me Melanie told on him because he didn't want her anymore and that clearly made Melanie angry. She made Miley lie too. Why do you think she was so fucked up? She was *reckless*, Samira, and she ruined that man's life. It was no wonder he was so goddamn deranged. Then it turns out that I stopped wanting Melanie and she was threatening to tell Roland that I'd taken advantage of her. Then she mentioned the money, threatened my sister, and like always, she took shit too far, and you don't fuck with my family. She threatened to sue Yvette, but Yvette didn't know shit. Yvette thought it was my money—my account. It was all on me, but do you think Melanie cared about that? Do you think she showed sympathy? No. She only wanted to hurt me, and she knew in order to do that, she had to attack my family—and that shit? That's what really pissed me off." He sat down beside me and I froze, pressing my back against the arm of the seat with wide, damp eyes. "When I found Calvin on Facebook, I set up a fake account and messaged him. I pretended to be a guy Melanie had accused too. We connected that way and he told me all these things about how if he could find her, he'd make her pay. Set her straight. So, I brought him to her. As soon as he was off parole, I booked a rental car for him so he could drive here. I told him how to find Miley and told him to have Miley text Melanie to so they could both be at her apartment. I was surprised he even showed up. Of course Melanie didn't show up for her sister and was even trying to pack up and run away, so I took matters into my own hands and brought her to him myself."

"But why? Why would you do something like that?"

"Because I was fed the fuck up, and if she was going to blow up my life, I wanted to blow hers up too. But I didn't think he'd *kill* her. Maybe just scare her, rough her up a bit, give her the reminder that she too had demons and needed to mind her own goddamn business. I even thought she'd keep the money going to my sister, let it be a secret between us. I mean, I assumed Calvin would demand money or do something to *ruin* her life, not *end* it. His crazy ass drove her all the way home and only God knows what he did to her before he actually killed her. Hell, I'm surprised he even made it that far with her." Dylan's Adam's apple bobbed again and he scratched the stubble on his jaw. "Didn't think he'd hurt Miley at all, but he did. He forced her to overdose. I was the one who found her body. I cleared her apartment. Scrubbed the hell out of it. Turned in those keys. At this point, Melanie was missing and hadn't come back to the mansion, Miley wasn't answering the phone, so I went to check things out. That's when I found Miley facedown on the table with a needle in her arm. My plan had backfired. Melanie was gone and he obviously had something to do with it, and I knew it could trace back to me if he'd fucked up or had gotten caught with her, so in order to throw the scent off the both of us, I changed Miley's clothes to something Melanie would have worn—which was much harder than I thought it would be, considering they had two very different styles. Fortunately, I did find something, and after that, I put her body in Melanie's car, which was still in the parking lot, and drove to the nearest cliff. It was tough to do it, but once I got Miley's footing right on the gas pedal, it handled itself. The car went full speed and drove right over the cliff."

"So that everyone would believe it was Roland," I said, heart pounding.

He scratched his jaw again, harder this time. "I needed the distraction. And to be fair, I thought they'd just rule it a suicide or at least look deeper into Melanie's history, find out about that Calvin guy and pin him before he could say a damn thing, but they never did. They automatically assumed Roland had done something to her since he was the husband and because he was still in proximity when they found her bruised up in her car. It appeared to be an open-and-shut case for the detectives. They couldn't get in touch with Miley, there were no other witnesses but me, and I wasn't going to mention Calvin or rat on myself, so all odds were stacked against Roland at that point. He seemed guilty as hell. Shit, even I started to believe he'd done it at one point." Dylan shrugged. "I guess it all worked out the way it should have anyway. It's not like Roland didn't have it coming to him."

I couldn't help my reaction to that. I slapped him, and his face turned with my hand. "I can't believe you! You know I can report this! I can tell Roland everything you just told me—that his life and his career went to shit because of *you*!"

"Yeah, and what good would come of that?" he demanded, eyes connecting with mine again.

I gave it a thought, staring into his dark eyes, and realized nothing good could come of it at all. Like he said, Calvin was gone, Melanie too, and Miley. All of them were gone . . . but they were gone because of *him*. All of this was because of something he'd started out of spite.

Now I understood why Melanie hated him so much—why she wanted so badly for him to go down and lose Roland's love. He was just as awful as she was, ruining people's lives and getting away with it. He set her up and caused her death. He may not have had the actual blood on his hands, but it was still on him. All of this stemmed from him.

"All of this because of his money," I breathed. "Yeah, Melanie and Miley are gone. The case is closed, but you can't just keep stealing from your cousin and getting away with it. Not after what you did to him."

"I can and I will, because if I got rid of one wife, trust me, I can get rid of another. And this time, they won't believe Roland had nothing to do with it. Two of his wives going missing?" He made a *tsk-tsk* noise. "They'll eat him alive."

"Wow." I choked on a breath. "You're fucking evil. Why would you do that to him? Hasn't he only ever been good to you?"

"Roland has everything. He's *always* had everything. And he was only good to me because he pitied me after my mother died. While my family suffered and we went broke to cover my mother's prescriptions and hospital bills, he just kept on thriving. Whenever we'd ask him for help, he always acted like he was too busy, or he'd ignore my calls and messages. And Aunt Cathy—that bitch never answered the goddamn phone. It wasn't until my mother died when he thought it was time to help me, and that never sat well with me. I lied to Melanie when she asked me about moving in. I told her my sister kicked me out to renovate and sell. Truth is, there was no house to sell. I was living with my sister in a one-bedroom apartment that we shared with my mother, but we were always planning on starting up a renovations company. I struggled with her to pay our bills. We asked him for help and he never gave it to us . . . not until it was too late. Not until my mother was *dead*. Even now, he isn't exactly *giving* anything to us. I had to resort to taking that shit because I thought he'd pay me more, offer to take care of my siblings sometimes, and the hospital bill debt. He never did. He just moved me in, let me have a room, made me his errand boy, and thought I would shut up and take it. *Fuck that*. He gave me access to everything he owned, so I took it. And I *still* take it. Melanie never canceled that bank account. She was too worried about escaping to do so. Right now, Roland thinks she set up the donations before she died, and because he felt so damn guilty about her death, he continues to make his contributions. To this day, he doesn't even question it and I know because I see the money hitting that account every month. Eventually, with you around, he might cancel it, but . . ." He shrugged. "I'll just find another way, I'm sure."

I heard a door shut behind me and flinched as I looked over my shoulder at Roland. He was making his way to us with a smile and three beers in his hands, clearly with good news in tow.

"Want to keep your marriage intact and Roland out of trouble?" Dylan asked. I focused on him again and he was forcing a smile, watching his cousin make his way toward us. "Then keep your fucking mouth shut. I'll stop taking his money eventually—once my brother and sisters are well taken care of too and I feel like it's enough. Until then, mind yours, and I'll mind mine."

Roland's footsteps came closer and Dylan stood up, accepting one of the beers he offered.

Roland sat beside me and handed one to me too, then he looked between us as Dylan sat, and asked, "Everything all right?"

I sipped my beer, looking from my husband to Dylan, who had one arm on the arm of the couch, a smirk on his lips. "Yeah, man. I'm all good. You good, Samira?"

I stared at him, wanting so badly to break the bottle in my hands and stab him right in the chest. He couldn't get away with this. Who did he think he was? He was such a smug bastard, so malicious, so conniving. I felt nothing but pure rage in that moment, thinking about all I'd gone through just to discover the truth. The *real* truth. And it turned out he was behind it all along.

But then I looked at Roland, who was smiling, happy as hell for the first time in a long time despite having a black eye and bruises, and all of that rage morphed into fear. And not fear for me. Fear for *my husband*.

He'd escaped the past—escaped Melanie and all the problems she'd dragged into his life. He was happy again, getting more endorsements and interviews, reclaiming his innocence and reputation. I couldn't put him through that all over again. Not when so much was going for him. Not over money. Not right now. And I couldn't have someone else he thought he could trust, destroy his life all over again. Someone had to protect him.

With that in mind, I put my eyes on Dylan's, and with my chin tipped and a subtle smile on my lips, I said, "Yeah. We're good."

Pro Caddy for Roland Graham Found Dead in Home

A Colorado man by the name of Dylan Parks was found dead in his home on November 13th, 2020. The Sageburg Police Department have ruled his death a suicide after finding his body on his couch with his throat slit and a pink pocketknife clutched in his hand.

A suicide letter with the words *I can't do this anymore. I'm no good for this world*, was found on the dining table, as well as the keys to what detectives later found out belonged to the home of professional golfer Roland Graham.

This comes only seven months after the shocking discovery of the body of Melanie Graham, Roland Graham's first wife, in a deep freezer on the property of former convict Calvin Thompson; as well as the discovery that it was actually the body of Melanie's twin sister, Miley Raine, that was found in the car that went over a cliff only three years prior. Thompson murdered Melanie Graham and Miley Raine and was shot dead with his own gun while fighting Roland Graham and Parks, who had discovered Calvin's criminal involvement with the sisters after digging up a news article in Graham's first wife's belongings.

Parks was Roland Graham's first cousin and golf caddy and worked professionally with him for three years. We asked Graham if he had any words about Parks and he told us, "Dylan was a great cousin and an amazing caddy, but not all of the choices he made were wise. Lots of his choices affected others, and his death really affects me right now. All I can say at the moment is that I loved him like a brother and that he will be missed."

At the time, Graham's wife was with him but had no comment.

Parks was thirty-six years old and leaves behind two sisters and a brother.

Dear Reader,

I'm so excited that I was able to share my thriller *The Wife Before* with you! This book was very exciting to write, but there are some heavy topics between the pages that I want to touch on.

As you know, Melanie suffered at the hands of an abusive relationship and before her death, she had a hard time coping with her unhealed past. I have witnessed up close (through relatives and friends), how toxic and mentally deteriorating an abusive relationship can be, whether the abuse is physical or mental. Whether it's a woman being abused or a man, these explosive relationships often result in pain, depression, and sometimes even death. That's why it is such an incredibly important topic to me, and why I want to discuss abuse in relationships openly. We all deserve to be loved and held in a safe space by the people we love. I feel for those who are suffering—those who want to get out but have no idea where to start. (And if this is you, please seek help from someone you trust or call a domestic violence hotline for assistance!)

After reading *The Wife Before* and diving into the minds of Samira and Melanie, you have witnessed the ripple effect of Melanie's childhood trauma and assault from a previous toxic relationship and how she dragged those issues into her marriage. You have seen that Melanie may have pretended to be okay as she got older, but that she never was—that she never felt safe and had been crying out for help for years but didn't trust anyone enough to get the help she needed until it was too late.

My goal while writing this thriller was to sink my claws into the complexity of relationships too. No relationship or marriage is perfect, of course, but I hoped to shine light on two things: Samira's relationship with Roland compared to

Melanie's marriage, and how even though it's the same man involved with both of these women, how different the marriages are, due to the women's different personalities and upbringings.

With that being said, I *really* hope you enjoyed my book as much as I enjoyed writing it. Abuse isn't a light topic and should be heavily discussed in our real lives, but please know this book is a form of escape and that I hope you had a fun, entertaining reading experience with it. If you'd like to join in on the social media buzz, please tag #TheWifeBefore or #ShanoraWilliams so I can join the excitement with you!

Sending love,

Shanora Williams